SHORTY IS IN *Love* WITH A REAL *One* 2

A NOVEL BY

SHVONNE LATRICE

$19.99
ISBN 978-1-966375-18-0
51999>

CHAPTER ONE

Khyle Luke

So when y'all niggas hop off the jet, you better tuck what's on ya neck and get the fuck from 'round here...

"Don't Come to LA" by YG came through the speakers, so Bella, Tasmine, and I got up to dance and sing along. Even though they weren't from Los Angeles, they loved some YG just like me, so they knew the words. As we moved our bodies with drinks in our hands, I felt Oden come behind me and kiss my neck, before going to the balcony to look over the party with his friends.

Suddenly, I heard people screaming from the first floor of the party, and before I could react, gunshots rang out. When I looked towards the balcony, I saw Oden collapse to the floor, blood seeping out the side of his mouth.

"No, what the fuck!" was the only thing I could get out before a crowd surfaced around him, knocking my friends and I backward.

Not wanting to be thrown into the background, I began barging my way through the people crowding around Oden, not giving a fuck who I bumped and how hard I did it. By the time I reached him, two men and one woman dressed in scrubs, were rushing up the stairs to get him.

"Where are you taking him?" I hollered as they lifted his body to put him on a stretcher. Although they were in hospital gear, something about it was strange. They didn't seem like they'd come from a hospital, not to mention they had gotten here way too fast.

"Go, Khyle! You can go with them!" Truman hollered to me, and then started back down the stairs.

Anton was trying to get the party under control, or maybe he was in search of the shooter, I'm not really sure. But he was running around the party like he was looking for something, and talking to a few shaken up people.

I didn't know who had come up in here shooting, but I really didn't care. I just wanted to make sure my baby was okay. Once I was sure he was good, then we could look into who the fuck tried to blaze him.

I followed the three people that were carrying Oden, out of the door and into this fancy van. They hooked him up to oxygen, and I sat there staring down at him as my heart beat damn near out of my chest.

He couldn't die right now, he just couldn't. I didn't know what the fuck I would do if Oden were taken away from me forever. He'd become everything to me in just a short amount of time, and I didn't plan on letting him go anytime soon. I wanted he and I to grow old together, have babies, and get married. Right now just wasn't the right time for him to leave the earth.

The truck we rode in made it to this big ass ranch house that seemed to only have neighbors 20 to 30 miles out. I followed alongside the three medical persons as they wheeled Oden in. His eyes were still closed which caused me to panic.

"When are his eyes gonna open?" I screamed as we entered this big cold room.

They ignored me as they began hooking him up to shit and making a fuss. I stood there not knowing what to say or do, because it wasn't like I could help them. I watched as they stripped him out of his clothing, while I made sure the female nurse wasn't being too touchy feely. He may have been on his deathbed, but I was still a jealous lover and proud of it.

"Give us a moment." She turned to me and escorted me out of the huge room that looked identical to a hospital one.

After she closed the door in my face, I stayed there frozen as if that would help me figure out what was going on. After realizing it'd be a while before I got back in there, I began walking aimlessly around the huge ass house, wondering whom it belonged to and if someone lived here. It was beautiful and nicely decorated. I could definitely see a nice little family living here, or a couple visiting for peace and quiet.

After tiring myself out from wandering all over the mini mansion, I laid down in one of the bedrooms, passing out after praying that God saved Oden.

A few hours later...

"Huh?" I woke up because someone was shaking me. When I opened my eyes, I saw it was that same female nurse wearing a warm half smile.

"Would you like to go into the room with Mr. Bishop?" she quizzed, handing me a cup with steam coming from it.

"Yeah, yes. Is he okay?"

"He's fine. He had on a vest, but the bullet did hit him pretty hard, bruising his chest. His body was in shock and that's why he kind of passed out," she explained, as I stood up, taking the mug from her.

I sniffed the contents and realized it was peppermint tea. I didn't care too much for peppermint tea, but I didn't want to be rude and I was a little cold.

"Why did blood come from his mouth?"

"It can happen if that area of your chest is hit with a really strong impact. But he's gonna be just fine, trust me."

"I'm sorry, what's your name?"

"It's Phoebe."

I nodded and followed her downstairs and into the room where Oden was. I could hear machines beeping, and the room was still ice cold damn near.

"Is there a way we can get some heat going?"

"No, sweetie. The cold air keeps the room sterile. I can bring you a blanket if you'd like, and there is a bed over here for when you get tired."

"Thanks."

She checked on Oden for a few moments, and then left out the room, leaving the two of us alone.

I walked closer to him, and sat on the edge of the bed to caress his beautiful head of hair. My eyes trailed his muscular arms, admiring the tattoos that adorned them. He was so unbelievably sexy, and he was all mine. It was so funny that he was still a head turner, even in a hospital gown.

I was so happy he'd made it out, that I stopped rubbing him to thank God. When I was done praying, I leaned down to peck his soft lips a few times. He opened his eyes for a hot second, but they closed right back as he groaned. I guess he was tired as hell and still in some pain.

Deciding to leave him be, I kissed his lips again before going over to the other bed in the room. I removed my sweater to reveal the thin tank top I'd worn under it, and then grabbed my tea and phone before getting into the bed.

When I checked my iPhone, I saw I had so many damn texts from my friends, and even some from Shayne.

Shayne: *Are you okay? Heard Truman's party got shot up.*

Me: *Yes, I'm fine. Goodnight.*

I turned my phone on vibrate, and then set it on the little table next to the bed. I polished off the tea, which for some reason was good as hell, and then laid down to fall back asleep. Tonight had been crazy as hell, but I was thankful that everyone had made it out okay.

CHAPTER ONE

Pilar Abraham

Four hours earlier...

Boy, maybe if you cared enough, I wouldn't have to care so much. What happened to our trust? Now you're just givin' up. You used to be so in love, now you don't care no more...

"I Care" by Beyoncé blasted all throughout the car, as my friend Adira sped to our destination. Although I couldn't relate to every word that Beyoncé sang, it was still resonating with me.

Just 30 minutes ago, as I was getting dressed to attend my boyfriend Truman's Christmas party, someone hit my phone with a picture of him hugged up on some bitch. I didn't believe it was anything, until right after the pictures came, a damn video of he and the girl kissing and shit was sent. I blinked back tears as I thought about the evidence that sat in my iPhone. I was hurt and still slightly in disbelief.

Truman had never cheated on me, and I did everything I could to make sure he never even thought about it. I cooked, cleaned, fucked, and sucked him whenever he wanted, and I even had my own damn money, despite the fact that he was paid. I knew bitches were on my nigga, the same way that they had a thing for his best friends, Oden and Anton, but I knew my baby didn't indulge. However, now I wasn't so sure if he'd been faithful all this time. I mean, you don't just go from being completely faithful, to kissing some random hoe in a party. At least she had better been some random bitch.

"Girl, what are you gonna do when we get there?" Adira questioned me, pulling me from my thoughts. I took a deep breath before responding because I didn't want to break down into tears.

"I have no idea, but somebody is gonna get fucked up."

"I told you his ass was doing dirt, Pilar, but you just didn't want to think your perfect ass man had it in him." Adira shook her head as she made a right turn.

Adira was that best friend that always gave it to you straight and never sugarcoated anything. I appreciated that about her, but I just hated her pessimistic attitude. She had no proof of what Truman had possibly been doing, yet every time he left the house, she swore he was going to meet another woman. She'd even followed him one day to see what he'd been up to, but it was all for nothing because she didn't find shit. I'm not quite sure when she started hating Truman, but it seemed like ever since he and I had been together, she carried a deep dislike for my man.

"Here, this is the address," I told her.

"I say we go to the club and meet some new niggas. My homeboy is having a little shindig at the Marquee tonight."

"Ain't nobody trying to be up in that crowded ass club, Adira. I like my space which is why I only club when my nigga is involved," I replied.

All I did was work, spend time with my man, and go to little events that he'd invite me to. Sometimes I wouldn't get that invite, but I wasn't tripping because I was the homebody type. If you looked at me, you would probably think I was an Instagram model that posted thirst traps for rappers on social media all day, but that wasn't me at all. I was just a regular Cuban and Black girl from New York that worked as a hotel manager out here in Las Vegas. All I wanted was a quiet life, with a husband who loved me, and some babies. I planned to have that with Truman, but finding out he'd cheated on me made me see him differently.

"Tell you what. If you hook me up with Oden, I won't say shit if you take that dog ass nigga back," Adira popped her gum as she threw her car into park.

"Truman told me Oden has a girlfriend," I spoke lowly, staring out of the window. Oden and his affairs were the least of my worries right now, and so was hooking him up with Adira's ass.

She replied, rambling about how she didn't care, but I ignored her as I got out of the car, carrying my new Gucci bag that Truman had gotten me last week for my birthday. Just thinking about how he took me to Switzerland and spent all that time with me, brought the tears back into my eyes as I walked up towards the house.

"This shit is jumping," Adira chuckled, swaying to the YG song that we could hear all the way outside.

"I'm Pilar, Truman's girlfriend," I told the bouncer guy standing by the door.

"ID?"

I blew out hot air and reached down into my purse to get my wallet. I showed Big Pun my ID, and once he shined his little light on it, he handed it back to me and gestured for me to go inside. I waved for Adira to follow, and as soon as we stepped in, some bitch dancing like a hoe on some random nigga bumped me. This was why I stayed my ass at home; the party scene just wasn't for me. I knew that was odd to hear coming from a 23-year-old, but I'd been that way for the longest.

I scanned the jumping ass Christmas party for my nigga, while Adira swayed next to me as if this was a joyous event. Finally, when I looked up, I saw Truman and his friends, Anton and Oden, walk up to the balcony to overlook the semi dark party. I smiled at my sexy man, admiring his tall skinny frame and gold diamond slugs that blinded me every time he laughed at something his friends said.

Truman wasn't my type at all when I first met him because I preferred muscular niggas. But I liked that he was tall as hell, 6'5, and that his demeanor was so cool and smooth. He may have been skinny, covered in tattoos, and rocking a scruffy beard, but it was sexy to me. I also liked that he didn't take any shit. My baby wasn't a punk by any means and would lay any nigga out for me and anyone else he cared about. I remember he beat the brakes off some nigga he claimed he saw looking at my ass, and I think that was the night I fell in love.

My thoughts were interrupted when I watched some bitch come behind him and hug him. The only time you hugged a nigga from behind was when you were fucking him, and on more than one occasion. I watched as he turned his face to the side, and she kissed his cheek. If I wasn't his damn girlfriend I would think this bitch was.

"Oooh shit, bitch, I knew it," Adira sucked her teeth. Reaching down into my purse, I pulled my little gun out and removed the safety. "Pilar! What the fuck are you—"

"She has a gun!" some people hollered.

POP! POP! POP!

I shot up towards the balcony with my gun, but when Oden dropped, I immediately regretted it. I was trying to hit Truman, but my aim was off because well… I'd never fired a damn gun. The whole party continued to panic, as I stood there frozen, not believing that I'd shot the wrong person. I also couldn't believe that Truman had me out here acting like I was Brandi from *A Thin Line Between Love and Hate.*

"Come on!" Adira pulled me towards the door, but before I turned away completely, Truman and I made eye contact.

While on the phone, he rushed down the staircase and over towards me as Adira pulled me out of the house. We didn't even make it to the car before Truman snatched me from her, and slammed me up against his black on black Range Rover.

"Fuck is wrong with you, huh?" he barked down into my face. He smelled and looked so good, which for some reason made me start to cry. "Get in the fucking car!"

"Let her go!" Adira yanked on Truman, and although he was skinny, she was no match for him. He gripped her bicep up and threw her ass, causing her to stumble off.

"In the car," he gritted to me as I watched some people roll Oden out and into a van. Some pretty girl with extremely long hair was running alongside him, so I guess she was his girlfriend.

Truman and I got into his car, and the whole ride home he made phone call after phone call, yelling at some people and talking calmly to others. The whole time I was praying Oden didn't die, because I wasn't trying to go to jail behind anybody, not even the nigga I loved more than anything.

We finally made it to our beautiful townhouse, and after Truman helped me out of the car, he snatched my purse and removed the gun from it. I wanted to ask why, but I knew it was probably for good reason. I clearly couldn't handle a damn weapon. I felt so stupid and even a little bit embarrassed.

"Explain yourself," he said as soon as he locked the front door. The lights in the house were still out, and neither of us bothered to turn them on.

"Explain *myself?*" I pointed into my chest. "Nigga, you need to explain your fucking self! Why are you all up on some bitch like you ain't in a damn relationship, Truman!"

"Wasn't all up on no bitch," he waved me off, sucking his teeth and plopping down onto the couch.

"Oh, so what is this? And this?" I asked as I stood in front of him, scrolling through the pictures for his ass.

He stared at each one with a calm expression, and once I was done, he looked up into my eyes and sighed.

"I had too much to drink, and she was in my fucking face, so the shit just happened. And what the hell were you doing there anyway? You told me you weren't coming this time."

"That's the only explanation you have?"

"Yeah," he scoffed, chuckling a little bit as he placed the couch pillow into his lap. I squinted my eyes, wondering where the Truman I'd known him to be had gone.

"Fuck you, Truman." I started towards the door.

"Pilar! Where the fuck you going?" he grabbed me and pulled me into him. I almost melted until I saw him smiling like this wasn't a serious situation.

"Don't worry about it. Worry about that bitch that you were kissing all in the fucking mouth!" My lip turned up after I spoke because the vision invaded my mind. No telling what else he was doing with her.

"Are you fucking serious right now? It was just a fucking kiss, and then you shot my boy, we're even!"

"Nah, nigga, we're not!" And with that, I yanked the door open and sauntered out. I glanced over my shoulder and saw him standing in the doorway, staring at me like I was a fool.

Tonight, I was just gonna go to a hotel to give myself a minute. My life had been turned upside down within minutes, and I just needed time to process… and time away from Truman.

14

CHAPTER ONE

Oden Bishop

A week and a half later...

I would be leaving the hospital tomorrow and I couldn't wait. I hated being laid up, not being able to work and shit. Thankfully school was out for winter, so I wasn't missing class or anything, but damn did I hate being immobile.

"Baby, let me buy your ticket home," I told Khyle who was lying with me in this fake ass hospital bed. I'm pretty sure they weren't as comfortable as this one.

"No, I wanna make sure you're okay. My family will be fine without me for a few more days, Oden."

"I know but—"

"Stop trying to convince me, I'm not gonna leave. Once I know you're okay, I will let my dad know so he can get me a new ticket."

"You told him what happened?" I turned to look at her.

"No, not really. I just said that you were really ill and I didn't want to leave you alone since you didn't have anybody out here to take care of you."

"Good," I sighed, rubbing my hand across my big ass hair.

I was still perplexed that my assailant turned out to be Pilar. I couldn't even be mad at her, because Truman was doing her dirty. I just wished her ass didn't come in on that violent tip, especially when she didn't know shit about a damn gun.

It was actually kind of funny that she tried to shoot that nigga, because Pilar wasn't that type at all. She was hella nice, and loved Truman's dirty drawers. She for real thought he was being faithful this whole time, which was astonishing.

Anton and I were still slightly in disbelief that Truman had even gotten caught. For as long as he'd been with her he'd been smashing other hoes, and Pilar didn't have the slightest clue. But now that she did know, she was staying in a hotel or with her friend, I don't remember which one Truman said. He wasn't tripping like that because he knew he had her wrapped around his finger; his words, not mine. I shrugged at my thoughts as Khyle caressed my hair.

"What are you thinking about?" she smirked.

"Pilar's ass. I didn't know she had a crazy streak."

"Really? I can't believe this is the first time she's acted out, because what she chose to do was so extreme."

"I'm glad you think so, because I ain't trying to have you shooting at me."

"Oh, best believe if I catch you doing something I'm stabbing you and that bitch." Her face turned serious, and even though I was a little disturbed by her statement it made my dick hard.

"You ain't gonna catch me doing shit," I responded, while caressing her exposed thigh. There was a silence, so I looked to see her face kind of twisted. "Fuck is your pretty ass frowning for?"

"You said I wouldn't catch you."

"Okay?"

"So you're saying that you're too slick for me to catch you cheating, Oden?" she moved from under my hand, and I just blew out hot air. I didn't feel good and I wasn't in the mood to have a petty ass argument with her. "Hello!" she nudged me.

"Is that what you think I meant, Khyle?" She shrugged in response and that irritated me. "Aight. Well, since you don't really know, then I will let you think what you want. And maybe this would be a good time for you to go home for Christmas break."

I could feel her looking at the side of my face as I flipped through the TV channels looking for something. I didn't watch too much live TV because I stayed on Netflix, Hulu, and other apps. And if I wasn't watching that I was playing video games. By saying that, I didn't even know what the hell I was looking for really. I needed to be home ASAP, where I could be comfortable. Fuck.

Suddenly, Khyle slid down the bed, and went into my boxers for my dick. I watched her with a stale expression as the TV lit up the otherwise dark room. She said nothing as she began to let her tongue travel over the tip. Placing my hands behind my head, I leaned back to enjoy the show, and to see how she was gonna make up for acting like an insecure ass little girl just a few minutes ago.

"Sloppy," I mumbled to her as she started to ease more of me into her sexy mouth.

I tucked my bottom lip in at the sight, and moved her hair out of her face gently so I could see everything. Her mouth got wetter, and just like I'd requested, she got nasty with it. I didn't like neat head; shit, what nigga did?

Grabbing a handful of her hair, I yanked her off me, and then forced her mouth back on it. I did that a couple times, and damn did that shit have me hard as a brick. Keeping my grip on the back of her head, I sat up so that I could control more of her movement.

"Get on the floor, Khyle," I demanded and she did as I asked. I swung my feet off the side, and as soon as she was on her knees, I had my dick back into her mouth. "I wanna cum in your mouth, baby." I clutched her hair and moved her up and down, sometimes slowly and sometimes fast. I loved this shit right here, and whatever I was mad at before didn't matter to me.

I pulled out of her mouth and let my dick swipe against her full lips before going back in. Shit. As she drenched my rod with her saliva, I began to breath heavily, knowing I was near. Pressing the head of my dick into the back of her throat, I let out the loudest moan because that shit always drove me crazy. I kept pulling her off my dick, and pushing myself back into her mouth, and she took every stroke like the little freak I was turning her into.

She sucked me off for a few more moments, before I was nutting all in her mouth. She tossed her head back to swallow, and as soon as she was done, I yanked her to her feet and bent her over the hospital bed, ripping off her thong.

"Uuuh," she gasped as I entered her from behind.

"Damn, you got this wet from sucking daddy off?" I whispered into her ear while slowly sliding in and out of her from the back. Baby girl was sopping wet, making a nigga weak in the damn knees.

"Mhm," she nodded, tucking her lips in.

I pressed her face into the bed, gripped her hips, and slammed into her, beating her pussy to a pulp. Hearing her call out so innocently was always a fucking turn on. I knew her walls weren't used to this type of treatment before she met me. I smiled watching her grip the sheets in her pretty hands, while crying out like she was being killed. Hearing myself slam into her was the shit, and watching her little ass move only added to that.

"Odeeennn!" she whimpered, releasing onto my pole.

She was so wet that I had to pull out, bend down, and just kiss it from the back. After swiping my tongue between her folds a few times, and gently sucking on her clit, she released her juices again. Turned on like crazy, I stood up and slid back into her from behind.

"You taste so good," I grumbled, ripping the back of her dress and sucking random areas on her back.

She was sniveling softly as I did so, while slowly winding my hips into her from the back. Once I was done licking from her neck to her anal cavity with my dick still inside, I straightened up and pounded her pussy until I was shooting up the club.

"I told you I would never cheat on you," I said as I kissed and licked on her ear, prompting her to shiver. My dick was still inside of her as her pussy throbbed. "Tell me you're sorry." I pushed into her some more even though she was already at the base. Her gasping made me hard again.

"I'm sorry, baby," she whimpered as I played with her nipples from behind. I didn't wanna pull out yet because she felt so good.

I sucked on her neck enough to leave a hickey, and then pulled out of her slowly. I rubbed my fingers against her drenched center, making her coo softly.

"Lay on your back," I instructed.

She stood slowly, pushed her ripped dress down to expose her naked body, and then laid on her back like she was told. After putting her legs on my shoulders, I slid back inside.

"You sore?" I asked and she nodded.

I just leaned down to kiss her nastily as I started to beat it up again. She was crying out into my mouth as I pulverized the pussy. I planned to be knee deep in her guts all damn night.

***

The next day…

I was finally back in my own crib and happy as hell to be. I couldn't wait to get back to work, because for some reason I felt like niggas had been slacking since they knew I was down for the count. I trusted Anton and Truman, but when it got down to it, it was obvious who reigned supreme, so when I wasn't around I was sure niggas would run amuck.

"Again, my nigga, I'm sorry," Truman sighed as we sat in my living room.

"Nigga, chill. She didn't kill my ass. You need to be apologizing to her. Has she come home yet?"

"Nope, but that's on her. I don't chase no bitch."

"Pilar just ain't no regular bitch, Tru," Anton chimed in, sipping the beer Khyle had brought to him.

She had the nerve to be cooking dinner for me and shit like she was my wife. I guess the hurting I put on that pussy all yesterday gave her ass some act right. I laughed as I watched her walk her now bowlegged ass through the kitchen. My baby could barely walk regular.

"Yeah, she's not, but I don't chase any type of bitch. I don't chase regular ones, special ones, handicapped ones—the list goes on. The moral of the fucking story is Truman don't chase no damn bitches."

Anton and I burst into laughter, and I even heard Khyle snicker. Truman was a fucking hand full for sure.

"So if she gets a new nigga, then what?" I looked to him.

"She won't. I got that lock on Pilar," he responded, lighting up a blunt. I watched Khyle open the sliding doors to ventilate my crib, before going back into the kitchen.

"A lock?" Anton frowned.

"Yes, nigga. You don't know shit about that lock yet, but Oden does. See, no matter what, Khyle ain't gonna leave him. Same goes for Pilar. Anton, you need to get a lock on that sexy one with them eyes, and stop knocking up the wrong ones."

I looked to Khyle to see if she'd heard, and I think she did because she was looking at us out the corner of her eye as she chopped something up.

I knew what Truman was saying, and I agreed to a certain extent. I knew Khyle would rock with me through thick and thin, but I damn sure knew that she would leave me if I fucked around on her, especially as much as Truman did on Pilar.

"I got Tasmine, don't trip. I just have to work out some kinks."

"She know about that strip—"

I ran my hand across my neck to let Truman know that Khyle could hear. I didn't want her feeling like she had to run and tell Tasmine about Anton's affairs.

"So everything is still straight with the shops, right?" I asked, promptly changing the subject. I could sense Khyle was getting uncomfortable with our previous one.

"Yeah, man, shit is even better. Ryan's ass got four cars shipped out last night," Truman grinned and so did Anton.

I had to sit up upon hearing that, because Ryan was the slowest nigga I had. For him to be getting four cars out, which was two more than expected, had me astonished to say the least.

"Ryan?' I bucked my eyes and they both nodded. "Shit, well maybe now that I'm back and better, he will get six cars out." We chuckled in unison.

This Christmas was gonna be fruitful as fuck.

CHAPTER ONE

Truman Morrison

Wanna show you how much I value what you say. Not only are you loyal, you're patient with me babe, oh, yes. Wanna show you how much I really care about your heart. Wanna show you how much I hate being apart, oh, yes.

Beyoncé's voice blasted over the private dance room I was in with that same chick Chiina I'd been smashing on the regular. She was pretty as hell, so was her body, and her pussy was even better. I knew I should have been out trying to get my girl back, but my pride was overwhelming right now. I did wrong, but I wanted Pilar to be the one to come back, to show that I was still in charge.

Today made two weeks since her ass had been gone, and she hadn't tried to hit me up or anything. At first I was cool because I spent my time working and smashing bitches by nightfall, but damn was that getting old. I missed my pussy, and having conversations with my bitch after she cooked for me.

"What's up with you?" Chiina straddled my lap, hooking my chin with her finger.

"Nothing. Why you stop dancing?"

"Because you weren't paying attention to me. You know I don't like when you don't give me all of your attention, Tru."

"My bad, baby." I groped her thick thighs as she pressed her pussy down onto my crotch.

"I can make you feel better," she giggled and got down onto the plush carpet. She reached for my zipper, and at first I was all for it, but I soon changed my mind.

"You good. Go out there and make your money. I'll talk to you later, Chiina."

"Okay." She rose to her feet with me, and I hugged her tightly into my arms. When I pulled away, she leaned her head back for a kiss, and I gave her a nice one.

Chiina was a stripper but she was one of the good ones. She was in college studying business, and stripping was her way of making ends meet. When I first met her, I thought she was just some hoe looking to come up off of the club owner, but when I got to know her I realized that she just liked a nigga. She was cool to chill and talk with, and when she ran across hard times, I would break her off here and there. I treated her a little better—no—much better than my other jump offs because them birds got no cash from me.

"Are you gonna call me for real, Tru? You always tell me you will but then I don't hear from you for days."

"I am baby, relax." I kissed her deeply one more time, making her pretty smile appear as she hugged my torso. The way she looked into my eyes let me know she had some deep-rooted feelings for me.

She knew about Pilar but she didn't. She thought Pilar was my ex that I wasn't sure I wanted to get back with. Yes, I told her this even before Pilar and I broke up. She was cool with letting me figure shit out, or at least that was what she told me.

I left out of Palace and once I got down into my car, I pulled out my iPhone to dial Pilar. That little devil on my shoulder was telling me to hang the fuck up and go back inside with Chiina, but my heart was telling me otherwise. I didn't love these hoes, but I loved Pilar.

"Yes," she answered, and I could tell she'd been crying but was attempting to mask it before picking up.

"You were crying, baby?"

"No." Her response was short, and only a few moments later she broke down.

"Pilar, where are you? I wanna come see you so that we can talk."

There was silence for a bit before she finally responded.

"I'm at my job, the Bellagio."

"Text me the room number, I'm on my way. And quit crying, baby. You know a nigga is crazy about you, aight?"

"Yeah," she sniffled.

"I love you, P."

"I love you too, Truman."

I hung up and a few seconds later, her text came through with the details. I turned up the Nipsey Hussle album I was listening to, and peeled out of the Palace parking lot, headed towards the Bellagio on the strip. When I got there, I gave my shit to valet, and then went inside to head up to the room number she'd texted me.

When I arrived, I knocked lightly, checking my lips in my phone to make sure Chiina hadn't left any remnants of her lipstick on me.

"Hey," Pilar opened the door.

She was wearing some shorts and one of them short tops with no straps attached. Her long hair was wrapped up into a donut thing on top of her head. She didn't have any makeup on, but my bitch was bad even without it.

"Sup," I leaned down to kiss her but she turned away, before backing up to let me into the room. "Damn, already?"

"Truman, stop. I know you didn't think you'd be able to just waltz in here and fuck me. Please tell me that's not what you're thinking."

"Aight, what's up? How can we fix this? How can *I* fix this?" I sat down on the bed. This room was nice as hell. I'd never been in this particular hotel, because I preferred staying in the Venetian or Caesar's Palace.

"First of all, I wanna know who the girl was that was all over you." She folded her arms, poking her hip out. My eyes trailed her sexy frame as I slowly glided my tongue over my lips. "Truman!" she snapped her fingers in my face.

"I don't fucking remember her name like that! Them bitches don't mean shit to me, Pilar! I told you that!" I was lying like fuck, because the girl at the party was Chiina.

"So you just put your mouth on random bitches all the time? Then put that same mouth on me?"

"I was under the influence, and the shit just happened, baby, I swear. Have I ever cheated on you in the past?" I pulled her down into my lap.

"No, but you looked so comfortable doing so it was like you do it all the time. And the way she was hugging you—"

"Pilar, stop. Now you're analyzing hugs? I don't know that girl from a can of paint, baby, and what I did with her was a mistake. I love you and I'm sorry for not coming to talk to you sooner. I felt like I didn't do anything wrong, and expected you to come back, but I apologize." I laid it on thick as fuck.

I mean, 85% of what I was saying to her was true. I did love her, and I did regret not coming to talk sooner, but I knew Chiina very well.

"Truman, I'm not the type of girl to forgive easily, but I know you and I trust that this was a mistake. However, if this happens again, I want you to let me go."

"I will, but it won't happen again so let's not even talk about that, Pilar." I rubbed her sexy thighs. "Who sent you that shit, anyway? The pictures and video of me?"

"Came from some burner number, probably using one of those apps," she shrugged.

I squinted my eyes, trying to remember who was all at my party, and who would have done some shit like that. It was definitely the work of some jealous ass bitch, but I'd have to muddle over that shit another time. Right now, I was horny for my girl.

I kissed Pilar's collarbone softly, while tugging her top down to expose her breasts. Once they were out, I cupped them and laid her on her back while sucking her nipples hungrily. She let out soft coos and moans every now and then, as I had my way with her. Reaching my hand down into her shorts and panties, I plunged my fingers into her, making her gasp and grip my arms.

"Truuuu," she whimpered, spreading her legs for me.

I sucked her nipples harder while finger fucking her feverishly. She was soaking my fingers more and more every time I slid them into her, and the feeling alone got my dick hard. Popping my mouth off of her nipple, I trailed my lips down her smooth caramel skin until I reached her waistline. Gripping her shorts and panties, I yanked them down and threw them to the side. I roughly pressed her legs into her stomach and latched my mouth onto her clit, sucking the life out of her. She was slippery wet already, and I enjoyed the taste of her when she was like that.

Allowing my tongue to dip into her hole every now and again, I brought it back up and collapsed my lips around her clit to continue to suck. I then entered her using my fingers, and began attacking her middle with both my mouth and hands. You could hear how wet she was. I loved how drenched her pussy got for a nigga.

"Ahh!" she screeched as she came, causing her body to violently shake.

Standing up, I slipped out of my clothes as she watched me, panting. Once I was naked, I flipped her onto all fours, and secured a condom on my dick. I didn't like to fuck raw, because with raw sex came babies, and I was in no position to be anybody's daddy. I had too much shit to do, too much life to live. Maybe one day though.

"Shit," I growled as I entered her.

I started off slow, allowing her body to get used to me. I was skinny, but you know what they say about us skinny niggas. I was not packed lightly down below, and I was proud of it. Being hung kept these bitches hooked on ya boy, and I wasn't complaining.

Once she released her juices from that slow shit, I started slamming into her. Smacking her ass so hard that I left a handprint, I spread her cheeks so that I could see myself ramming her shit. Her nice round ass was moving about as I pounded her from behind, slapping her ass and biting her back. Pilar loved that pleasure and plain shit, and so did I.

"I'm gonna cum, Tru!" she yelled out, placing her palm flat against the bed.

"Me too baby, damn."

I wrapped her hair around my hand, and pummeled her until she came again and I filled up the condom.

"Don't you ever keep that pussy away from me for that long, Pilar," I panted, rubbing my hands up and down her smooth back.

I slid out of her, and then turned her onto her back so we could kiss. I needed to get back on my 007 shit if I wanted to keep my girl and have my lifestyle. I got lazy with it for a second, and got caught slipping. Never again though.

CHAPTER TWO

$\mathcal{I}$ was finally back in California with my family for Christmas break. Half of the time I planned to spend here with my family had been spent over in Vegas with Oden. I knew he didn't need me per se, but I wanted to be there for him while he was ill. Also, I just loved being around him, so any excuse I found to do so, I was gonna use.

My mom needed me to get some things from Target like eggnog, a tree blanket, and some new Christmas mugs, so currently that's where I was. As I pushed the cart through the store, admiring other things I didn't need, my phone buzzed. I looked down to see it was Oden, and the biggest smile crossed my face. I loved that he hit me up all the time. Opening the text, I saw it was a picture of the bulge in his sweats.

Baby: *He misses you.*

The caption read.

Me: *I miss him too. I will be back to him soon enough.*

I was still sore from the bedroom beat down he'd given me two nights ago, but I was always willing to get some from Oden. He'd completely changed sex for me. It was a task that I thought women only participated in to please their partners and procreate. But now, I was in it for the pleasure just as much as Oden. One thing that did stay the same was the emotional aspect I got from it. Every time he and I slept together, I felt this closeness to him.

Baby: *I wanna be inside you so bad right now. Send me a picture of it.*

Me: *Oden no, and I'm not at home.*

Baby: *When you get home, FaceTime me. Be naked, and I want it to be the FIRST thing I see.*

Me: *Okay nasty.*

I placed my phone back into my purse, and continued to pick out some mugs that I thought were cute. As I was doing so, I heard the laughter of some girls. I ignored it at first, but when it got louder, I looked to my right to see Jacqueline, the bitch I told Brian to stay away from.

"Oh hey, Khyle. I thought you left the state for school," she cocked her head.

Jacqueline had been a hoe since I first met her, and that was back in sixth grade. I remember she got caught in the bathroom letting these boys finger her at that time. She was always popular from middle school all the way up until high school, but there was a reason for that. She was the hoe popular, and I was the regular popular. No one preferred the former, but Jacqueline seemed to love that her pussy was friendly. On top of her being a whore, she was really pretty, with her smooth dark skin, long curly hair, and curvy frame. She was a nigga's dream: beautiful and an easy lay.

"I did, but there is this thing called Christmas break, where school is out and you get to come home. It's really nice. Maybe if you had chosen to do something with your life, you'd know what I was talking about."

"No need to get upset, boo. You have a new man, so you shouldn't be mad at me over Brian." She toyed with her necklace. I couldn't quite make out what it read.

"Ain't nobody worried about Brian. If I was, I wouldn't have broken up with him."

"Damn, you sure did break up with him. I was in his bed that night, and I made him feel much better about it."

My brows dipped as I listened to her. That nigga had her in his bed that night? What if I hadn't decided to break it off with Brian? I would have been getting played. I mean, yeah, I was kind of doing the same thing to him, but what if I wasn't? For all he knew we were good, yet he had this skank in his bed, and at that time of night?

"Well, I'm happy for you guys, Jacqueline. Brian isn't really a prize."

"Hmm, he isn't? I have a future doctor for a boyfriend, and umm, what is your little boo?" she fake pouted.

"Fine as fuck," her homegirl jumped in, making me wonder how she knew what my nigga looked like. She stuck her phone out so that Jacqueline could look on it.

"Damn, he is fine. Better hope I don't make a trip to Vegas because I wouldn't mind seeing what that dick is like."

"Bitch, you couldn't fuck my nigga if you paid him. Only niggas that want that bottom of the barrel ass pussy are thirsty ass niggas like Brian."

I bumped her shoulder as I walked past her, making my way to the food area. I prayed that she tried to retaliate because I hadn't beaten a bitch's ass in almost a year.

I got everything I needed and funny enough, as I was checking out, I saw Jacqueline's whack ass in the line next to me. I turned my back to her so that I wouldn't even pay her any mind. I had a new man, so I wasn't about to be in here fighting over Brian, but if she touched me it was on. I wanted to enjoy the time I spent out here in my hometown for Christmas, and as enjoyable as delivering an ass whooping would be, it wasn't on the agenda.

After leaving Target, I stopped by Starbucks to get drinks for my sister, my mother, and myself. My dad didn't drink lattes, coffee, or tea of any kind, so he always declined. I smiled as I thought about that. I missed the little things about my family, shit that I wouldn't think twice about usually.

When I pulled into my parents' huge driveway, I texted my mom so that she'd tell my dad I needed help. He never answered his phone, and if he did, it would be hours later. As I waited, sipping my pumpkin spiced latte, I saw the front door open and Brian appear. He was smiling and talking with my father as they approached the car. I was so stuck on seeing him, that I didn't realize my father was waiting for me to open the trunk.

"Sorry," I said, getting out of the car after my dad knocked on the trunk of his Mercedes.

"Sup," Brian smirked, draping his arm around my shoulders to pull me into a hug. I was literally frozen so I couldn't reciprocate.

Brian helped my dad get all the groceries, and I grabbed the tray of drinks to bring them inside, still perplexed. I couldn't believe my parents had allowed Brian to come over, knowing Oden was my boyfriend. Had they lost their fucking minds?

I waited until Brian left the kitchen, and once he did, I pulled the divider closed and turned to glare at my mom who was preparing chicken, and then at my dad who was mixing up some kind of drink.

"Why the screw face?" Shayne quizzed, shoving a cookie into her mouth.

"Really, Mom? Dad? Why is he here?" I whispered, checking over my shoulder as if I'd be able to see Brian.

"He just came over looking for you, and what was I supposed to say, Khyle?" my mom responded as she heavily seasoned the chicken.

"Uh, how about 'she's not here, come back another time'? Anything to get him to go home."

"Khyle, we've gotten close to Brian so even though you two are no longer, that doesn't give us the right to be an ass to the kid. Now, that also doesn't mean I think you made a bad choice, because like I said, he's a bit of a weasel, but the kid is okay and I can't be rude," my father explained.

I just nodded, and glanced at Shayne who shrugged, while chewing on her cookie.

Exiting the kitchen, I spotted Brian in the living room watching television. He was texting on his phone, and by the look on his face, the conversation was intense.

"What are you doing, Brian?"

"Watching this old football game," he chuckled lightly.

"No, what are you doing *here?* Why would you be coming to see me? Shouldn't you be spending time with Jacqueline?"

"I came to see you because I miss you, Khyle. Everybody ain't like you, baby. They can't just move on and forget people."

"I haven't forgotten you, Brian." He made me feel bad for a moment. "I told you it just happened and—"

"And you didn't expect it. Yeah, I don' heard that rehearsed ass story enough times, Khyle." He shook his head. "Forgive me if I'm having a hard time letting our three-year relationship go."

"Brian, don't act innocent. I know you've been hanging out with Jacqueline."

"Hanging out, not fucking her and trying to be in a relationship with her."

"Oh really? Then why was she in your bed with you when I called you to break up? Don't even try to deny it because I heard her in the background," I lied to see if he'd admit it.

"She wasn't in my bed, she umm, she was in my room because she needed my notes for that class we have together," he spoke with his eyes staring at the TV, making it obvious he was lying. He always looked at something else when he wasn't telling the truth.

"At 2am, she came to your house to get some class notes? And what class do you have with Jacqueline?" I smiled, slightly finding amusement in this horrible lie.

"Art… class."

I couldn't help it, so I began laughing at this nigga.

"So wait, you have an art class with Jacqueline that is so difficult that she would need to borrow your notes at two in the morning, Brian? Do you hear yourself?"

"Khyle—"

WHAM!

I slapped the back of his head hard as fuck.

"How long have you been sleeping with that bitch, Brian?"

Rubbing the back of his head, he started to lie again, but I smacked his ass a second time so he'd know I wasn't fucking around. I only cared because I knew he was fucking her before I even went to Vegas, but I wanted to hear him say it. If I'd never met Oden, I'd still be with this lying ass nigga.

"Aight! Aight! I just started fucking her like a week before you broke up with me. Before that, she'd given me head here and there, but nothing else because I didn't need it. And since you said you didn't like giving me head, I thought you wouldn't mind— ah! Khyle, stop!" he screamed, once I punched his arm hard as fuck, repeatedly.

"What the hell is going on in here?" my dad entered the living room.

"Come on!" I yanked Brian up by his skinny arm and started towards the back of the house.

"Khyle, you cannot go into your bedroom with him alone, you know that," my dad called after me.

"We're going to the den, Dad."

He nodded and watched us for a little bit to make sure.

"You thought I wouldn't care?" I questioned Brian as soon as we'd gotten into the den. "So what if I didn't like giving head, that's no reason to cheat!"

"Baby, I'm sorry. It only happened a couple times. And I ended up fucking her because I'd been without it for so long. You were in Vegas, and then when I came to visit you, you were on your period so I couldn't get any."

"You're a little ass boy, Brian. Seriously. Is that all you think about? Sex and head?"

"No, and you know that, but I have needs, Khyle. And at the moment, you weren't there to fulfill them."

"Disgusting," I scoffed, shaking my head while staring at the big beautiful piano in the den.

"You honestly think your little Vegas gang banger isn't fucking another bitch while you're out here right now?"

"He's not."

"Woooow!" Brian burst into laughter. "That nigga got yo' head all the way fucked up, huh? You honestly think that nigga can go without sex the whole time you're here, Khyle?"

"We do other things, like FaceTime naked—you know what, why am I explaining myself to you? I know my man, and he is not doing anything."

"I bet you thought you knew me too, huh?" Brian grinned, before kissing my forehead and leaving out.

I watched him, unsure of what to think about what had just gone down. For some reason, I felt like he'd won that argument, and I didn't like that at all.

CHAPTER TWO

Shayne Luke

Lloyd and I had been chilling heavily ever since our date. I'd never had such good dick and conversation to match in my life. I felt like I was in love with that nigga already, but I knew it was just because it was new. I was kind of starting to want a relationship with him, but I wasn't too sure if he was on that tip as well. I hadn't seen him mention another girl or anything, so shit, maybe he was trying to lock me down. What I was sure about though was that I needed to end things with Pierce's ass.

Pierce tried to come back to Los Angeles for Christmas with me, but I told him my parents felt like they were losing me and wanted my sister and me to themselves for a while. Of course, he bitched and moaned, so I agreed to let him spend Christmas Eve and Day with the family. I rolled my eyes as I thought about it, while sitting in the kitchen with my mom and sister. And since my dad left out to go chill by the fireplace while listening to jazz music, I wanted to use this time for some girl talk.

"So, remember the guy I told you about?" I questioned the room.

I'd already mentioned him to Khyle, but she didn't know as much as my mother. They were both like my best friends, but after embarrassing myself in front of Khyle with Oden, I wanted to be sure Lloyd was the real deal before boasting about him.

"Lloyd?" my mother smiled before dropping a few pieces of chicken into the skillet to fry.

"Lloyd? Who is Lloyd?" Khyle cocked her head.

I sipped my latte to hide the smile that wanted to burst through. It did nothing to help though, because as soon as I set it down I was grinning.

"The guy I mentioned when we came home for Mom and Dad's anniversary party. Anyway, I think I'm gonna break it off with Pierce. Lloyd and I are getting pretty serious."

"Serious how?" Khyle sat back, folding her arms across her chest. I knew she was suspicious because of my behavior with Oden, but this was not the same case.

"So serious that he's coming down here tonight to see me, and is gonna stay for the rest of the week. He said he has some time off."

"Wow, can we meet him?" my mother quizzed.

"No, not until I break it off with Pierce. I don't want Daddy embarrassing me and saying some shit in front of Lloyd."

"Well, honey, I thought you said Lloyd knows about Pierce and is okay with the situation." My mom threw her kitchen towel over her shoulder, before placing the piping hot fried chicken into a basket like always. My stomach grumbled at the smell.

"And he is okay with it, but he won't be okay with Daddy running his mouth about Pierce and I all night. So, once I get that situation squared away, I will bring him by as my new man. Like Khyle did with Oden." I looked at my sister who was blushing at the sound her boyfriend's name. I admit it was still hard to believe that thee Oden Bishop was my little sister's man.

"Oden, that was a really nice boy. He reminded me a lot of your father when he was young. James is still like him, but he's calmed down a lot," my mom smiled as she reminisced.

I admired my parents' marriage because it was so obvious how in love they were. My dad treated my mom like she was the greatest thing in the world, and my mom treated him the same in return. I wanted that someday, and hopefully I would get it with Lloyd.

"Well, I hope Oden will put a ring on it like Dad did," Khyle chuckled, and so did I.

"He will. You have my DNA, Khyle, and that's all you need to be able to get a husband. These guys can't resist us," my mom joked, making the three of us laugh in unison.

We continued to converse with one another until dinner was ready, then the four of us ate together after I fetched my dad from the den. Afterwards, I ran a nice hot bubble bath, and soaked good in this new bath milk that made my skin soft. I wanted to be perfect for Lloyd tonight.

By the time I'd finished bathing and spreading lotion all over my body, my phone was jumping back to back. I smiled, knowing exactly who it was. I was bummed when I grabbed my phone though, because

I saw there were just texts from Alanna, Marisol, Pierce, and a funny meme from Khyle. Plopping down onto my bed, I decided to go ahead and ring Lloyd to see if he was out here and settled yet.

I called him three times but I got no answer, so I just slipped into my nightshirt and got under the warm covers in my big bed. I texted while lying down, with Alanna, Marisol, and Pierce until around midnight, when I fell asleep. I hated when Lloyd did stuff like this.

An hour later...

"What the fuck," I grumbled, patting the bed for my ringing phone. When I located it, I picked it up to see Lloyd's name. "Hello?"

"Heyyyy, baby, I hope you weren't sleep."

"Are you joking? It's…" I glanced at the time on my phone before putting it back to my ear. "…It's 1:23am, Lloyd, of course I'm sleep."

"You mad, shawty?" he inquired in a low sexy tone, his southern accent apparent as hell. I'd grown to love that shit.

"Kind of, yeah."

"I'm sorry. Can you come through and see me or what?"

"Tonight?"

"Yep."

Sighing, I asked, "Where are you?"

"At the Montage, on Canon Drive."

"In Beverly Hills?" I sat up, throwing my warm comforter to the side so I could climb out of my huge bed.

"I believe so, yeah."

"You better be happy I live in Beverly Hills, nigga, or you wouldn't be seeing no fucking body tonight," I ranted, pulling a few items out of my drawers and stuffing it into my new Gucci bag my father got me.

"Right," he chuckled. "Text me when you get here, baby."

I hung up the phone and then went into the bathroom within my room to brush my teeth. Once I was finished, I changed into a tube dress, despite it being nippy outside, and then grabbed my jacket and sneakers before leaving.

I made it to the Montage Hotel in no time since the streets were pretty clear, and after texting this nigga, he came all the way down and outside to get me.

"You could have just given me the room number," I said once we got onto the elevator.

"I know, but I wanted to come get you, make sure you were good."

"Thanks."

We got to his huge ass room… no, this shit was an apartment, not a damn room. I was a bit taken aback because I knew he had a little bread but damn, this nigga was doing it big like he was a drug dealer or some shit.

"Damn, Lloyd."

"I know, I said the same shit. I used my boys' travel agent and this is what she booked me. Oden told me she only dealt with nice shit so I was prepared to blow some bread. And since I'm gonna be here a week, I thought why not."

"You damn right why not."

I dropped my purse in the living room and started looking around with him following me. I was in love with this shit. I planned to lay up with him in it until Pierce came out here too.

"Want some?" Lloyd held up a bottle of champagne when we got back into the bedroom portion. I nodded my head, still smiling and taking in the scenery.

He poured the drink into the glasses, and then handed me one. I took a sip and just closed my eyes to enjoy how smoothly it went down. I could taste how expensive this shit was.

See, this was the life I was supposed to be living, not that bum shit Pierce was on. He could find another bitch to struggle with because I had every intention on experiencing the good life with Lloyd Gardener.

"Be right back. Be naked when I return." Lloyd kissed my cheek and hit the lamp. I stared out at the balcony, and just giggled with excitement.

"Ooh!" I jumped when I felt something vibrate.

I scanned the bed, and then finally spotted Lloyd's iPhone going ape shit. I looked towards the direction he'd gone, before finishing what was in my glass and setting it on the nightstand next to me. Grabbing the phone near the foot of the bed, I pressed the home button to see Lloyd was a very popular guy. There were so many notifications on his home screen that you could scroll for 10 minutes straight. After seeing random shit from Instagram, to text messages, Snapchat, and phone calls, I scrolled back up to the top to see who was hitting him up this late.

"Elodie, huh?" I mumbled, and slid my thumb across his screen to see if I could guess his passcode. To my surprise, the phone just opened, so he didn't have a lock code.

I immediately tapped the text-messaging app. When I did, I saw he had 150 unread texts, but right now I was interested in what Elodie had to say. Checking to make sure Lloyd wasn't on his way back yet, I hit their conversation thread to read.

Elodie: How long are we gonna be apart Lloyd? You can't just come to Birmingham, fuck me, and expect me to not think we're getting back together.

Elodie: Hello nigga?

Elodie: Lloyd, please… I can't even sleep.

"Fuck you doing!" Lloyd snatched his phone from me, face balled up like a fist. I was speechless after reading what Elodie had to say.

"Who is that?" I whispered, feeling pain from my heart all the way down to the pit of my stomach. Whomever she was, she was someone that loved him and I didn't like that. He never mentioned anybody special when we had our conversations.

"She ain't no fucking body." He climbed into the bed after removing his boxers. "I thought I told you to be naked, Shayne."

"You went to Birmingham a week and a half ago, is that when you fucked her?" I was still speaking lowly and slowly because it was the only way I could keep my voice from shaking. I clearly liked him more than I thought.

"Shayne, you live with a whole 'nother nigga, do you really think you can question me?" he spoke sternly, as he slowly turned his head to face me. His dark skin was so smooth, going perfectly with his scruffy but neatly trimmed beard. I watched him in awe as he scratched his short curly hair and exhaled.

"I don't want to be with him and you know that, Lloyd."

"So what? The point is that you live with him, and I'm sure you're fucking him, so please don't question me. You and I are friends and that's it, shawty! And don't interrogate me ever again while you're currently going home to another nigga every night!"

Because he was right, I had nothing to say. I just got off the bed to change into my short nightgown, before tying my hair up and getting under the covers. Lloyd watched me the whole time. I just turned my back to him once I was in the bed, and stared straight ahead.

I heard him moving around, until finally he was pressed up against me. His hands ran up my thigh while he kissed on the nape of my neck. Once he reached the waistband of my thong, he pulled it down slowly while sucking on my neck like a vampire.

"Move, Lloyd," I moaned once he started to run his fingers across my pussy from behind.

"Don't be mad, Shayne. I'm here when you want me, it's your call."

"Lloyd— ah!" I gasped once he lifted my leg and thrust into me. He gripped my breasts through my nightgown as he pushed himself further inside of my body. It was so thick and long.

"I'm here when you want me," he repeated, dipping his hand between my legs to play with my clit.

He continued to hump me from behind while stroking my button gently, and before I knew it I was cumming. He lifted my left leg, which was on top, for more access, and then started slamming into me, forcing me to cry out while gripping the sheets.

"Fuck," he grunted against my ear as he pounded me feverishly. "You know your pussy is good, that's why you act like that. Fuck!" he grumbled again, moving in and out of me with precision.

I was too busy exploding again to answer.

A few moments later, we both sang our cries in unison from releasing. He slowly pulled out of me, and touched my pussy from behind to see how wet I was. Flipping me onto my back, he dipped down under the covers and began sucking my center like his life depended on it.

I knew exactly why Elodie was blowing him up; she'd been dickmatized just like me.

CHAPTER TWO

Oden

Money don't talk, it just look good. Put me in a suit and tie, still I look hood. Designer hoes, Atlanta hoes. Couple bougie bitches from the west coast…

Anton, Truman, and I sat in the VIP of the underground strip club of Palace, watching about five girls dance to "Giuseppe" by DJ Mustard. There was so much damn money on the floor it was ridiculous. Me and my niggas were acting out for the Christmas season. We had bottles, weed, and plenty stacks of money. This was how we celebrated Christmas because none of us really had family like that to actually celebrate or party with.

Anton had his mom but not only was she sick with HIV and sluggish, but he felt like she was back on drugs and didn't want to deal with her. A part of me felt like she got the disease from drugs and not from Anton's father, but I would never say that aloud. I mean his dad was smashing prostitutes while his mother was out binging on drugs with my mom, so who knows.

Truman only had his dad, who was just a bitter old nigga that despised his son because Truman's mother died during childbirth. As for me, I didn't have anybody and it had been that way ever since my grandfather died. And even though I had Khyle now, she was in Los Angeles with her people.

As I stared the women down, allowing the liquor and weed to sink into my system, one of the ladies working the club named Cara knocked on the door. I waved for her to come in, and she smiled shyly as she neared me. I was gone as hell, so all I could offer was a lazy smile back to her.

"Mr. Bishop, there is a man out front claiming that he's your father."

"What?" I sat up, feeling like I was sober all of a sudden.

"Yes, he said his name is Ossie Bishop." She glanced down at a piece of paper in her hand before making eye contact with me again.

I closed my eyes and looked at one of the girls dancing hard with her eyes on me. I wasn't even looking at her really, more like through her, as my mind processed all kinds of thoughts. That was definitely my pops out there; one, because that was his name and no one knew it, and secondly, because he always came around during this time.

"Mr. Bishop?" Cara got my attention.

"Uh, yeah, I'll be out there in a second, Cara. Make sure I have someone to escort me through the front," I responded, exhaling heavily.

Since opening this club, I realized bitches were way too touchy and bold. I learned the hard way when I decided to walk through the club floor just to peep the scene, causing an army of females to swarm around me. I had to pull my gun out in order to break free and get back to my damn office. So now, it was pivotal that I had someone escort me if I was going to be walking through the club. I for real understood what celebrities went through.

"You good?" Truman tapped my chest lightly.

"Yeah, yeah, I'm straight. I'll be right back, I'm gonna use the restroom."

"Nigga, it's one right there," Anton pointed to the one located in this particular section.

We had different VIP rooms with different price points. This one we were currently in was the Kingdom VIP, which ran for seven grand on the weekends, and four grand on the weekdays or during day parties.

"I prefer the one in my office because it's mine."

I left out and met up with Scott, the guy who was going to get me down to my dad. We made it through the front with ease, and once I spotted Cara, I saw that nigga, Ossie. I waved him towards me so he could come over to the side of the club so it wouldn't bring so much attention. People in line were already calling my name like they knew me, and I wasn't in the damn mood.

"Son," Ossie slurred and stumbled up to me. I gripped his bicep and yanked him around the corner, making him fly into the side of the wall.

"Fuck you doing here, man?" I gritted as if I didn't know why he was here.

"Oden, it's Christmas time and umm, I was wondering if you had a gift for your old man."

"Yeah, but you got mine?"

"I did, I did, I swear I did, but umm, Sherry, you remember Sherry, right? Well, she had it last and I looked and looked before I came here—"

"How much you need?" I tucked my lips in, attempting to hold in my anger. I didn't understand why I loved this nigga.

"You own this place, huh?" He tilted his head back to take it all in before looking back into my face.

"Yeah, along with Tony and Tru."

"Looks like it's doing pretty well. So umm, I just need $2,000 to get myself back on track. You know I'm trying to get this monkey off my back and umm, that costs money." He licked his extremely dry lips.

I chuckled angrily before reaching into my pocket for a knot of cash. Double-checking my surroundings, I began to peel off some money before pressing it into his hand.

My father was a good dude growing up, had a basketball scholarship to UNLV and everything. I still have the newspaper clippings my grandfather showed me of him, and to say he was going to be great was an understatement. That was until he met my mother, Staci, a wild girl who was into all kinds of shit, but beautiful as hell. My dad became so wrapped up in her and what she liked to do, that eventually he was doing drugs just like her, lost his scholarship, and got kicked out of school for the drug use.

Granted, when my mother met him she was an occasional user,

but somehow them coming together turned them both into full-blown drug addicts. My mom stopped long enough to carry and deliver me, only because of my grandfather, but then resumed doing drugs five months after I was born.

My mother died, getting high with Anton's mother one night, and my dad kind of fell into a dark hole after that. I mean, he'd always been a druggie, but he'd always been better than her until she left the Earth.

Now he was nothing but a bum who slept outside, and only visited his son around wintertime for some cash. I'd tried helping him, but it always backfired. Either he would relapse as soon as he left rehab, or he would betray me in ways that were unforgivable. All in all, I just couldn't deal with him closely anymore. However, I hated to see him suffer, so when he asked me for money I gave it to him.

"Thanks, and once I get it together, I'm gonna pay you back," Ossie snapped me from my thoughts.

"I know," I nodded as if I believed him.

We stared at one another for a few moments, and for a second, I actually saw someone genuine who wanted to be a good man. A tear slipped from his eye, but he just laughed it off. Without another word, we walked away from one another.

That encounter fucked up my whole damn mood, and I didn't feel like I'd had any weed or liquor, even though I'd had plenty. As Scott escorted me back to my closed off section with my boys, I powered my phone off. For two hours straight, Anton, Truman, and I got twisted as hell, partying with the strippers, and when it was time to go, I had to call my driver. I didn't drive tonight because we'd all planned to get hammered in the first place. But thank God we were all going to the hoe crib, so there wouldn't be multiple trips.

"Nigga, didn't you just get out of the doghouse with Pilar?" Anton smirked at Truman as Truman kissed on and finger banged some bitch in the Escalade limo.

Anton had his arm draped around Amethyst, and Ice aka Keesha, was kissing all over my neck. I was gonna tell her to stop, but I was super close to blacking out, so saying anything sounded exhausting. All I did was move away from her occasionally.

"Nigga, what about that pretty eyed bitch you're fucking with?" Truman sneered, removing his hand from the girl's pants.

"She's not my girl yet, but when she becomes my girl, best believe I'm gonna be Heathcliff Huxtable in this bitch," Anton joked, making us laugh. I believed him too, because whatever shorty did to him had him on her ass tough. I caught Amethyst looking a little bothered by Anton's words.

"Hey," Keesha cupped my chin and turned me to face her.

"Hey," I responded, biting down on my lip. I was never getting this drunk and high in my life again. A nigga felt like he needed a wheelchair.

During the rest of the ride, the six of us chilled and made conversation. Finally, we made it to the hoe crib, and Keesha was damn near pulling me out of the car.

"Damn, wait," I slurred, stopping to pick my iPhone up since I'd dropped it. I powered it on, and stuffed it into my pocket before it booted back up all the way.

Truman used his key to get in, and the six of us went our separate ways into the rooms we usually used. Keesha raced to the back, with my wrist clutched tightly in her hands, and once we got into the bedroom, she pushed me into the chair and closed the door, locking it. I let my head fall back against the plush ass chair, as she rubbed her hands up and down my lap.

"I missed you, Oden."

"Yeah?" I spoke with my eyes closed, head still tilted back against the chair. I couldn't even keep the shits open so I gave up.

"Hell yeah."

"Yo, you gotta go, Keesha," I slurred.

I listened as she unbuckled my pants, and jumped a little once her hand reached down into my boxers to grab my dick. I chuckled a little because I could hear either Anton or Truman fucking the shit out of one them hoes already. The girl was crying out, and the headboard was banging the wall.

"I don't wanna leave O—"

"Please, shorty." I pushed her hands lightly. She finally let go, and sat back on the carpet. "Now leave, I'm tired and you know I'm married." I stuffed my dick back into my boxers, and let my head fall back. Married? Yeah, I was gone.

"Okay," she mumbled.

There was silence for a little bit as I started to drift off to sleep in the comfy La-Z-Boy.

Suddenly, I felt Keesha trying to reach for my dick again, as my phone began buzzing in my pocket. I pulled it out to just glance, and almost jumped out of my skin when I saw Khyle's name. Answer it? Don't answer it? I ain't know what the fuck to do.

"Move, move," I nudged Keesha off of me and stood up, fixing myself. "Don't say a got damn word. Told yo' ass to go," I said, teeth clenched as I answered the phone. "Khyle," I panted.

"Why are you out of breath?"

"I uh, heard my phone ringing so I ran to get it. What you doing up this late, baby? I miss you." My fucking sentences weren't even making sense right now. "Go!" I mouthed to Keesha and pointed to the door.

"What?" Keesha whispered, twisting her face up.

"The fuck out of here!" I shouted but in a low tone, waving wildly towards the door.

Keesha sucked her teeth and got up to leave angrily. I locked the door just in case, and then climbed on top of the bed.

"Ahh! Oh fuck!" one of the girls that either Truman or Anton were fucking screamed out.

"What the hell is that, Oden?" Khyle quizzed.

"Nothing. What you doing up so late? You better not have been out giving my pussy away." I was trying my hardest to sound sober even though I was ready to black out.

"Of course not, Oden," she giggled. "I'm in my bedroom. I missed you so I thought I'd call you all late like you be doing me when you can't sleep."

I just chuckled at her, and let my head fall against the pillow as we continued our conversation.

I didn't do anything, but oddly I still felt scared as fuck that Khyle would think I did. I didn't have any more strikes to get, so if she thought I cheated she would leave my ass for real. I wasn't trying to lose my baby when I didn't even do anything. I just needed to relax.

CHAPTER TWO

Tasmine Randall

Christmas Eve…

It was Christmas Eve, so my parents' home was completely covered in Christmas lights, with big ass blown up snowmen and Santa Clauses in the yard. It was snowing, but it looked nothing like the movies you see on ABC Family. The snow here in Louisville wasn't very much, and it was even a little disgusting in my opinion. I wished we lived somewhere, where the snow piled up and looked all pretty and white like in the films.

Currently, my sister, Tasia, cousin, Mia, my parents and I, were all sitting in our living room with the huge Christmas tree. There were so many lights and ornaments that I was getting a damn headache, but I would be lying if I said I didn't enjoy the Christmas season and all its extravagance. And I was happy to be home with my family after spending Thanksgiving in Vegas, even though my Thanksgiving was the shit. I sighed happily as Anton crossed my mind.

"So what are the niggas like over in Nevada?" Mia asked. My mom had just passed out glasses of homemade eggnog to the room, before going to sit by the fireplace with my father.

Making sure my parents were out of earshot, I replied, "They're nice, very nice. I think I've even found my first boyfriend."

"What? Who is this?" Tasia smiled, wiping her milk mustache from her lip.

"You know who it is, but Mia, it's this guy named Anton Nickerson. He's dark skinned, tall, has the right amount of muscle, and he's phenomenal in the bedroom. Not only that, but he has his own place, car, and money."

"Oooh, damn, bitch. Does he have any friends?" Mia questioned excitedly. I noticed Tasia appeared to have something on her mind.

"Yes, he has two that I know of, but they both have girlfriends."

"So! You know I don't care!"

Mia was telling the truth too. For as long as I'd known her, she'd only messed with guys who were in relationships. I think it was because she was scared of commitment and she knew that an already taken man wouldn't want anything but sex from her. However, it did backfire more than a few times, where the guy dumped his girlfriend thinking he was gonna be with Mia, only for her to let them know it wasn't happening. She for real turned niggas into bitches, because at least two of them threw a brick through her window and spray painted *thot* onto her car.

"I'm sure you don't, but no. The one named Oden is dating my roommate Khyle."

"Oh, the pretty one with the really long hair?" Mia frowned. "Is that really her shit?"

"Yeah, it is."

"How do you know?"

"Because her sister has the same hair length, and she let me play in it once, when I put in some cornrows. It's hers, Mia," I chuckled.

"Oh, okay. She seems cool. I always see y'all two and that other pretty bitch, on Snapchat together."

"Yep, that's Bella." I turned to look at Tasia who was still silent. "Nothing to say? You of all people should be happy for me. You knew how much I loved me some Anton after we visited Las Vegas."

"He's not like your *boyfriend* though, right?" Tasia looked deeply into my eyes like she was praying I said no.

"Well, no, but it's definitely headed in that direction. We literally talk all damn day, and spend most of our free time together, if I'm not with Khyle and Bella."

"Even while you've been here on break?" Mia inquired.

"Yep. He texts me good morning every morning, and once I reply, our texting is nonstop. Unless I get busy or he gets busy, but the break is never long, maybe an hour or two."

"The reason I'm asking is because this Instagram famous stripper is claiming him like he's her man," Tasia finally spilled the beans.

"Excuse me?"

"Let me show you." Tasia unlocked her iPhone and began tapping a few things before handing it over.

"Sexy Amethyst?" I read her username with a disgusted tone. "Mrs. Nickerson," I nodded as I read her bio. She had other shit in it, but that was what caught my eye, especially the diamond ring emoji she had next to it.

I scrolled through her pictures, which were mainly of her in her stripper fits or showing off her ridiculous ass body. She was a beautiful girl too, with a deep mocha complexion like Anton, and full lips. Her boobs were definitely fake, but they looked better than a lot of boob jobs. They weren't all spaced out, looking like they were headed towards her back to have a meet up with her spine.

I didn't see any pictures of her with Anton though, just one where he was standing near her, and she snapped a photo of herself, only catching his sexy ass side profile. She captioned it, *My baby could be a model, huh?*

"Well?" Mia pulled me from my investigation.

"I don't see anything but his last name in her bio, Tasia." I handed the phone back to my sister.

"No, hold on." She scrolled through as I gulped down some of my eggnog, hoping she'd come up with nothing. My stomach felt weird and I was suddenly sad as hell. I was also embarrassed because I'd been bragging about this nigga and it was blowing up in my fucking face already. "Here." Tasia put her phone back in my hand.

It was a video of Amethyst holding her iPad smiling, so I tapped it for the sound after refreshing it, so that I could get it from the beginning.

"Babyyyyy! What are you doing?" she laughed into her iPad,

which was shown partially so we'd see Anton's name. I guess she was using the iPad for a voice call, and her phone to record the video for Instagram.

"Playing the game, I told you," the guy replied, sounding just like Anton. It could be anybody though.

"Anton, it's rude to play the game when I'm on the phone."

"And I told you I would call you back if you let me be for a minute," he answered.

It was him. This nigga was fucking with this bitch. And I knew she recorded this video to show off so everyone would know she was fucking with Anton Nickerson.

"No, I would miss you too much so I'll just chill on the phone," she pouted playfully into the camera for her followers.

That was the last thing she said before the video restarted. I passed it back to Tasia after reading the caption, *He ignores me but I love him.* Tasia handed it to Mia who was itching to see it like, she didn't just hear when I watched it.

If the bitch, Amethyst was claiming she loved him, how long had they been messing around? And he told me I was the only girl he talked on the phone with, but clearly that was a fucking lie. What if she was his bitch and I was the side? I probably couldn't even be mad at her. And then all these baby mamas he had, what the hell was I thinking fucking with a nigga like him? I'm so damn stupid, and that's why shit like this happens to me.

"I mean damn, so you gon' fuck her ass up or what?" Mia asked as Tasia cracked up. Mia was always fighting somebody.

"No, what if she was his girlfriend the whole time?"

"This video was just posted last week, Tasmine."

"So, the caption says she loves him, meaning the relationship started well before that damn video, Mia. And even then, I'm not fighting over him, he's barely mine."

"So you're done with him?" Tasia inquired, staring at the side of my face.

"Yep. We can be cordial because he's a cool dude, but as far as us coming together as a union, hell no!" I shook my head repeatedly. I was boiling with anger right now.

Anton and I had plenty of talks about what we expected from us talking. I didn't want there to be any confusion, so I explained to him that I wanted a relationship eventually. I didn't mind having fun, but I wanted it to lead somewhere. He straight up lied and told me that was exactly how he felt, and that he, at some point, wanted to be my man.

But damn, he wasn't my man. And we never discussed any boundaries on what we could and couldn't do while 'talking'. I was so confused. I didn't want to end things with him, when he was only having fun and thought his actions were okay since we're not exclusive. But then again, I didn't want to keep talking to him, if he knew what he was doing was wrong but still did it.

"You good, Tas?" Tasia rubbed my back.

"I'm perfect. So this guy, Josiah you've been talking to." I fully turned towards my sister, changing the subject. "Tell me about him."

I couldn't continue discussing Anton or Amethyst any longer. I would get to the bottom of that shit though, face to fucking face.

CHAPTER THREE

Bella Bacigalupi

Christmas Day...

This morning went by great. My parents, my brother, Brandon, and I opened gifts together and just had so much fun doing so. It felt good to be in their company, and to just be able to make one another smile with our gifts.

Another upside was the fact that Dean wasn't around me talking shit, groping me, telling me what to do, or just all around annoying me. I was starting to hate him and I didn't want to hate someone who had done so much for me emotionally. And that alone was part of the reason why I couldn't really choose Santino over him, regardless of how badly I wanted to.

"Well, I'm gonna go take a shower." I rose to my feet, grabbing some of the gifts that I could carry to take with me.

"Okay, mija. How many waffles would you like though?" my mother questioned as my father helped her stand up.

"Two if they're regular, but three if they're chocolate chip," I smiled, kissing her before continuing up to my room.

"Ma, please don't make chocolate chip," I heard Brandon's bratty ass complain. As much as he pissed me off with his antics, I was happy he was here, and had even gotten him a gift.

Speaking of gifts, last night Santino gave me the prettiest necklace I'd ever seen. It was a simple gold chain with a gold heart attached, covered in diamonds or what at least looked like diamonds. Although small, the fact that he gave me something so special was everything to me. Dean claimed he had a gift that he would give me today, but who knows. And I didn't care if either boy gave me a gift, but the fact that Santino bought me something so romantic made me blush at the thought. Not to mention the horrible but adorable poem he put in the box with it. I closed my eyes as I sat on my bed, reminiscing about the way he made love to me after gifting me.

I replied to all my Merry Christmas texts, and the Snapchat that Khyle had sent me, before turning the shower on along with some music. I could never get ready without music, no matter the genre. Lately, I'd been obsessed with Christina Aguilera's Christmas CD, so that was what I played this whole season.

I brushed my teeth, flossed, and rinsed with mouthwash before hopping into the shower and using my lavender body wash. Once I was finished I got dressed, but as soon as I laid down on my bed to toy with my necklace, there was a knock at the door.

"Yes?" I propped myself up on the bed.

"Honey, I have your food and Dean is here," my mother beamed, walking in with a grinning Dean. He looked nice, like always, and he was carrying a gift bag.

Tucking my necklace under my sweater, I got off the bed to get the tray of food from my mom, and kissed Dean on the cheek as she left.

"Merry Christmas," he stuck the bag out to me.

"Merry Christmas," I replied with a mouthful of waffles.

I set the tray to the side, and took the shiny red bag from him. There were all kinds of pretty tissue paper covering whatever was in it, so I threw it to the side to see something that looked like a white cloth, and something else in a box wrapped in plastic. Pulling the white cloth thing out, I realized it was a onesie for a baby.

"There's more," he smiled.

I reached back down into the bag and saw the box wrapped in plastic was a pregnancy test.

"Dean, what— what is this?"

"Motivation," he chuckled, sitting down next to me and rubbing my thigh. "I told you I wanted a baby and I think it's time we start practicing."

"Dean—"

"Your birth control? Where is it? Is it the pill form or what? I never see you take pills so I looked it up to see if there were other kinds."

I wasn't even on birth control, and I had no idea where he'd gotten that from. He only fucked me raw once, against my will.

"Dean, I'm not having a baby right now, or anytime soon. I told you I wanted to finish school and work for a couple years. I'm 18, I can't have a baby."

"Come here."

He pulled me closer to him, and began kissing on my neck sloppily. Suddenly he stopped, and reached down my shirt to expose my necklace.

"Dean—"

"Who the fuck gave you this bullshit?" he toyed with it, lowering at me. "Who gave it to you?!" he shouted in my face, making me jump.

"Nobody! I-I bought it for myself when I went to the mall, Dean. Ah!" I yelped when he gripped my jaw and squeezed on it roughly. It hurt so bad that I couldn't even close my mouth.

"You better not be fucking with somebody at that damn school, Bella. You know me, and you know I don't play any fucking games." He threw me backwards by my face.

"Dean!" I screamed when he yanked the necklace from around my neck and broke it. I couldn't help it so I began to cry.

"Oh what, you love the muthafucka that gave you this, Bella?"

I didn't respond as I continued to cry, so he threw the necklace down at me. When I examined it closely, I saw that it was indeed broken, making me sob even harder than before. Dean was about to say something, but my door burst open and there stood my father. My dad was tall and stalky, due to him being a mixture of Black and Italian. He was big and very crazy, especially about me.

"Why the hell is she crying on the floor?" my father hissed, shooting daggers at Dean who appeared to be scared out of his mind.

"Sir, I—"

"Get yo' ass out of my house before I fuck you up," my dad cut him off.

"Andre," my mother appeared with a look of pure confusion written all over her face. She watched me as I rose to my feet and plopped down onto the bed.

"Sorry, sorry, sir." Dean slipped past my parents and darted out to leave. My father followed him to make sure. At least I hope that was why he followed him.

"Honey," my mother half smiled before coming in further and closing the door. "What was he doing to you?"

"Nothing, Mama."

"Sweetheart, your cheek is bruising already." She looked me over with sad eyes. "Tell me, Bella."

"Nothing, Mama! We got into a little argument and that was it! You guys didn't have to kick him out like that!" I sniffled.

"Bella, who gave you this?" She picked the beautiful broken necklace up out of my hands.

"Santino."

"Santino? What are you doing talking to that boy, mija?"

"He's not the same anymore, Mama. He's grown up, and he's nice to me. He—"

"Are you sleeping with them both?"

"Kind of. I only did it once with Dean since I've been back, and Santino and I have been doing it a nice amount of times at school."

"Oh my gosh, mija!" She placed her hand on her forehead as if she were gonna pass out. "Bella, that is not how I raised you. I don't want you having sex at all, but I especially don't want you being a whore."

"I'm not a whore, Mama," I began crying some more as I let her words sink in.

"I know, baby, I know you're not. But you cannot date them both. This whole time I thought Dean was good to you, but now I'm not so sure. But when I look at you I can see that you love Santino, you always have. I don't like him, but for some reason you can't seem to let him go emotionally."

"No," I shook my head, feeling pitiful as I began to sob violently.

She pulled me into a hug and rubbed my back gently. "Shhh, Bella. It's okay to love someone who has hurt you before. But listen," she made me sit up and then wiped my tears before kissing my cheek. "You make sure Santino works for you this time. He needs to know that he can't just break your heart and get you back whenever."

"I'm trying."

"I see that you have this pretty necklace here. But what I want you to do is stop lying down with them both, especially Dean because you don't love him."

"But he helped me at that time, Mama, you know that. I owe him!"

"You don't owe another human being anything, Bella! And don't ever let me hear you say that again! If you owe anyone anything it's me, because I carried you around for forever inside of my body, and then spent a decade pushing you out!" she grinned, and picked my hand up to kiss the back of it.

"Please, no delivery stories, Mama."

"I'm not gonna go there, maybe another time. But you don't owe Dean anything. It was nice of him to be a shoulder to lean on, but that doesn't obligate you to be his fiancée. If anything, you'd be helping him by letting him go be with someone who loves him."

"Mama, I don't know—"

"Bella, listen to me, mija, get rid of Dean now. Even if it doesn't work out with Santino, do you honestly want to marry Dean?"

"No."

"I didn't think so. Take my advice, I have experience in this." She stood up.

"You had two guys at once?"

"Well, I had a few men after me, and even one who was much nicer to me than your father, Bella. But I loved Andre and so I chose him. I could have easily married the other guy but I didn't love him, and I knew no matter what he did, I would never be happy with him and I would always love your father."

I just nodded slowly as I thought about what she'd said.

I had the exact same feeling she did. I was head over heels for Santino, always had been, but I was scared of being with him again. Last time, I was so depressed when we broke up, and I never wanted to be in such a dark place again. I didn't like the hold Santino had on me; it was too powerful.

"Want some tea, mija?" She grabbed my tray of food to take it.

"Yes, please. I'm gonna lie down. If I'm sleep when you come in, please wake me."

"Okay."

I laid on my pillow and stared out of my window for a little bit, before finally drifting off.

That night...

I woke up to my phone ringing, and picked it up to see it was Santino. I looked around my room, and saw my tea sitting on my nightstand, probably cold as ice. The ringing stopped, and when it did, I saw Dean had text me 20 times. Typing my code into my iPhone, I went into our text conversation and quickly scrolled through, seeing all of his apologies and bullshit. I was about to tell him we needed to talk, but Santino called me again.

"Hello?"

"What's good, Bella? I miss you."

"Do you?"

"Yeah, a lot. I think about you all fucking day, man," he replied in a low tone as if he were thinking when he said it.

"Sanz, I umm, I had sex with Dean last week."

I wanted to let him know because he begged me not to. I tried to keep Dean off for as long as I could, but he was starting to get suspicious with all of my excuses.

"Wow," he said before chuckling angrily and exhaling. "You fucked him, even though I asked you not to?"

"I tried, Santino! I was running out of ways to keep him off of me! He was gonna start getting suspicious."

"So what, Bella! That's when you tell his ass that you don't wanna be with him no fucking more!"

"I can't just do that! I don't even know what we're doing!"

"You don't? Really? I've told you hundreds of fucking times that I wanted you back but you're still on your bullshit! The only person that doesn't know what we're fucking doing is you, mami!"

"Okay! Okay! I'm gonna do it, but I just need time—"

"Fuck out of here," he laughed angrily again. "Did you like it when he fucked you, Bella?"

"What kind of question is—"

"Did you like it when he fucked you?!" he roared so loudly that I jumped, even though he wasn't in my face.

"No! No, of course not! I just laid there until he was done."

"Condom?"

"Santino—"

"Did he strap up or nah?"

He was so angry that I was thanking God the answer was 'yes'. He'd probably kill me if Dean and I didn't use one.

"Yes, we did. He's on this thing of trying to get me pregnant, so I made sure to. I always use protection," I half lied. Dean always strapped up, minus the time he forced himself on me during Thanksgiving break.

"Bella, on my muthafucking life, if you fuck him again I'm killing his ass."

I simply nodded as if he could see me, as I stared at my lavender painted walls. My mom was right, I needed to choose, because shit was getting out of hand.

CHAPTER THREE

Back at campus…

School would be starting this coming Monday and I was not ready. This was the longest Christmas vacation I'd ever experienced, and I loved it. I was happy that I was able to spend half with my family, and the other half with my baby. We'd caught up on plenty of sex, which had me feeling refreshed and vibrant.

"Let's go to the strip club tonight," Bella said.

She was lying on her bed, texting. When I got a glance, I saw Santino's name at the top. I thought it was funny because they both literally just got here yesterday, and they felt the need to text nonstop already.

"How, Bella?" Tasmine quizzed.

"Easy, we're 18."

"You gotta be 21, baby girl, did you forget?" I looked to her before sipping my iced tea from Starbucks.

"No, to see niggas you gotta be 21, but to look at women you only have to be 18. Y'all didn't know that?" Bella frowned.

"No, you did?" I smiled, thrown off by her knowing that.

"No," she chuckled. "But Santino told me when we were talking about strip clubs. So sexist that guys can get in to see the opposite sex at just 18."

"Well, what strip club, and I'm not trying to see any bitches?" Tasmine chimed in.

"Me either, but no good parties are popping tonight so I thought, why not? We'll just dance to the music and shit, we ain't gotta get no damn lap dances."

"I'm down. Oden is working tonight anyways so I hadn't planned on going over there."

"Bitch, don't make us seem like a second choice," Bella playfully sucked her teeth. "Now we should go to Palace. Maybe if y'all two bitches tell the guy at the door you fuck with the owner we can get in for free."

When she said that, Tasmine rolled her eyes. I noticed she hadn't mentioned Anton once, and I didn't see her texting him like she usually did.

"We can try it," I shrugged, looking down at Bella who then smiled. "How did you get that bruise, baby?" I asked, lightly touching her cheek.

"Ran into something back home," she giggled and then rolled off of her bed. That was the third time I'd seen a bruise on her, and it was always whenever she came back from Arizona. "Aight, so let's start getting dressed around 8pm. It's $15 if you come before 9pm, and $40 after. So just in case they don't let us in off the strength of Oden and Anton, we won't have to pay that much."

"Cool," I nodded, watching her inspect the bruise.

She caught me looking and smiled uncomfortably before saying, "Nothing a little makeup and shit can't fix, chica."

Some hours later...

Perry pulled up to Palace, and you could hear the music from inside already. I didn't expect it to be jumping this early in the night, but shit, I guess they called this place Sin City for a reason.

Niggas really partied from sun up to sun down over here, and the majority of shit was open for 24 hours. Las Vegas was definitely for people who loved the nightlife, and enjoyed turning the hell up until the wee hours of the damn morning.

I loved living here. Just the smell of the air made me want to be free and get into shit. I enjoyed how liberal the town was, and how everybody and everyone stayed ready. I for real made a good choice coming to school in Vegas.

"Everybody good?" Bella quizzed after touching up her lipstick in the mirror.

We all wore dresses tonight, because we wanted to match in a way. One of us wearing pants wasn't gonna work, not even Perry who whined about it being too cold. We wanted to look sexy but simple, since we were all involved in one way or the other. Yes, all of us. Perry let us know that she met someone while on Christmas break. I wondered if he was like her, or if he was the opposite, meaning more outgoing. I laughed to myself as the thought of Perry and a mute ass nigga dating, entered my mind. That would hands down be the quietest sex in history.

"Damn, damn, damn," some dude with a gold silk shirt ran his tongue over his teeth as he eyed each and every one of us.

We ignored him like we always did these thirsty niggas, and proceeded to the front.

"Get ready. I hope you have a speech prepared," Tasmine whispered into my ear before laughing. I prayed that I had some clout to get us in this club, because I for real didn't want to come up out of my $15.

"Sup, pretty ladies," the bouncer smiled. "I need y'all at the end of the line right there," he gestured to my right, and when I looked, I saw it was wrapped around the building.

"I'm Oden's girlfriend, Khyle, and my boyfriend said that I don't have to stand in line or pay any club fees so…"

"And that she and her friends get a VIP table," Bella chimed in, and he looked at her with an attitude filled expression.

"Girlfriend? I ain't know anything about Mr. Bishop being in a relationship. Khyle you say?"

I wasn't too sure how I felt about that statement, but I assumed that Oden wasn't politicking with his doormen like that for them to know anything about his personal life.

"Yes, Khyle."

"Let me see if someone can get ahold to him."

The bouncer spoke into his earpiece, and then asked us to step aside as he and some other doorman collected money and stamped people's hands. Some girls were chuckling at us, I guess because they thought we'd been turned down. I was gonna say something, but I didn't want to get all in their asses and then the bouncer not be able to get ahold to Oden for us to gain entry.

"Not answering, Ms. Khyle," the bouncer looked to me and shrugged.

"I will call him."

I pulled my phone out and dialed him, but it just rang and rang until his voicemail picked up. I tried it again but the same thing happened. The bouncer knew I couldn't reach him, and I could tell he felt bad for me. I knew he thought I was some side chick who believed she was Oden Bishop's girlfriend.

"Call Anton," I looked to Tasmine and she shook her head 'no'.

"I can't, Khyle."

"Tell you what, you pay the 15 and I will let you in without having to stand in line. That's the best I can do right now baby."

"Fine," the three of us said in unison as Perry stayed quiet.

We paid him 60 bucks, which I was seething about, let him check our IDs, and then entered the club. It was already dark, and people were dancing everywhere. The stage was huge, glittery, black, and shiny with a disco like light twirling above it. Some girl was currently twerking against the pole, with it pushed in between her huge ass. I turned my lip up in disgust at the sight.

Pull up real fast, on my curve. 0 to 100 when I swing and I swerve. See them niggas hate. But they never say a word…

"Nasty" by Kid Ink blared over the strip club as the girl continued to shake her ass and do tricks. Niggas were doing the most as they threw large amounts of money on the stage.

"Damn, I'm in college for the wrong thing," Tasmine joked, making us giggle and nod.

"What the fuck do we do up in here?" I asked, because I felt stupid.

We were just walking around and standing in different spots periodically, as niggas tried to get at us with every turn. It was nothing like the parties we went to, because only a few people were dancing to the music in the middle of the floor. Don't get me wrong, the place was packed out already, just in the wrong areas.

"I see you turning these niggas down, maybe you're looking for something different," some girl dressed like a boy approached Tasmine.

"No, no thank you," she replied, pursing her lips. We just laughed and moved away.

As we walked, I spotted another lesbian dressed like a dude getting a lap dance from some thick stripper. This place was wild as hell.

"Hey," someone called out and I turned to see that same bouncer who let us in. He nodded his head down towards the table he was standing next to, gesturing for us to sit there. "Can't get you a VIP because they're booked, but a table is the next best thing."

"Thank you," the four of us responded happily before sitting down.

As we danced in our seats and made meaningless conversation, some girl walked up to the table of guys next to us. She slid into one of their laps, and then began dancing on him after a while.

"She's in my English class," Perry spoke up, pointing to the girl.

"For real?" I bucked my eyes and Perry nodded.

"Yeah, her name is Keesha. She's a senior now, but she failed freshman English when she first enrolled so she's taking it now."

"Damn, how do you know all this, Perry? I know you didn't ask because you barely talk," Bella joked as we giggled.

"No, she was talking to someone else who asked and I overheard."

"Shirley Temples for you ladies," some scantily clad waitress placed the red colored fizzy drinks in front of us.

We thanked her before she left, and all ate our cherries from the top at the same time. I looked around and spotted the waitress talking to that same bouncer before he walked outside, so he must have sent the nonalcoholic drinks over.

"Oh, hi, Perry," the Keesha girl stopped at our table. She was folding up the money the guy gave her, and sweating profusely.

WHAM!

The guy behind her smacked her ass so hard it made my ears ring. Before she could say anything, some big nigga yanked him from his seat, dragged him towards the exit, and threw him out like they did Jazz from Fresh Prince. I could tell Keesha was slightly embarrassed and kind of over it.

"Hey, Keesha," Perry finally replied. "These are my friends Tasmine, Bella, and Khyle."

I noticed when Perry said my name, Keesha stopped scanning the table and zoned in on me. I kept looking into her eyes as well, because I wasn't sure why she was so intrigued by me or my name.

"Khyle? Are you fucking with someone named Oden?" she cocked her head. Her question gave me that queasy feeling in my stomach that I always got when other women spoke his name. It was due to my fear of them telling me something I didn't want to hear.

"He's my man, baby girl." I ran my manicured pointer finger across the necklace he gave me, bearing his last name. "So yeah, I fuck with him."

"Oh wow, me too," she chuckled, prompting me to rise from my seat. My friends did the same, even Perry, but she did so to calm me by placing her hand on my shoulder. "Chill, ladies. Don't get mad at me, Khyle. I didn't know you were his bitch like that. I knew he fucked with you because I heard him mention you, but he made it seem like he was single."

"No, I'm sure he made it clear who I was, boo. Don't try to come up to me and convince me that anything is going on with you and my nigga. If he did fuck you, I'm sure it was before we got together. And baby, I know the dick is bomb, but you have to get over it at some point."

She giggled, covering her mouth, being all dramatic and shit. I'd grown to hate her damn laugh.

"You're right, the dick is good, that's why I've been bouncing on it all winter."

Before she even finished, I'd tossed my drink into her face, and began climbing over the table to get her.

"Khyle! Khyle!" I heard my friends yelling, pulling me down from the tabletop as Keesha laughed and backed away, letting my drink drip from her face. I knew she was embarrassed and trying to save face.

"Get the fuck off me!!" I hollered at my friends, getting down from the table.

Once they let their guards down, I slid across the table and started wailing on that bitch. She grabbed a handful of my hair as I punched her repeatedly, and we ended up falling onto the floor. I didn't care about her pulling my hair. I was relentless with my punching, which eventually forced her to let go.

"Khyle!" I heard Tasmine scream.

"Oh my gosh!" someone else yelled as some niggas laughed and commented as well. I drowned everyone out as I pounded this stupid bitch's face in.

"Cut it out!" some nigga growled as he yanked me up, but not before I kicked that hoe in the face with my stiletto.

The commotion continued as he carried me outside and sat me down. I tried to run back in but he stopped me immediately, and held me until my friends came out.

"Move, nigga!" I barked, snatching my arm from him and storming towards Perry's car. When I got there, I looked in the window to see my hair was fucked and I had a scratch on my neck. It was nothing compared to what I did to that hoe though.

"Khyle, girl, I would have helped but you were murdering the bitch!" Bella smiled. I didn't respond as I waited for Perry to unlock her car.

"Wasn't she? Her whole fucking nose and mouth were covered in blood. My bitch got hands!" Tasmine chuckled as we got into the car.

Again, I said nothing as Keesha's words circled my mind. The fact that Oden fucked every bitch in Vegas with a pussy had me believing that slut.

"No, Perry, drop me off at Oden's house, please."

"Tonight?" she asked. "What if he's—"

"Perry, please, just take me."

I wanted a fucking explanation, and I wanted that shit tonight!

CHAPTER THREE

Oden

Some niggas bang the C some niggas bangin' the P. I'm really in the streets you other niggas is weak. On my mama and the hood, fuck around you'll rest in peace…

"Five fucking Maseratis shipped out tonight, bro!" Anton hollered excitedly as Truman dipped through Las Vegas with the music blasting.

We had the windows down, letting the air hit us as we smoked on some of the best weed I'd ever had in my life. I was happy as hell, too, about getting that many cars shipped out. Usually three was a job well done, so five was unheard of almost. My bank account would be swelling like a muthafucka in a short couple of days.

After stopping to get some food from Del Taco, we went to our townhouse community. Truman dropped Anton off near his, and then drove me around to mine.

"We gotta celebrate this shit I feel like," I said as I opened the door.

"I'm down. Let's go to Palace."

"Nah, we need to have like a fucking yacht party in Los Angeles or some shit."

"I'm down, you know it," he nodded.

I dapped him up and then climbed out of my car feeling high as hell. I was sure that I was floating right now.

"I said, the homies in the Cutlass on E, down for whatever cuz the homies roll deep. Finger on the trigger, bandana 'round the Mac. Ridin' through the hood with a cup full of 'gnac." I sang The Game's "Da Homies" to myself as I slipped the key into my doorknob. "Oh damn, hey baby."

I spotted Khyle sitting in my dining room in the dark, with her back to me. She didn't respond to my greeting, so I locked the door and walked up behind her to lean down and kiss her cheek. She moved from me slowly, and kept her neck bent until I moved away. I sat down adjacent to her, and placed my hand on her thigh, which she also moved.

"What's good, baby? You straight?"

"Did you fuck someone named Keesha?" she quizzed and my heart dropped as I thought about the night she tried to suck me off.

"Cool little minute ago, but that was before we officially got together, Khyle. Why? Where is this coming from?"

"I met Keesha tonight, and she told me how you two had been intimate before."

"Well… yeah," I shrugged.

"So you haven't touched her since before we got together, right, Oden?"

"Nah, I haven't even seen her, actually," I chuckled nervously. Her stare was intense as hell, and she looked a little scary because her hair was disheveled, and her mascara had run down a little bit. But like always, she was beautiful as ever.

"How haven't you seen her when she works in your club?"

"I mean I've seen her, but I meant like I haven't seen her outside of work and shit. Like a party or something." I was starting to sweat bullets with this interrogation. I knew if I told her the truth and said Keesha came to the hoe crib but nothing happened, she wouldn't believe me.

"So why would she tell me that she's been bouncing on your dick all winter?"

That stupid lying ass bitch, I thought.

"I don't know, Khyle. The bitch is fucking lying. Maybe she's mad because I haven't touched her ass in a long time."

"I just find it odd that she chose to say she did it during winter, a time where I was away from you for a significant time period."

She was scaring the shit out of me because of how calm she was.

"Because winter just passed so it makes more sense for her to choose a season that's close. It's actually still winter, baby," I snickered but she didn't crack a smile.

"Let me make sure I understand, Oden Bishop. Keesha slept with you before we got together, and hasn't since. Yet, she knows I'm fucking with you, and heard you mention me which means she's been near you since we've been together."

"No."

"Then how does she know my name?"

She was confusing the fuck out of me.

"I may have mentioned you before we got together, baby. It's not like I didn't know you before everything was official. It's possible that I mentioned you beforehand, and she heard, and umm, she remembered."

"The night I spoke to you and some girl was moaning, who was that?"

"Some bitch the homie was smashing in the next room, Khyle. If it were me, it would have been louder, don't you think?"

She stared at me, silent, blinking every now and then.

"So you went to the hoe crib with your friends while they fucked bitches and you what, sat there watching a Disney movie?"

Fuck, how the hell was I gonna explain why I was at the hoe crib with the homies while they smashed bitches?

"Hello!" she barked, slamming her hand onto my wooden table.

"Aye, bring that muthafuckin' 10 to a 2, Khyle! I was at the hoe crib with them because I was the one who drove to the club that night, and so I umm, drove them to the hoe crib so they could smash. And on my way out, you called me so that's why you heard it."

"How were they gonna get home from the hoe crib?" she cocked her head.

"They could call an Uber."

"So then why couldn't they call an Uber to take them from the club to the damn hoe crib, Oden? Oh no, let me answer that. It's because each of y'all niggas had a bitch, and y'all all brought them there to fuck! And *you* fucked Keesha!"

"No Khyle— Aye, what the fuck!" I threw my hands up to block as she started raining blows on me. Once she punched my ear, I was mad as hell so I gripped her arms roughly.

I was about to get in her ass for putting her hands on me, but once I pinned her wrists to her sides, she broke down crying. Dropping into the chair at the table, she placed her head down into her arms and sobbed like her life was over.

"Khyle, baby, I didn't have sex with Keesha." I kneeled down next to her and rubbed her smooth thighs.

"Oden, stop lying!" she cried, picking her face up which was drenched by now.

"I didn't—" I stopped myself because I felt the need to come clean. "Khyle, I was drunk and high as hell. I did bring her to the hoe crib, but nothing happened. She was trying to suck my dick even though I told her ass to go. She finally gave up though when I barked at her ass."

"Because I called?" she sniffled.

"Yeah," I answered and she just dropped her head to bawl some more. "But I'm happy you did because it woke me up so I could make her leave for real."

"You promised!" she shoved the shit out of me, but her strength was no match for mine so I didn't move much.

She rose to her feet so I did the same, trying to stop her from getting around me to leave.

"Khyle, come on. Don't leave me over this shit, baby. I ain't do nothing! She tried to fuck me but I kept her ass off!"

"Move, Oden!" she screamed and pushed me again. She got frustrated when she realized she wasn't strong enough.

"Khyle, stop." I snaked my arms around her waist to pull her in closely and kiss her full wet lips. I then trailed the kisses to her cheek, and then onto her neck.

"Oden, you promised," she whispered, making me feel like shit again. I wished she would stop saying that, but this was no one's fault but mine. I had no business being in that room with Keesha, regardless of the fact that nothing happened. "I don't wanna be with you anymore."

"Khyle, no, you're tripping right now. I get that you're mad but I'm sorry. The bitch did not get anything from me! She touched it, trying, but I stopped her! And the only reason she touched it was because I was under the damn influence!"

"So now every time you're drunk you get a pass?"

"No, but damn, this one shouldn't count. I would never cheat on you, and this shit doesn't count!"

"You honestly think I believe that you had that bitch in a bedroom and didn't fuck her? That you fought her off? Nigga, please!"

"Nothing happened, Khyle! I didn't cheat! This does not count as cheating. I have to fuck, or kiss, or at least get a damn hand job to cheat."

"And you probably did, so let me go, please."

"Nope."

I began kissing and sucking on her neck, while groping her ass.

She was pushing at me, but I kept going in on her neck because I knew it was her spot. Backing her into the wall of my dark dining room, I reached under her dress, and slipped my hands down into her panties. She was soaking wet but still trying to push me off. I picked my head up to suck her lips as I ripped her panties off like they were nothing.

"I said to stop," she whimpered lowly as I ran my fingers across her wet center.

"Damn," I mumbled at the feeling.

I gripped her body against mine using my right arm, and went back to sucking on her neck while pushing my sweats down some to reveal my dick. Once it was out, I used that hand to go back between her legs and toy with her clit. She was so drenched down there that it was crazy, and I could no longer hold back the urge to be inside of her.

"This is rape, Oden! I said to move!" she pushed my chest with her small hands but it did nothing.

"Ain't rape, this is my pussy. And look how wet you are," I whispered just before lifting her and bringing her down onto my dick, making her gasp. "Fuck," I groaned against her ear once I was inside of her.

"Uhh, uhhhh!" she called out under her breath as I brought her up and down my dick. I pressed her against the wall some more, making her legs spread wider. "Oden," she sniveled as I pounded her center slowly.

She felt so damn good, and I didn't know if it was just because she had some good ass pussy, or if it was because I felt like I was gonna lose her.

"I'm sorry," I whispered against her lips as my dick slipped in and out of her. "I'm sorry for letting her come home with me."

I pulled the top of her dress down with my teeth since it had no straps, and once her beautiful nipples were out, I began flicking my tongue over them as I wound my hips into her. She came only a few moments after, as she watched me suck her nipples hungrily. Once I'd had enough, I crushed my lips against hers and we kissed passionately as I fucked the shit out of her. My tongue was so far down her throat that I thought I would choke her. The feeling of her running her fingers through my wild curly fro was the shit right now.

I pulled away a little bit, and then grasped her body tightly as I bounced her on my dick feverishly. I watched her perfectly round breasts move slightly, which prompted me to take one of her nipples into my mouth again.

"Ahh! Ahh!" she cried out sexily.

I sped up my strokes, pummeling her snug and sopping wet middle, until I filled her up with my seeds.

"Fuck," I panted against her collarbone before kissing it.

Once I caught my breath, I pulled out of her, and placed her to her feet before putting my dick up. I knew her legs weren't strong enough for her to run off, so I wasn't worried.

Dropping down to my knees, I opened her legs and started feasting on her already super wet pussy. She stood there crying out and massaging my hair as I sucked on her clit. I lifted her a little to place her legs on my shoulders, and pressed my face into it so I could slurp, suck, lick, and kiss with precision. Once her moans became high pitched, I prepared myself for her release. She came, and I just stayed down there lightly kissing, before standing to my feet.

She was even weaker than before, so I scooped her up and carried her to the bathroom with me. We showered and fucked again, before going to my bedroom to lie down. I fell asleep with her wrapped in my arms, feeling like I'd accomplished something by getting her to stay.

That was until I woke up in the morning to see her gone, and the necklace I gave her sitting on my nightstand. Fuck my life…

CHAPTER THREE

Anton Nickerson

That Monday…

My mind had been elsewhere all damn day, to the point where I couldn't even pay attention in class. I'd spent the whole damn time checking my fucking phone to see if Tasmine had replied to any of my texts, but there was nothing. I'd even called her yesterday, which I would have never done with any other girl, and she didn't answer and never returned my call. I almost popped up on her ass, but I felt like it wasn't even that damn serious. I was strongly rethinking that shit though.

"Sup, Tony!" someone shouted and I just nodded my head up without even looking, as I approached my car.

I was beyond confused by Tasmine's cold shoulder shit because I didn't know what the fuck I had done. The last time I saw her we were good, shit, so good that we fucked all night. Maybe she found another nigga when she went home for Christmas break. If that's the fucking case, I'm gonna be hot as a muthafucka because I had first dibs on her fine ass.

"Bullshit," I mumbled as I cranked my car.

As I was about to pull out of my parking spot, I saw her walking across another parking lot with Khyle. She was smiling, laughing, all happy and shit like she was good without having seen me in a long ass time. Opening my door, I climbed out, locked it, and then jogged across the way until I caught up to them.

"Tasmine!" I gripped her arm, and her smile immediately faded upon seeing me.

"Yes?" she removed her arm from my grasp.

"Where have you been? What's up?" I frowned down at her, confused as to why she was acting like everything was fucking normal.

"I've been in Kentucky, Anton. And then I came back last week, why?"

I glanced at Khyle, who rolled her eyes and walked off. I hoped her ass hadn't convinced Tasmine to leave me alone just because she dumped Oden's ass. I ain't have shit to do with their problems.

"What the fuck do you mean why? You haven't seen me texting and calling yo' ass nonstop damn near? Tell me your damn phone is broke!" I didn't mean to yell at her, but I was angry as hell already, and she was making it worse by acting like I was tripping.

"Oh yeah, I've just been busy with … shit."

"Alright," I chuckled and turned around. I didn't even care anymore. If she found a new nigga, more power to her ass.

"Tony!" she called after me.

"What?" I turned around with a look of disgust. She was annoying me by this time, and I didn't have shit else to say to her ass.

"I just think we should be friends instead of whatever we were trying to do. I feel like that would be best for the both of us."

"And why is that?" I folded my arms across my chest.

"Because I don't think I'm really what you're looking for, and I don't think you're ready to be what I'm looking for. So, I believe being friends will prevent us from disappointing one another, and it will make sure we can be cordial down the line."

I heard her but her eyes were telling me something else.

"That's really how you feel?"

"Yeah, I do. And I think you agree with me."

"Nah, actually, I don't agree with yo' ass at all. And I don't believe you either. Good luck with that new nigga you got back home."

"Tony! Anton!" she called after me as I walked off.

I didn't even turn around to look at her ass because there was no point. I was done with her and had nothing else to say. On the bright side, at least I fucked, right?

∗∗∗

Later that evening...

I was sitting on my couch eating Raising Cane's, and catching up on *Empire*. People swore by this damn show, and since I was free tonight, I thought I'd see what the hype was about. I planned to use this free trial of Hulu very much.

So far it was pretty good, and the music was actually listenable. I usually hated music based movies and TV shows because the music was too trash and too damn consistent throughout. I'd read that Timbaland produced the music for the show though, so it was no surprise that they had some low-key hits.

As I took a huge bite out of my Texas Toast, my phone began ringing. I hated that deep down I hoped it was Tasmine calling to tell me she'd changed her mind. Why was I so on this girl? I got the pussy so I should be able to keep it pushing. I guess it was because she was different from the women I was used to, and she kind of reminded me of my mother during the rare times she was on the good foot. Some women just have that wife factor built into them, and I saw it in Tasmine. Whatever nigga she got when she went back home had definitely lucked up.

I saw it was Amethyst calling me, and after pondering for a little bit, I went ahead and answered.

"Sup," I picked up.

"Hey, I don't work tonight. What are you doing?"

I sighed, wondering if I should tell her that I was free, or lie and say I had some shit to do. Don't get me wrong, Amethyst was cool and very sexy, but I had a feeling she was getting the wrong idea about what we were doing. She was always trying to talk on the phone with me, and because she was cool, I agreed a couple of times. Not only that, but when she came over to the hoe crib a few of times, she would make little comments that I didn't like. I remember she mentioned something about being happy she didn't see any female products in my bathroom. In my opinion, it shouldn't matter because she definitely wasn't my woman. I don't know, maybe I was just being paranoid, but I was praying this girl didn't think I was about to be her nigga.

"I'm doing something right now, but I will be home in like an hour," I replied.

Since I was at my real home, I needed time to get to the hoe crib. Also, I wasn't about to hop right up just because she called; I was in the middle of an episode of *Empire*.

"Okay, should I bring some food?"

"I ate already, but thank you."

"Just making sure. Don't want my baby being hungry," she giggled.

I opened my mouth to just come out and ask her what she expected from this, but I just decided to drop the issue.

"Thanks, see you in a bit."

I relaxed for a little bit longer, finishing my food, and when I was done, I took a quick shower before leaving. When I got to the other spot, I saw her car sitting there already. Before I even cut my engine off good, she was climbing out.

"Baby!" she shrieked, running up to me and hugging me.

"Hey," I chuckled at how excited she was.

I led her into the apartment, and cut the TV and lights on so that we could see. She set her purse on the coffee table, and then removed a bottle of champagne and two flutes which were wrapped in tissue paper.

"What's all this?" I frowned, plopping down onto the couch and removing my hoodie.

"All this? It's just champagne, Tony."

"True," I nodded, feeling like I was being too paranoid.

She sauntered into the kitchen and rinsed the flutes, before coming back out. I opened the champagne, and then she took the bottle from me to begin filling the glasses up. As I brought the glass to my lips, I saw her staring at me with a weird ass smile.

"I love stuff like this, just being here with you, sipping champagne, and not having hundreds of people around. It's nice."

That was it, I had to get shit straight. Maybe if I asked, she would ease my mind and tell me what I wanted to hear. I felt it was better than holding it in, and having her throw bricks through my car window later because I 'cheated'.

"Amethyst, baby girl, you know I don't want a girlfriend, right?"

Her face went from happy to sad instantaneously. She looked like a wife who had just found out her husband was leaving her. Snapping out of it, she cleared her throat and then set the flute onto the coffee table, blinking constantly like something was in her eye.

"No, no, I knew that. I'm not looking for a umm, boyfriend either, so we're definitely on the same page."

"We are?"

"Yeah, of course we are. Where is the bathroom again?"

"Straight to the back."

I watched her with dipped eyebrows as she nervously got up and rushed to the bathroom. Her mouth was saying one thing but her body language said otherwise. However, I was going off of what she said from out of her mouth. And I was happy we felt the same way about our situation.

CHAPTER FOUR

Shayne

"You coming to bed?" Pierce walked into our dark living room, and stood there staring at me. I was watching something on television, not paying attention obviously, and sipping wine.

"In a minute, Pierce. It's only 9:30pm."

"Aight." He made his way over to me, and leaned down to peck my lips lightly. I felt him looking down at me on the couch for a few, before turning around and leaving.

I was starting to feel bad for being so distant with Pierce, but I couldn't help that my mind was occupied with Lloyd. He was all I thought about. I think it was the fact that he was here one day and vanishing the next. His mysteriousness attracted me to him. It made me yearn for his presence and his touch; not to mention, the nigga was fine as fuck. I sipped my wine and rocked my head from side to side to loosen the crook in my neck. Just thinking about Lloyd had me stiff as hell.

I looked down at my phone when it buzzed, but then rolled my eyes when I saw it was only a text from some nigga I never stored. I couldn't tell you his name if you put a gun to my head. My phone stayed being blown up, but I only looked forward to talking to one person.

"Fuck it."

I set the wine down and picked my phone up to dial Lloyd. I'd texted him earlier and we held conversation for a nice little while. Then he told me he'd call me later, but he hadn't yet and that was around 4pm. I was so anxious to hear his voice and be around him.

I got no answer, so I tossed my phone to the side angrily. I was bored, lonely, and missing my boo. I hated being in this position. I wanted to be Lloyd's girl, and be with him all the time, but I knew while I had Pierce I couldn't do that. And I couldn't just dump Pierce because he took care of me. Yeah, I'd just gotten an okay job in the Harrah's hotel show, but it wasn't enough for me to have my own place, car, and still get my nails done and shit. I felt like Pierce had a hold on me because of his financial support.

Standing up, I grabbed my jacket from the coat closet, and then got my keys and purse. Leaving the apartment slowly, I jogged across the little parking lot to get to my car. I was gonna go hang out with Alanna since I didn't have shit else to do. Right now, anything was better than sitting up in the house staring blankly at the damn television.

I made it to Alanna's about 10 minutes later, and parked right near her townhouse. Getting out, I hit the alarm, and checked my surroundings as I neared her spot. After dropping my keys into my big beautiful Gucci bag, I banged on her door like I was the damn police.

"Alanna!" I hollered, but got no answer. I knew she was here because her car was parked outside.

Lifting the huge flowerpot to my left, I grabbed the spare key and used it to unlock her door before putting it back. When I walked in, all of her lights were on, and soft music was playing. I spotted two wine glasses sitting on her floor by the couch, and two plates on the counter in the kitchen.

"My bitch is finally getting some dick," I chuckled lowly as I crept to the back.

"Dive" by Usher was playing in her bedroom, and since the door was cracked I could see that it was dark inside. Moving closer since I was a fucking freak and wanted to see some shit, I peeked in. My happiness immediately faded upon seeing her riding Earl Jr. like that nigga didn't drop and dis her as if she meant nothing. Not to mention, he was currently engaged to the woman he low-key left her for.

"Really, Alanna?" I burst into the bedroom and they both scrambled to cover themselves, before she cut the light on.

"Shayne! Are you serious?!" she shot daggers at me, right as I shot some at Earl Jr.'s ass.

"No are you serious?! Why are you fucking this nigga after how he did you!"

"Aye, mind yo' business, bitch!" he had the nerve to bark at me.

"Shayne!" Alanna shrieked as I started whacking that nigga with my big ass purse. He was doing his best to block me, but I was fucking him up.

"Nigga, who are you calling a bitch?!"

"Stop, Shayne!" Alanna yanked me back and tossed me towards the bedroom door. "Get out! Who I sleep with is none of your business!" she panted, glaring at me.

I couldn't do anything but shake my head at her before turning on my heels to leave. Before I left though, I chucked her bottle of body spray at Earl Jr. and it hit him dead in the bottom lip. Right when I approached the front door, Alanna gripped my shoulder and turned me to face her. I couldn't even look at her though because I was so disappointed.

"Shayne, he and I are working on getting back together."

"Why?"

"Stop shouting. And it's because we love each other. I'm not like you, I can't be with a man for years and just leave him because he did something I didn't like."

"It's deeper than that with Pierce and you know it."

"Regardless, I love Earl and I have for a very long time. I've been with him since he and I were 16, Shayne. I have tried to date but I just can't."

"Alanna—"

"Aye, Lana, I'm gone." Earl Jr.'s bitch ass came walking out buttoning his pants. I will agree the nigga was sexier than a muthafucka, but the way he fucked her over could never be forgiven in my book.

"No, baby, she's leaving. Just go back to the room," she begged him like some weak bitch.

"Yeah, nigga, I'm leaving."

I snatched the door open and slammed it hard as fuck behind me. Pouting like a brat, I stomped to my car and climbed in. I stared out of my front windshield wondering where the hell I could go at this time of night. I was wide awake and not ready to go home and get in the bed with Grandpa Pierce just yet. I knew Lloyd wouldn't answer me, so I wasn't gonna make a fool of myself by calling him.

Nibbling on my lip as I pondered, someone finally came to mind. Someone I knew would always be down to have a good time.

"Heeeeyyy," Marisol sang into the phone once she answered.

"Hey, what are you doing tonight?"

"Was gonna go out, but I heard the function I planned to go to was ratchet and you know that ain't my style. I'm staying in. Why? You have somewhere for us to go?"

"No, I was looking for somewhere."

"Why don't you come here? I have a pool, Jacuzzi, plenty of liquor, weed, and blow if you're into that."

"I'm not into blow," I giggled lowly as I cranked my car up. "I will be to you soon."

"K."

I thought about Alanna's stupid ass the whole way over to Marisol's. She was just so fucking dumb. She knew what type of nigga Earl Jr. was, yet, she still let him into her bed. That muthafucka hadn't talked to her in almost a year, but now that he wants her back, she's welcoming him with open arms? I sucked my teeth at the thought as I turned into Marisol's complex. That was what I hated about Alanna, she was too fucking meek when it came to these niggas. She let them treat her like shit. Well, she let Earl Jr. treat her like shit, I don't know of any others. But ain't enough love in the world for me to let a nigga dog me like that.

"Hey, baby," Marisol answered the door in her bathing suit.

One thing I could say about Marisol was that she was beautiful. I also like that she played no games when it came to these niggas. It was refreshing to be around someone who had the same mentality as me as far as these fuck boys out here. I knew she would never let Earl Jr. do her like he was doing Alanna.

"Hi," I spoke dryly as I walked in, scanning her place like I'd never been there before.

"Where are you coming from? Home?" She walked into her kitchen and began pouring some stuff into a blender. I sat at her bar to watch her.

"No, Alanna's."

"She didn't wanna come over with you?"

"No, I walked in on her fucking Earl Jr."

"Earl Jr.? Why does that name sound familiar to me?" She cocked her head and began blending up the margarita. This bitch stayed ready to turn up.

"Earl Marsden Jr., he's a professional football player and Alanna was his girlfriend for years before he got drafted and dumped her."

"Ohhh, right, I remember her whining about him one night when she got twisted with us. Isn't he engaged?"

"Girl, yes, but they're working on getting back together she says."

"Wow, ya girl needs to invest in a backbone. That nigga would be working harder than Santa's elves trying to get back into my bed. Now, I will fuck a new nigga in a hot second, but a dude who did me dirty and broke my heart? Nope!"

We laughed in unison as I nodded in agreement.

She finished making the margaritas, and then we went into the backyard where the Jacuzzi was. I stood there at the edge, and just watched her get into it. I didn't have a bathing suit, so it was just gonna be my feet tonight.

"Get in," she chuckled, sipping her drink.

"I'm not soaking my clothes, Marisol."

"I have something you can change into afterwards, boo."

Sighing, I stood to my feet about to get in, but stopped myself. Pulling my shirt over my head, I threw it to the side and then removed my sweats. I'd rather get my bra and panties wet, because once I got out, I could just throw my clothes on and drive home commando.

"Have you dealt with Oden recently?" I questioned her, allowing the warm Jacuzzi to soothe my muscles.

"Girl, no, not since he got with your sister. But you know Ice that strips at his nightclub? She told me she fucked him recently."

My eyes were wide as hell because I almost couldn't believe it. The way that nigga was talking, it sounded like he never planned to step out on my sister. I will be honest and say it did bother me a little bit though. I wasn't gonna say shit to Khyle about it because I was sure she wouldn't believe me, and then she'd tell Oden. I didn't want any problems with his crazy ass at all.

"You serious?"

"Yeah, girl. She told me because I had heard she got her ass beat by your sister. And not only that, people haven't seen them together, your sister and Oden. So word is that it's over."

"Girl, you are dropping bombs on me tonight." I gulped down some of my margarita. This shit was strong as hell, but that's my fault because I told her to add extra tequila.

"That's what I said when I found out. They claim he's working overtime to get her back, but Oden doesn't seem like the type."

"Damn."

"So how are you and Lloyd's sexy ass?"

"We're perfect."

I liked Marisol, but I still didn't trust her enough to be telling her the problems I had with Lloyd. Knowing her, she would go after him.

"Good. Hopefully I get me my own thing. The single life has been fun but I'm over it."

"I'm sure. I've never liked to be alone."

It got quiet as we just relaxed in the Jacuzzi tub and downed our drinks. Once we polished them off, she refilled our glasses since she had the blender pitcher out here. We kept drinking until the blender was empty, and by that time I was feeling good as fuck.

I closed my eyes and let my head fall back, resting against the concrete, as I danced subtly to the music playing in my head. I heard water moving, and then I felt Marisol's hand run down my flat stomach. Picking my head up, we made eye contact as she moved closer, kissing me gently. I should have stopped her, but it was something about kissing a woman. Her lips were much softer than a man's, and I enjoyed that… on occasions.

As we tongued one another down, she pressed her body closer into mine, standing in between my legs. My back was up against the Jacuzzi wall, allowing the bubbles to massage my drunken body. Marisol's hand traveled down into my underwear, and I gasped when she inserted her fingers.

"Fuck," I mumbled against her lips before we resumed kissing. She'd only been fingering me for a hot second and I was already on the verge of cumming.

She proceeded to make me cum a couple times in the hot tub, before we moved the festivities into the house. I knew she was the right person to call tonight.

CHAPTER FOUR

$\mathcal{I}$t was only 7:30pm, but I was lying in bed already, freshly showered. I didn't want to do anything but sleep, cry, and do it all over again. I couldn't believe what Oden had done to me, especially after all the talks we'd had. I explained to his stupid ass that I wanted loyalty, and he promised me over and over he was all about that.

The worst part about it though was that I believed what he'd said. I actually thought that some 24-year-old entrepreneur who was wanted by every girl in Nevada damn near, was gonna be good to me. I swear sometimes a nigga can have you so gone that you'll end up living in fool's paradise instead of just visiting.

I bet you thought you knew me too, huh?

Brian's words kept replaying in my mind. It made me sick to think about how I stood there and defended that scumbag ass nigga, and he was cheating on me the whole time.

I touched my neck to feel where my necklace used to be, and just shut my eyes to let the tears fall. I honestly felt like my heart had been snapped into two, and my chest literally ached sometimes during the day. And to make matters worse, it seemed like everyone knew about us. I saw all the bitches on his social media asking him if it was true that he was single, but he never responded. He didn't usually reply to them anyways.

I had the lights out already since Tasmine wasn't in the room, and soft music playing from my phone. As I wept softly on my pillow with my body in the fetal position, I wondered if I would ever recover from this. Before I knew it, I had dozed off.

Around 11pm that night...

I felt like someone was holding me, but I knew it was a dream. However, when I opened my eyes, I could still feel their strong arms holding onto me for dear life, as if they were trying to stop me from going somewhere. The embrace felt good, prompting me to rub my hands over their forearm. Once I came to my senses and realized someone was in my bed, I turned my head to the side to see that wild curly fro. I immediately became repulsed by his presence despite how handsome he was and how good he smelled.

"Move," I nudged him, trying to knock him off of my small bed.

He stayed silent as he grabbed ahold of my wrists and pinned them above my head, while climbing on top of me.

"Khyle, I'm sorry, baby," he whispered, looking down into my face. His eyes were so sad, almost as if he were about to cry, but I didn't care. If he really had strong feelings for me, he wouldn't have cheated on me with some stripper.

"Tasmine!" I screeched, hoping she was in the room. How did this nigga even get in here?

"She's not in here, she went out with Bella and Perry. I told them I needed to talk to you and for them to leave."

I was angry at them just that quickly, for allowing him to come in here and be with me. They knew everything, yet they helped his ass out.

"Get off me, Oden. I swear if you touch me sexually I'm going to the campus police to tell them you raped me."

I was dead serious right now. If he thought he was gonna sleep with me, he had another thing coming, in the form of rape charges.

He cocked his head and just looked at me for a few. Even in the dark, you could see how fine he was.

"So you for real don't ever want to be with me, even though I'm telling you nothing happened in that room." I'm sure it was a question, but he said it more like a statement.

"I don't. Maybe you should go find Keesha."

"I don't want Keesha, I want you."

"No, you don't want me. Let my fucking wrists go!" I yelled loudly.

He was still on top of me, in between my legs, and holding my wrists above my head. The fact that I wasn't strong enough to break free and claw his face like an alley cat, infuriated me.

"I do want you, baby, badly as fuck."

"No, you don't," I started to cry and hated myself for it. "I left my boyfriend for you, I betrayed my sister for you, I stopped talking to my best friend for you, I didn't go home for Christmas in order to spend time nursing you back to health, and I even fought in public like some hood rat for you. I did everything you wanted to keep you satisfied, even FaceTiming you to help you get off while I was away. And you couldn't even keep it in your pants for the three weeks that I was gone, Oden? Yet, you expect me to believe you want me."

"I do, Khyle, fuck. And I did keep it in my pants! Why don't you believe me? I did not cheat! I promised you I wouldn't!"

He let my wrists go, and wrapped his arms around my body to hug me while he kissed on my neck. I used that opportunity to try and push him off with all my might, but what he said next weakened everything in me.

"I love you, baby, I'm in love with you. You can't leave me like this… over nothing."

My body froze as he rubbed up my shirt to grope my breasts. He then brought that hand down to get my panties off, before yanking my shirt over my head. I laid there naked, replaying his words in my head over and over, as I watched him get off the bed to undress himself. He got back in, and placed my legs over his forearms, before pushing his long thick dick into me, making me whimper in pain slightly. Once he was inside of me, he lowered his body closer to mine, and began to tongue me down hungrily.

I'd fallen for the bullshit yet again.

***

The next afternoon…

I left Oden in my dorm room this morning after showering and brushing my teeth, so I could go to class. He'd texted and called me a few times, but I didn't answer. I wanted him to leave me the fuck alone. I prayed that his ass was gone when I got back because I'd just gotten some food and I wanted to eat it in peace.

As I was walking towards my dorm hall, I spotted Tasmine. I rushed up to her, and she smiled when she saw me. I didn't get a chance to get in her ass this morning because like Oden, she was knocked out.

"Tasmine, why did you let Oden in the room last night?"

"Let him? You think I let his big ass in the room?" she raised a brow, and I just chuckled because I knew she was telling the truth. "I walked into the room, and he came in right behind me, ignoring me as I told him to bounce."

"Well, thanks for trying."

"What happened? You were sleep when I left, and right when I closed the door, I saw the light from under the door go out."

"He held me until I woke up, and I tried to get him to leave but…" I began shaking my head, hoping the air would dry my eyes so the tears wouldn't fall.

"What, Khyle?" she pushed my hair behind my ears.

"But he told me that he loved me and like an idiot, I fell for it." I covered my face as I sobbed because I was embarrassed. I hated crying in front of people, because I despised sympathy.

I heard her drop her books to the ground before pulling me in for a hug. She rubbed my back, as I cried into her shoulder.

"You're not an idiot, Khyle. You have strong feelings for him, so of course him telling you that was gonna make you soften up."

"I had sex with him, and now I feel like I need to take one million showers. I feel yucky, knowing he slept with that whore and was still able to touch me after."

"I thought he said she just touched it?"

"That's what he says but I don't believe that. All three of them brought girls home to smash, it was obvious."

"Yeah," she looked off and nodded.

I knew she was thinking about Anton. She wouldn't tell us why she had suddenly decided to stop talking to him. I knew it wasn't because of that night Oden cheated on me, because she had cut Anton off before I told her about it.

"Well, I don't wanna hold you up, and I'm starving so, I will see you at the room."

"Okay, and there is a function tonight, you coming?" she smirked, allowing her pretty eyes to beam.

"You know what, yes. I think it will be good for me to get out and shit."

We went our separate ways, and I let out a sigh of relief once I reached Dayton Hall. I was famished and ready to pig out before my math class later. I swear I loved my dorm hall, but I hated that it was so far from every damn thing. Actually, all the dorms were in a sense, but mine seemed to be the furthest.

I entered the building and took the elevator up to my floor. As I made my way down the hall, I spotted Oden standing by my door in jeans, sneakers, and a hoodie. He had the hood pulled over his head, covering his hair, and you could really see how handsome he was when all of it was out of his face. That's not to say he wasn't scrumptious with it all wild and shit.

In his hand was a bouquet of roses, and they were so vibrant and beautiful. Everything was perfect before me, except hoe ass Raquel conversing with him as she leaned up against Perry and Bella's door, since he was against mine.

"Excuse me love birds," I said.

Oden's smile faded as he moved out of the way to allow me to open the door to my room. He tried to follow me in, but I turned around and stopped him.

"Khyle, let me talk to you."

"I don't wanna talk, Oden. I am busy and you need to leave."

"I bought these for you."

He handed me the roses in the most beautiful vase I'd ever seen. Taking them into my hand, I stared at them in disgust as if they were him. They were no longer pretty to me. Pulling them from the vase, I threw them into his chest, letting them fall to the floor. The hurt in his eyes when I did that almost prompted me to apologize and hug him, but I couldn't.

"You need to leave. And you need to never talk to me again," I spoke slowly so that I wouldn't cry.

"Khyle—"

"Listen to me, read my lips, whatever. I don't want to be with you, Oden Bishop. I do not care if you love me, because I don't love you. There is nothing that can be said or done to change my mind, so give it up."

Raquel stared with her jaw on the floor and her eyes wide as saucers.

Oden looked at me with squinted eyes, which only made him sexier, as he licked his full lips. He then turned away, and proceeded to walk down the hall without another word. As I watched him hit the corner, my heart began to beat out of my chest almost. I slammed the door, and just slid down it, crying so hard that my body jerked. I hoped I wouldn't regret my decision.

CHAPTER FOUR

Truman

$\mathcal{I}$ was sitting inside of my office within Palace, just going over some paperwork. I wanted to look at the numbers and see where we needed to maybe improve and focus on some more so that every part of this place could bring in as much money as possible.

Right when I was finishing up, I heard a light knock at my door, so I yelled for the person to come in. Our offices were deep within the club, so nobody really came back here unless it was for an emergency or some shit like that, which was rare.

"Hey," Chiina walked in smiling. I swear she was the prettiest bitch in this club, outside of it, too, if you didn't count Pilar.

"Hey, what's wrong?" I sat back in my chair and clasped my hands together.

"Nothing, really. I just wanted to know if you would be free for dinner tomorrow. I'm off and I was thinking we could go get food."

"And you want me to pay?" I rose to my feet, rounding the corner of the desk.

"Umm, I didn't think about that part—"

"I'm fucking with you, baby. Don't ever go out with a man who wouldn't be willing to pay for your meal. You're too fine for that."

Chiina was the first girl I ever had some low-key feelings for that wasn't my damn girlfriend. I usually fucked these hoes and threw them to the side like it was nothing, but Chiina deserved better than that. The more time I spent around her, the more I wanted to be there for her and shit. I liked that she had a good head on her shoulders like Pilar.

"Okay, well then what do you say about dinner tomorrow, your treat?" she smiled shyly.

"Sounds good. You gonna spend the night with me?"

"Of course, Tru. I always want to spend my nights with you." She moved closer to me, and stood between my legs as I leaned on my desk.

I let my hand run down her thick hips as I licked my lips, imagining all the nights we shared together. Chiina was a pleaser, and I loved that about her. Anything I wanted she was down to do. Shit Pilar wasn't fucking with, Chiina was more than happy to oblige.

Bending her over my desk, I pulled her thin bikini panties to the side, after unbuckling my jeans and revealing myself. I dropped down to my knees and ran my tongue along the length of her pussy slowly. I didn't eat bitches out that weren't Pilar, but Chiina had that good shit. I loved tasting her and listening to her soft moans as she caressed my hair. All in all, fucking her was everything a nigga could want and more.

"Tru," she whimpered as I sucked on her clit from the back.

She was getting wetter and wetter as I made love to her center with my mouth. I just closed my eyes to savor the taste and the moment as I went ham. Spreading her cheeks so I could get more access, I snaked my tongue into her hole, before bringing it back down to flick over her button feverishly. Latching my mouth back onto her bud, I vacuumed it into my mouth until she came long and hard, trembling.

"You like when I eat that pussy, huh?" I smirked, turning her to face me before I slipped my tongue into her mouth. She simply nodded before I did so.

Placing her up onto the desk, I entered her slowly and pumped a few times before pulling out to get a condom. It took strength from every muscle in my body not to continue fucking her raw, but I didn't want any kids, and Anton had a nigga paranoid. Granted he always strapped up, but still. And I wasn't used to fucking raw either. I only did it once with Pilar, then drove her ass to get a Plan B that night. And only newly, I would fuck Chiina for a few moments with no cap but nothing more.

"You don't have to," Chiina said, referring to me using the condom.

"I do, baby."

"Oooh!" she gasped as I slid back inside of her. I sucked on her neck as I pumped in and out, while gripping her round ass in my hands.

"Damn, Chi," I grumbled against her soft cheek as her pussy held my dick in a chokehold.

Lifting her up off the desk, I slammed into her repeatedly as she whimpered and whined like she always did. I loved hearing that shit.

A few more hard pumps later, and I was nutting all in the condom. Chiina always shortened my stamina when we got together.

We kissed for a little bit before I let her down, and then we made our way to the bathroom within my office to clean up. As we were coming out of the bathroom, Pilar barged into my office with her face balled up. I swear I felt my balls shrink and go back into my damn body. It seemed like I was staring down at Michael Myers from them damn slasher films.

"Pilar, calm down." I placed my palms out to her once I saw her panting like a crazy person.

"Why are you up in your office with this bitch, with your pants partially unbuckled, Truman?" Pilar hissed.

"Truman, why is she here? I thought y'all broke up?" Chiina chimed in. Fuck my fucking life right now, dog.

"Oh, we're broken up, Truman?" Pilar folded her arms.

Before I could respond, she charged me and started fucking me up. Her punches weren't that hard, but she was landing every single one of them muthafuckas no matter how much I tried to block her. Finally, I was able to grab her wrists, and when I did I saw Chiina walk past me in attempt to leave.

"Chi—"

"Don't be trying to get her to stay!" Pilar shoved me backwards. "You know what Truman, fuck this. I'm too good for any of this shit. Y'all can have each other."

Pilar stormed out and I was right on her heels, going down the stairs and barging through the crowded club of people, hoping I didn't lose her. When we got out to the parking lot, I grasped her arm to spin her around, and she snatched from me.

"I'm done. I told you the next time something happened I was done with you." She shook her head as tears streamed her face.

"Pilar—"

"Done, Truman! Go back inside and try to get that bitch back, because it's no point in trying to get right with me."

I stepped towards her, but she decked me between the eyes, and unfortunately that one hurt. I wasn't even sure how she reached up that high, considering I was a tall ass nigga and she was on the shorter side. As I stood there dazed and confused, I watched her get into the car I bought her and speed out.

"Fuck!" I shouted.

"Truman, baby, I got you!" some hoe yelled that I ignored before slipping back into the club.

As I made my way back through to get to the back staircase, people tugged on my shirt and gripped my shoulders, pissing me off. I saw exactly why Oden had someone escort him when he had to get through here. Finally making it back to my office, I saw Chiina sitting on the sectional in my office, staring down at her feet.

Closing the door, I said, "Baby, I am so sorry about that, she—"

"You lied to me, Truman."

"I…" I couldn't even think of anything to say because I'd been caught.

"I'm gonna go."

She rose to her feet and started towards the door, but I grabbed her and pulled her into me. She was so young, only 19, and I could tell that she was inexperienced with relationships. And shit, as tight as the pussy was the first and every time I fucked, she could have been a damn virgin. This stripper life just wasn't for a good girl like Chiina.

"I'm sorry for lying to you, baby girl. I didn't know how to break up with her, so I just didn't do it. But now that this has happened, I'm free," I half lied.

I had every intention on getting Pilar back, but I didn't want to lose Chiina in the process. I was all fucked up and doing fucked up shit constantly. I felt like my life was spiraling out of fucking control right before my eyes, and I couldn't do anything to stop it.

"So it's just me and you?" she smiled up into my face as I cupped hers.

"Just Truman and Chiina." She giggled innocently just before I pressed my lips against hers. "Go get dressed so we can get out of here."

"Okay." She darted off.

As soon as she left, I dropped down onto the couch and sighed dejectedly. Hopefully this was as bad as Pilar's and my relationship would get, because I really couldn't deal with anymore bullshit... my bullshit.

CHAPTER FOUR

Santino D'Stefano

One Week later…

"*H*er pussy kept drying up like every three strokes my nigga." My teammate, Trevor, sucked his teeth as he told us about some girl he fucked a couple nights ago.

"Aye nigga, that ain't her fault, that's you," I chimed in.

"Hell nah, man. I'm good as fuck in bed. Back home in Philly, all them jawns know the deal. I'm famous for delivering this good dick," he joked.

"Not if she's drying up," Huelo replied.

"Man, fuck y'all. Once y'all get a bitch that dry up on you, I don't wanna hear nothing."

"Nah player, that shit ain't gonna happen to me. Every time I'm in, it's sopping wet, trust me," I assured him as we walked towards our dorm hall.

We'd just finished our workout, and all I wanted to do was take a shower and go see pretty ass Bella. She was all I fucking thought about, and I was determined to get her to leave that Dean nigga in the dust.

"So Bella got that wet wet?" Trevor smirked.

"Mind ya business, man. Don't even think about her in that way." There was no smile on my face anywhere because I was dead serious.

"It's hard not to, she's pretty as hell. And niggas be wanting to know what's up with her and shit. Ain't like she claiming you."

"Don't remind me," I scoffed.

"What about Khyle? I heard she was done with Oden, dumped that nigga in front of a hallway full of people," Huelo snickered. He'd had a thing for Khyle since he saw her back at Blueberry Hill.

"Yeah, I heard that shit too. I'm pretty sure it's true because I used to see that nigga in Dayton Hall all the time and now he's never there. And Khyle be looking all sad and shit," I answered.

"Because she needs some dick in her life. I can handle that for her," Trevor licked his lips, making Huelo and I laugh.

"Nah, nigga, I've been waiting on that pussy to free up for the longest, so I got first dibs," Huelo let Trevor know.

"Well, if she don't wanna fuck with you, can I slide in and try then?"

"You know what, yeah. But only because I know she kind of likes me already, so she's definitely gonna wanna fuck with me," Huelo smiled cockily.

The three of us entered Dayton Hall, and then went into our dorm rooms. Huelo and I were roommates, and Trevor and my other teammate, Connor, were next door to us so we shared a bathroom.

Once inside the room, I immediately went for the shower because I didn't want to wait until after these niggas had gotten in. After cleaning myself up, I changed into some boxers, gray sweats, socks, and a wife beater, before grabbing my phone to call Bella. As I was about to, another call came through.

"Aye, let me call you later," I answered.

"Okay, but I'm here in Vegas, Sanz, and I wanna see you. I didn't the last time and my friends were on my head about it. Don't embarrass me this go 'round," this chick named Leena whined.

I sighed in response, rubbing my hand over my face.

Leena was this girl from my hometown in Scottsdale. I'd been fucking her pretty much whenever I wanted to before coming to school here in Nevada. Since becoming closer to Bella, I haven't touched her, but I have texted her here and there.

Whenever she wanted to chill, I would think of a reason not to though. I was focused on getting Bella back right now and that meant that Leena needed to kick rocks. Plus, I was only smashing and nothing else. I just let her think she had them girlfriend privileges because I didn't have anybody serious at the time. But since that was no longer my situation, she needed to back that ass up, Juvenile style.

"What you doing tonight?" I asked, cursing myself out silently as Huelo laughed.

"We're just having dinner in the Paris Hotel, you should come by. I will text you the restaurant. We might go to the club after."

"Aight. I may just slide through the dinner thang, but I have shit to do so I can't really stay long, Leena."

"We'll see about that, baby. I love you, okay?"

"Okay."

That's how we always got off the phone. She would tell me she loved me and throw okay on the end, and I would reply with an okay. She wasn't complaining about the shit, so I wasn't gonna change it.

"I'm gonna go see Bella."

"Damn, two in one day, Sanz? I need to get like you. Well, that's if Khyle don't wanna marry me."

"Trust me, Huelo, she won't," I taunted, before snatching the door open and heading to Bella's dorm room. I loved that we lived in the same building, because it was almost like living together… sort of.

I knocked lightly when I got to her room door, and a few short moments later, Perry answered, pushing her glasses up.

"Hi, Santino," she beamed up at me. She was the shortest, skinniest girl I'd ever seen.

"Hey, is Bella in here?"

"Who? Oh, yes, she is." Her smile dropped and she stepped back, holding the door open for me.

I spotted Bella sitting at her desk, typing on her new laptop, so I approached her and kissed her cheek gently, making her smile.

"Hey you," she chuckled, standing up to lock her arms around my torso.

"What's up? What you doing?"

"Working on this paper due in three weeks. You know how slow of a writer I am, so I need to do it little by little instead of waiting."

"True." I pecked her full lips and then gazed down into her eyes.

"What?"

"Nothing."

"I was thinking we could go to the movies tonight. Sound like fun?"

Fuck.

"Baby, I can't tonight because I have to be up pretty early in the morning. But what about tomorrow night? Friday is when all the new movies come out anyway."

"Where do you have to be early in the morning?"

"Uh, workout… football."

"Y'all are still practicing even though it's basketball season now?"

"Yeah, I have to keep my body conditioned, Bella. I would be no good come football season if I don't train this whole time."

"That's why I don't play sports. I like to eat and watch TV too much," she laughed and so did I.

"Well, luckily your body is sexy already and you don't have to do anything to it."

"Yeah," she stuck her tongue out and twerked a little bit, making my dick wake up instantly.

I relaxed with Bella for a little while longer, and noticed Perry looking at me weirdly every now and again. She was so fucking strange, man, and I hated that my girl had to be in a room with her. I was praying that she got someone else next year because I low-key couldn't deal.

After leaving Bella's room, I went to mine and got dressed in some black jeans, a black short-sleeved button up, and some all-black Nike Huaraches. I slipped my black baseball cap down onto my head, and then spritzed a little cologne before grabbing my wallet, phone, and keys.

"Getting all dolled up for Lisa?" Huelo shoved a handful of popcorn into his mouth. I hated the smell of popcorn and didn't get how niggas fucked with that shit.

"Shit stinks my nigga, leave the door open. And her name is Leena. Now, would you shut the fuck up before one of these nosey bitches overhear and run tell dat."

"Leena, Lisa, who gives a fuck. Bitch ain't sucking my dick." He placed a weight against the door to keep it open.

"She ain't sucking mine either, at least not anymore she's not."

"Until tonight. Wait until tonight, girrrlll!" he began singing Bobby Womack's "If You Think You're Lonely Now".

I just scoffed and walked out the room as he cracked up.

Leena and her people were having dinner at Martorano's, this upscale ass Italian restaurant inside of the Paris hotel. I didn't plan to stay long at all, I just wanted to show my face so she would stop complaining about not seeing me when she visited Vegas.

This girl had never come to Vegas this much before I moved here, but now it seemed like she was here once a week. And it wasn't like she couldn't come before because she was currently 23 years old, while I was 18, meaning she'd been of Vegas age for a minute now. Last time she came to my damn game with a sign and shit, almost getting me caught up with Bella. Bella even asked me about her, but I played dumb like a muthafucka.

I walked through the Paris hotel, admiring the French feel of it. It definitely made me want to travel. Paris was a place you took a significant other to, someone like Bella.

As I approached the podium inside of Martorano's, I asked the lady if she had a table for Leena, and she escorted me over. At the table sat Leena and her two best friends, Ellie and Crystal.

Crystal was finer than a bitch, making me mad I went for Leena first. She had a body that bitches went to the doctor for, and a face that bitches envied. Leena was fine too, but her ass was kind of flat which I wasn't too fond of. However, because her face was so pretty, nobody cared about the fact that she was lacking in the behind area. But Crystal, maaann, I was still waiting to see a flaw.

If Bella and I don't work out, which won't happen, the next time I run into a pretty girl, I'm gonna wait to see all of her friends first before making a move.

"Ladies," I greeted them before sitting down next to Leena. Crystal smirked at me like she always did, letting me know she wanted the dick. Damn was she a looker, but she had nothing on Bella Bacigalupi.

"Sanz, you coming to Chateau with us Saturday?" Crystal questioned, running her tongue across her full lips.

"Did you forget my baby is only 18," Leena chimed in.

"Oh damn, I did forget. You'd never know just from looking at him."

Everyone chuckled lightly except Ellie, who didn't care for me too much. I ain't know why, I mean, I had an inkling, but she had been giving me the cold shoulder like that since the first day I met her. She was kind of ugly though, with her pale skin, fried brown hair, thin lips, and a body that was comparable to a bag of laundry. She wasn't fat, but her body was just weak as fuck and shaped weirdly, if that makes sense.

I ended up being a little hungry, so I went ahead and ordered some food as well. The four of us, well the three of us, made conversation, as we ate the bomb but expensive food. Once the bill came, I only paid for Leena, Crystal, and myself, since Ellie wanted to be a bitch to me and shit. I usually wouldn't have paid for Crystal, but because she was so bad, I did.

"Excuse me."

I got up because I had to pee like a fucking big dog. When I got inside of the bathroom, I rushed up to the urinal and began pissing. I heard the bathroom door open, and when I glanced over my shoulder, I saw Crystal.

"Need help?"

She walked up to me, turned me to face her once I was done, and began stroking my dick. He was coming to life in record time, but luckily I came to my senses.

"Move, Crys, you know I'm with Leena."

I really meant Bella, but I didn't want to start any shit right now. Not to mention I didn't want them knowing who Bella was. They were a messy ass crew, and I knew if they approached Bella on some bullshit, she would kick me to the curb. Even though she was still with Dean and low-key giving me the run around, I still didn't want her thinking I had someone.

Crystal sucked her teeth before saying, "The way you dodge her calls and barely text her back? She didn't even get to see you last time we came, unless you're counting the game we went to."

"Crystal, maybe when you're not with her. Come out here alone."

I was gonna say anything to get her out of my face. Best believe if I didn't have Bella I would have been knee deep in that pussy by now.

"Deal."

I nodded as I zipped myself up, before going to wash my hands. I grabbed a towel to dry them, and then grabbed the door handle with the napkin to hold it open for Crystal. I walked out behind her, and almost shit my pants when I saw Perry.

I didn't even know this bitch left the dormitory if it wasn't for class. I mean, she would go places with Bella, Khyle, and Tasmine, but I'd never seen her on her own, especially in a damn hotel on the strip.

"Perry," I laughed nervously.

"Hey," her eyes followed Crystal all the way back to our table. "Who was that, Santino?"

"Old friend from back home."

"You guys always go to the bathroom together?"

I was a bit taken aback, because I'd never heard her talk this much.

"She kind of ended up in the wrong… one," I furrowed my brows. Perry nodded in response, but I knew she didn't believe me. She didn't say much but she was smart. "Perry, how about we keep this between you and I?"

"Why should I?" she folded her skinny arms across her nonexistent chest.

"Because telling Bella something like this would hurt her, and I didn't even do anything so it'd be pointless."

"I don't know that you didn't do anything. You could have been in there having sex for all I know. Telling Bella could help her."

"No, it wouldn't."

"I'd like to see a movie tomorrow, Santino."

"Okay?" I frowned down at her. My damn neck was starting to hurt because she was so fucking short and I had to look down.

"And I want you to take me."

"You know I have plans with Bella for the movies tomorrow night."

"You could cancel them and take me, or I can go ahead and tell Bella that I walked in on you having sex with this girl." She nodded towards the table Crystal, Ellie, and Leena were at.

"And I'll just tell her that you're lying."

"Who would she believe though? The boy that got her pregnant and deserted her, then proceeded to sleep with every girl he came in contact with? Or the quiet, honest Perry with no reason to make anything up."

Damn, she had me.

"Fine, Perry—"

"Good. I will let you know the details tomorrow afternoon in your Instagram inbox." She walked off through the restaurant and out onto the casino floor.

Was I for real being blackmailed by meek ass Perry?

CHAPTER FIVE

Perry Washington

"I think we should put curls in your hair," Raquel smiled at me through the mirror we were looking into.

Raquel stayed next door to Bella and I, and since she lived in Vegas like me, we'd ran into each other a couple times during winter break. We started hanging out a little, but I didn't want Bella, Khyle, and Tasmine to know because they hated her due to her thirstiness for Oden. It was easier to hang out with her during winter because the ladies were back in their hometowns, but now I had to pretty much sneak around.

After spending time with her and her roommate, Siena, I have realized that they were pretty annoying. All they talked about was Oden, how cute he was and anything else they could think of. I wasn't too boy crazy, I just had a few crushes here and there, so I really didn't get why they felt the need to obsess over one man. It made me uncomfortable when Khyle was still dating him, but now that she wasn't, I felt a sense of relief.

"But before I curl your hair and Siena does your makeup, we

need some information." Raquel walked around the chair I was in to face me, and then folded her arms as she leaned up against the sink.

Raquel and I kind of had this deal. If she would help me become more appealing to the opposite sex and actually get someone I liked, I would give her inside information on Khyle and Oden's relationship. I hated to do that to my friend, but it's not like we were that close. Khyle seemed to prefer Bella and Tasmine over me anyway, which I didn't like. I was invisible when I was with them, but Raquel and Siena didn't make me feel that way at all.

"Now that Khyle and Oden are broken up, has she said anything about getting back with him?" Sienna came and stood next to Raquel.

"Well, umm, no. Khyle made it very clear that she isn't interested in being back together with Oden. I even watched her delete pictures of them off of her Instagram."

"Are they still in her phone though?"

"Possibly. I-I'm not sure. I just know that they're gone off her profile. And by the way she talks, I'm pretty sure that she's not interested in being back with him."

"I tried talking to him the day she disrespected him in front of everyone, but he wasn't really trying to chat with me," Raquel ran her fingers through her long curly hair. Her eyes were so big that I was sure if someone patted her on the back they'd fall out.

"Because Oden is the type that needs to see pussy first and then he will open up more." Siena licked her lips and giggled as if she knew what she was talking about firsthand.

They continued talking about Oden like they knew him, like

always, as my mind began to drift. I didn't want to go out tonight with Santino because he was with Bella and she was my friend. I mean he was very attractive to me, but that was as far as it went.

Raquel and Siena told me to go out with him, and once I did, they would introduce me to someone else that I would love. I didn't understand what Santino had to do with it, but I realized these two were just jealous of Bella, Tasmine, and Khyle. It's like they got off on the fact that Santino would be out with me behind Bella's back. I knew this was shady, but again, my feelings came first. I was gonna do what I needed to do to get someone to love. And if my friends didn't want to help me, I would find someone who would.

I couldn't figure out how to get Santino to go out with me though, so I started following him every time I could, to see if I could catch him doing something. I lucked up yesterday evening when I caught him with that girl inside of the restaurant. I smiled and sighed as I looked in the mirror, while the girls fixed me up.

They curled my hair and did my makeup, while blasting that same mumbo jumbo rap music that Khyle, Bella, and Tasmine always listened to. I didn't understand why someone would want to listen to such disrespectful songs. I didn't find pleasure in hearing a man call me the B word, or mention my female genitalia every other sentence.

"Yea my bitch, drop it down for me. Take it to the room, she go down on it. Ayyyyeee!" Raquel and Siena sang in unison as I panicked. Raquel still had a section of my hair wrapped up in the curler as she twerked, so I was scared it was gonna burn it out. Not only that, I was afraid Bella would find out I was in here with them because they were so loud.

"Hey, can you—"

"Okay, so look," Raquel cut me off. I wasn't talking loudly enough anyway I guess. "Go on this date with the nigga, and make up some stuff about Bella to piss him off so he'll dump that bitch." Raquel removed the curler from my head. *Thank you, Jesus.*

"Make up some stuff? Like what?"

"Like that she fucked another nigga while you were in the room."

"But she didn't—"

"Keyword, *make up,* meaning lie, Perry!" Siena rolled her eyes as she shook up the lip-gloss in her hand. I really didn't want that on my lips because of her promiscuity, but I figured the germs died when they hit the air.

"And fuck the nigga if you can," Raquel added, and then hi-fived Siena as they let their tongues hang out.

"Okay," I nodded as they finished fixing me up.

I wasn't losing my virginity to Santino, but then again, maybe he would be an okay choice. Bella seemed to like having relations with him. She always thought I was asleep when they did the do, but how could I be asleep when she was screaming the whole time? Not to mention him panting her name like some forest animal when he was getting close to… close to… finishing.

Lord, help me tonight.

⁕⁕⁕

I made it to the theatre and felt so naked. The girls had me in the smallest dress in the world, which was hard because I was pretty petite. As I walked up towards the entrance of Regal Cinemas, I repeatedly yanked my dress down because I felt like my butt was exposed. I spotted Santino leaning up against the front of the place with his hands shoved into the pockets of his dark jeans. He had on a hoodie and some black Chucks. I felt so overdressed.

"Hey Sanz—"

Before I could finish, he yanked me around the corner where there were no people. He pressed me into the wall of the theatre, and I stopped breathing for a second.

"I want you to listen, Perry, and listen well. I may be a football player that gets straight A's but that doesn't mean I won't fuck some shit up, especially when a bitch is trying to punk me," he gritted. His gorgeous face was balled up just like a piece of paper. "I don't know what kind of issues you got and I really don't give a fuck either, but if you tell Bella anything, I will make sure you disappear."

"Disappear—"

"Yes, disappear, vanish, gone without a muthafucking trace. D'Stefano, my last name, meaning my father has ties to the Italian mafia, mami, and all I would need to do is snap my fingers for them to make you take a dirt nap."

His breath smelled good, minty. Yeah, that's how close he was in my face, despite him being over six feet, and me being 4'9 1/2.

He had scared the shit out of me, and nothing or no one was worth my life. I wasn't really sure if he had ties to the Italian mafia, but I wasn't gonna be the girl to find out. I'd let the next person do that.

"I'm sorry, Sanz—"

"Save it. Keep your mouth shut, I liked you better that way."

And with that, he walked off, away from the theatre.

Standing there feeling dumb for a minute, I finally lifted myself from the side of the building, and trudged back to the car like I was carrying a ton of bricks on my back. I sped straight back to the dorms, and rushed to get into my room before Raquel and Siena saw me. I mean, they were right next door, so it was easy for us to run into one another.

I rolled my eyes as the rap music from inside my room blasted because I knew what that meant. When I walked in, I saw Khyle, Tasmine, and Bella all dolled up and ready to go somewhere. I wondered what Santino told Bella to get out of the movie date. It must've been something good because she wasn't sad or anything.

"Where the hell did you go?" Khyle smirked, walking over to me in a white dress that was cut out between her breasts and around her navel. Oden was very stupid to cheat on her, but guys are naturally dumb.

"Out with that guy I umm, told you I met." I began gathering things for a shower.

"Ooh yeah, when the hell are we gonna meet him?"

"Soon. It's still new. I want to make sure everything is real before I introduce you guys. Don't wanna embarrass myself."

Khyle just nodded before brushing her long hair in the mirror as I watched her closely. She looked over at me, catching me gaze at her, and just smiled softly. How embarrassing.

"Well roomy, you might as well stay dressed and come party," Bella said as she put on mascara. She loved mascara, had a drawer full of them. Even the days where she went without makeup, she threw on mascara.

"No, I'm tired and I have some things to do."

"Party pooper," Tasmine joked, fixing her jean shorts.

"Pleeeaassse, Perry! It'll be fun!" Khyle pleaded, flashing her beautiful smile. She was honestly the prettiest girl I'd ever seen in person.

"Fine," I half smiled. I was suddenly anxious to hang out with Khyle.

"Good, let's go!" She took my hand into hers and pulled me out the door as Bella and Tasmine followed.

My hand began to sweat as Khyle held it, and my breathing became a bit shallow. I think tonight I was gonna have my first drink…

CHAPTER FIVE

Tasmine

The four of us were riding in Perry's car, on our way to the party. I was happy that she agreed to go, not only because she needed to get out more, but because we were about to call an Uber. I hated paying for anything that I could get for free.

We pulled into this shopping center because tonight, the party was in this hookah lounge that someone Bella knew had booked. Bella seemed to know everybody, and I think it was because she was so outgoing. Not to mention she was beautiful, so niggas were always gonna invite her somewhere or give her information about a party.

"Have any of y'all ever smoked a hookah before?" Khyle questioned, as we walked up towards the entrance.

"Nope, but I heard it doesn't do shit like get you high or anything," I replied.

"IDs, ladies?" the guy standing up front questioned, locking his hands down in front of him. He took this job way too seriously, and it made me laugh.

"How old do you have to be?" Bella inquired.

"Have to be 18."

We all let out a sigh of relief as we dug in our wristlets for our IDs. We handed them over, and after he shined his light on them, he returned them to us.

Walking into the place, the music was so fucking loud that it was hurting my ears. It was probably because the speakers were in the corners of each room, sitting on top of these stands instead of elevated. There were tables surrounded by nice velvet couches, and the people who were sitting down had this big ass thing sitting on the table with some shit attached to it that they were smoking out of.

"You got somewhere for us to sit?" Bella walked up to some random guy who I assumed was the one throwing this party.

"Of course. I'm Rico, ladies," he hugged us all lightly, before leading us to an empty table.

He left for a little bit, and then came back with some lady who was holding what everyone else had on their table. She started doing some shit to it, and once she was done, she stood up straight and smiled.

"So here are some mouthpieces guys. Just put your mouthpiece on when it comes around to you, and then inhale. The flavor is pineapple."

They have flavors? I thought.

She and Rico walked off, and I just had to catch him grabbing her ass. It was obvious how he was able to book this spot.

"Guess I will go first." Khyle grabbed the wire like thing sticking out of the platinum tower, and placed her mouthpiece on it. She inhaled, and then tilted her head back to blow the smoke out. "Perry?" Khyle looked to her right.

"Perry!" I nudged her ass since she seemed to be spaced out, staring at Khyle.

"Huh? Oh yes." She took it, put her mouthpiece on, and nervously inhaled before choking like crazy and cracking us up.

We continued passing it around, and the rumors were true about this not doing shit to you. I didn't get why people did it, because I couldn't even really taste the pineapple, and the only effect I was starting to feel was being light headed.

"Word Is Bond" by YG came on, and I chuckled because I knew Khyle was gonna dance since she was obsessed with him. She wasn't the only one though, because I'd noticed this place was kind of like a party all of sudden.

The three of us stood up to dance along with Khyle, as Perry sat there like always. She just watched Khyle dance along, not taking her eyes off of her. Khyle saw her, so she grabbed Perry's hands and made her stand up so she could dance too, but her shy ass was not having it. I swear everything she did, well didn't do, was hilarious to me.

As we continued to party, I noticed I didn't think about Anton once. Usually he would have crossed my mind, no, stayed on my mind the whole time, but tonight it wasn't really like that. Tonight was gonna be a good night, but what I kept seeing that was strange, was Perry watching Khyle hard as hell like she was preying on her. But that was weird ass Perry for you.

***

Some hours later...

"Oh my gosh! Who knew that would be so fun!" Bella shrieked, making me laugh.

"I know, I was just thinking the same thing."

It was around 1am, and we were just leaving that hookah slash party. After awhile, it was a full on packed function with everyone dancing crazily, and drinks being passed around. No one had to get their ID checked and that was my type of party. We were gonna go to Blueberry Hill, but Khyle wasn't feeling well, so we just went to Del Taco across the street from the school.

"You good?" I rubbed her back as the four of us stepped off the elevator.

"I think I'm gonna throw up," she replied as we rushed down the hall.

The four us entered Khyle's and my room, and stood by as Khyle burst into the bathroom to throw up. She'd only had three drinks so she couldn't have been throwing up because of that. I'd seen her toss back way more and not vomit.

"You think the hookah made you sick?" I frowned.

"I'm not sick," Perry spoke up. This was the most I'd heard her ass talk in one damn night. She glanced at Bella who was watching Khyle intensely.

"Did you always use a condom with Oden?" Bella quizzed, walking into the bathroom with Khyle.

"Oh God," she mumbled as Bella rubbed her back. "I'm gonna take a shower guys, I will talk to you later." She rose to her feet and flushed the toilet.

Bella just nodded and walked out with Perry on her heels. Once they left, Khyle came out of the bathroom to brush her teeth. I just began removing my jewelry as the room stayed silent. After she flossed and rinsed, she turned to face me, leaning against the sink with a glum expression.

"Will you come with me tomorrow to the clinic? If I'm pregnant, I want to get rid of it."

"Of course I will come. But Khyle, are you sure? You haven't even had a chance to think about whether or not you wanna keep it."

"I can't!" she yelled, tears in her eyes. "What would I tell my father who thinks I'm still a virgin, and expects me to remain one until marriage and get a degree? Or my mother, who waits for me to mess up just so I can be *normal* as she calls it. And where would the baby live, in the dorm with me? Or maybe with its cheating ass father who I haven't seen or talked to in forever."

"Okay, okay, we will go in the morning. Set your alarm."

She nodded her head and then went into the bathroom to shower. I was one of those people who didn't believe in getting abortions, but I understood where she was coming from. The baby was a blessing, but not too much good would come from it right about now.

The next afternoon…

Khyle and I had just come back from the clinic and she was definitely pregnant, four and half weeks to be exact. She'd had some spotting so she didn't realize that her period hadn't come. Anyway, the doctor gave her a pill, but told her to take it once we got back. Now we were in the room with Bella, staring at one another as if this was an old western film.

"Did you regret getting an abortion?" Khyle asked Bella.

"Yes and no. Sometimes I wish I'd kept it because I *am* gonna have kids in the future, and for some reason I feel like that baby I aborted is gonna be wondering why I didn't keep him or her. But on the flip side, I knew having a child at 15 wasn't the best decision."

"I never even thought about getting pregnant all those times we did it without a condom. It just flowed, we weren't thinking about anything else. That was my problem, though; I let him get into my head," Khyle sighed.

"Are you at least gonna tell him?" I quizzed, and she shook her head 'no'.

"Fuck him! All he's gonna do is try to use that as a reason to get back with you," Bella rolled her eyes.

Although I agreed with her that Oden would try to use that as a way to get back into a relationship with Khyle, I knew if he found out she aborted his kid, he would flip the fuck out and it wouldn't be pretty.

"Yes, and I know for sure he will be able to convince me to keep it by filling my head with all that bullshit like he used to. Yeah, fuck that. I don't want to be tied to him in any way." Khyle tossed the pill into her mouth and gulped some of her Starbucks iced tea to down it. "Guess I should go put one of these pads on, huh?"

"Yeah," Bella and I said in unison.

Once Khyle went into our bathroom, I turned to Bella and said, "She should have told him, Bella."

"He'll live, Tasmine. He wasn't worried about her when he was sticking his dick in that Keesha bitch, so why should she worry about him now?"

"I know, but he's gonna go insane. You know he's out of his mind, you've heard the same stories I've heard. Remember when he kicked that guy's ass at that party for touching Khyle on her waist when he tried to get by?"

"So what, Tasmine! He's not gonna beat Khyle up. What's the worst that can happen? Huh? He goes off on her and tells her he's done? So what, they're done already!"

"I guess you're right," I nodded.

Somehow, I felt like Khyle would regret making this decision on her own, but it wasn't my body and it wasn't my life.

CHAPTER FIVE

Oden

Few days later...

My living room was dark with only the TV on and some low music that I sang along with every now and then. I had a bottle of brandy sitting on my coffee table, as I took my second blunt to the face. After placing my lighter down, I slipped my free hand down into my boxers for comfort, and just stared at this nigga JJ act a fool on *Good Times*.

This was pretty much how I ended all my nights, acting like a bitch over Khyle. I've wanted to go and see her plenty of times, but I decided against it. Her throwing the flowers at me and giving me that speech was enough to make me wanna choke her ass up a wall, so I thought it was best that I just stayed away from her. I just couldn't wait until I didn't think about her ass anymore, because that day had yet to come. I'd fucked more bitches than I could count while being broken up with her, and it still didn't help.

"This nigga is stupid," I chuckled lightly at *Good Times*, throwing back the rest of the brandy in my cup and refilling it.

As soon as I plopped back against the couch, my iPhone began ringing. Frowning, I looked down at the screen to see Truman's name flash across. It was a little after 1am, so it must have been some shit that had gone down for him to call me. Usually, this nigga was smashing some hoe at this time.

"What's good?" I held the phone between my cheek and my ear as I took another pull on the blunt.

"The dealership got shot up tonight, and they tried to set it on fire but the shit didn't work my nigga."

I was too high and drunk for this shit.

"Wait, when?"

"Like 20 fucking minutes ago, man!"

"Are you sure? How do you know this shit, dog?" I was rushing back to my bedroom to hopefully find something to throw on.

"Doobey just called to tell me, nigga. He and his people were working on the cars underground when they heard these fucking machine guns and shit."

Thank God no one knew we had a chop shop underground.

"Fuck. Aye, come get me, man. I don' got high as a giraffe's pussy and a little tipsy too. And I don't wanna have an Uber dropping me off." I ran my hand down my face, before moving my big ass hair out of the way.

"I got you."

We hung up and I set my phone on the dresser so I could slip on some sweats and a t-shirt. I grabbed my hoodie, and then some socks and sneakers. As I splashed cold water on my face in the bathroom, I wondered who the hell would do some shit like this. I mean from the outside looking in, it was just a regular dealership, so I knew it wasn't some random nigga that came at my shit like that. They'd have no damn reason to.

Walking out of the bathroom, I went to my kitchen to down a huge bottle of water, hoping it would pull me out of being super cross faded. By the time I was done, Truman was calling me again to let me know he was outside of my spot.

"Where are you coming from?" I asked him once I got in the car. He lived in my same townhouse complex, but he took way longer than expected, letting me know he wasn't at home.

"You know Chiina?" he questioned.

"Nigga, from Palace? You still fucking with her? Tru, she's an employee."

"So! Don't act like you ain't never smashed an employee of the club before my nigga." He pulled out of the complex.

"I know but damn, I guess I'm just surprised that you're still smashing her. You don't usually double dip my nigga."

"I know, but she's different. And now that Pilar stopped fucking with me, I'm really laid up under her."

"Damn, so we both lost our women."

"Khyle ain't hit you?"

"Nope. And I ain't hitting her ass up. It clearly ain't meant. I'll let her fuck with these weak ass niggas for a bit. She'll be missing a real one soon."

"Yeah right. You know damn well if you even think she's about to bust it open for another nigga you'll be on her bumper."

I just laughed in response because he was right. I hadn't heard shit, and I had definitely been asking. All I was told was that some nigga named Huelo was interested. It had better stop there though, at just an interest. I couldn't imagine another muthafucka getting my pussy. That shit made my head hurt just thinking about another nigga fucking the shit out of Khyle like I did.

We finally pulled up to my dealership, and I just shook my head looking at the busted up windows, and the sad attempt at trying to burn the place down. Truman and I exited the car at the same time, and just walked around the place, seeing what else was broken. Thank God they'd only shot it up, failed to burn it down, and then left.

"I'm trying to figure out when one of us made an enemy," Truman kicked a huge piece of glass.

"I'm wondering the same damn thing my nigga. I ain't had beef with anybody in a minute, shit, I ain't even had an argu—"

"What?" Truman frowned when I stopped talking.

"That nigga Billz."

"Montgomery?"

"Yeah, nigga. Remember that night we shot his boy and his bodyguards?"

"Yeah, but he didn't see us, and the people that could have snitched were murked as well, so I'm confused."

"Nigga stepped to me about his Wraith, Tru."

"Why you ain't say shit?"

"I thought he was bullshitting." I started out of the dealership, headed to Truman's car. I was pissed just thinking about this being Billz's work.

"Maybe he was just bullshitting. I mean, how do we know he had anything to do with this shit?"

"We don't, but I'm sure as hell gonna find out."

***

I was leaving one of my classes, ready to take my ass home and nap. My head was throbbing like crazy because I got so high and drunk last night. After checking out the dealership, Truman and I went to his crib and got drunk than a muthafucka with some Patrón straight. That was a bad idea because I was feeling the effects of it as we spoke. That's why I hated clear liquor.

"Hi, Oden," someone called out to me as I pulled my hood over my head, stuffing my hair into it.

"Hey, umm…" I pointed to her with squinted eyes, waiting for her to tell me what her name was because I had forgotten. Shit, maybe I never knew it. She looked familiar though.

"Raquel."

"Right, Raquel." Yep, never knew it. "Nice to see you again."

She grabbed my arm to stop me from turning around, and I stared down at her hand to let her know to stop touching me. She let me go.

"I was just wondering if maybe we could hang out together or something. When you're free, because I know you're a busy man."

"Hang out where?"

"Uh, I don't know, anywhere. We could go eat, to one of UNLV's many parties together, the movies, I mean, it's a lot to do in Vegas."

My fucking head hurts.

"I'm not really going on dates and shit at the moment, baby girl, but thanks for the offer."

"You're not going on dates? What does that mean? I know you're single now so aren't you looking for something new?"

"Actually, no. Right now I'm just fucking, so if you wanna go to dinner, or a movie, or a party as a couple, you need to for real look elsewhere. Only place I will take you is to my bed, and the closest thing you'll get to a movie is getting your face put in the pillow."

She just looked up at me without saying anything, so I took that opportunity to turn to leave. She grabbed my hand this time to stop me.

"That's cool. That sounds like more fun anyway."

"Wow, so you—"

I choked up on my words as I watched Khyle walk by with some big Tongan nigga that I assumed was that Huelo guy. She looked good with her hair hanging down her back, tight jeans, and a short top that showed her flat stomach. She glanced at me periodically, then at old girl before looking back to Huelo and speaking.

"Damn, no 'hi'?"

Yeah, I took the thirsty nigga approach with my words. I was desperate.

She straight looked at me like I was the stupidest nigga in the world, before pushing her hair behind her ears and walking off with that Tongan nigga. Tucking my bottom lip in and nodding, I turned my attention back to Rachel.

"You know where I live?" I inquired, referring to the hoe crib.

"Yeah, at the Wyatt apartments, right?"

"Be there tonight around midnight, unless that's too late for you. You got any friends?"

"For Tony and Tru? Of course."

"Nah, for me. Unless you're not into that." I knew this girl would do anything to get in my bed, so I wasn't worried. She was one of those bragging types, the ones that only fucked with certain niggas to say she fucked them. I didn't understand females like that, because it only made them look like a hoe. I'm not really sure how they thought it made them look though.

"Umm, yeah, I have a friend."

"Cool, see you later Rachel," I grinned.

"Raquel."

"Right."

And with that I walked off.

Fuck Khyle. I was tired of her ass dissing me. I was done with her, finished, finito, but I was gonna show her better than I could tell her.

CHAPTER FIVE

Bella

"Hey, Perry, can I use your computer to print something?" I asked my roommate.

Perry came back with a printer this semester, and it was hooked up to her laptop. It was like a luxury having a printer in the room, because you didn't need to walk all the way to the library just to print shit.

"Sure." She powered her computer on for me, and then typed in the password before bringing it to my desk. She then carried her stuff into the bathroom for a shower.

I saw her browser was up already, so I just clicked it. She had Khyle's Instagram page up which was kind of weird. Not that she was looking I guess… but because she could just go on her phone and do it… why use the computer?

Anyway, I went to the Gmail website so I could log into my account, and once I did, I downloaded the paper I'd emailed to myself and clicked print.

While waiting, Perry got a text message on her computer. It was from an un-stored number, but Santino's name caught my eye. Looking over my shoulder to make sure she wasn't around, even though I could still hear the shower water, I minimized the Word Document I was printing and clicked her iMessage app. I then tapped the conversation that had the blue dot next to it.

1+ (702) 555-0933: Has Santino called you? You've been distant since you guys' date.

1+ (702) 555-0933: Perry!

I didn't know who to be madder at, Santino or this fake ass bitch that I thought was my fucking friend.

Slamming her laptop closed after my document finished printing, I stood up and made sure to put it away nicely before it got messed up during our brawl. About 10 minutes later, Perry came out of the bathroom in her nightshirt with her hair all wet.

"Something wrong, Bella?" she furrowed her brows all innocently like she always did. Wasn't anything innocent about this bitch.

"Yeah, why the fuck are you going on dates with *my* nigga, bitch?"

Her mouth opened and closed, like she couldn't think of the right thing to say, and I just shook my head with an evil smirk.

"Bella, it wasn't my idea. It was someone else's idea that wanted to hurt you. I only did it because they were gonna help me with something. But Santino didn't even—"

"Tell me who the fuck put you up to this before I beat your ass, Perry."

"She umm, she…" her face dropped but then she brought it back up to look into my eyes. She then just pointed over her shoulder with her thumb, to let me know it was either Raquel or Siena.

"Wow. You better be telling the truth." I stormed into the bathroom and banged on their door. Since we shared one, it was easy as fuck to approach these hoes.

They used to live next door to Khyle, but for some reason when we came back from Christmas break they were in the room next to Perry and I, and the people who used to live next to us moved next to Khyle and Tasmine. I'm thinking it was because Khyle and Raquel despised one another.

I honestly didn't know what problem Raquel and Siena had with me. I knew they despised Khyle because she was Oden's girlfriend, but what did that have to do with me? Maybe since I was Khyle's friend, they chose to try and fuck me over too. But they were about to regret that shit right now.

"Yes?" Raquel snatched the door open.

WHAM!

I punched her and she stumbled back, falling onto her ass. Siena got up off her bed as I barged in past Raquel. As soon as I got in Siena's face, we started boxing. She was no match for me, and I was actually surprised because of all the shit she talked. You would think this bitch had hands.

At the moment, she was lying back on her bed yowling while I fucked her up. By the time I decided to leave her be, Raquel started coming for me, so I served that bitch, too, like I was a waitress in a restaurant. She was a little better, slamming me into the wall next to the sink, which hurt like hell, but only angered me more.

"Stupid bitch!"

I began swinging on her, and after seeing she couldn't hold her own, she started backing up until we were in the bathroom. She slid on the water that Perry had trailed, so I straddled her and kept going in.

"Stop! Siena! Help!" she called out.

Siena didn't want this fade again so you best believe her ass was like Helen Keller to Raquel's cries for help.

"That'll teach you to fuck with me or my nigga, you ugly bitch." I kicked her ribcage and then stormed back into my room, shoulder-checking Perry since she was in the bathroom doorway.

Perry was looking down at a crying and beat up Raquel like she'd never seen it before. Only reason I didn't beat her ass was because I could tell she'd been taken advantage of. Also, she was almost half my size so it wouldn't have been a fair fight.

"I'm sorry, Bella!" she called after me as I grabbed my phone and left the room to go handle Santino's ass.

I didn't know if I would get into trouble for beating up Siena and Raquel, but I prayed that I didn't get kicked out of school.

As soon as I got to Santino's door, I beat on it roughly with an open hand. Not but two seconds later, he was snatching it open wearing the sexiest frown. He was shirtless, showing his tattooed and muscular chest.

"What the fuck is wrong with you?" he hissed.

"You went out with my roommate, nigga?" I barked loudly as

hell, and the people in the hallway were tuned in. All they were missing was the popcorn.

"Get yo' extra'd out ass in here!" Santino yanked me into his room and slammed the door. "I didn't go on a fucking date with nobody."

"Oh yeah? Because Perry said you did, and I know she's not lying. Is that why you all of a sudden couldn't take me to the movies, Sanz?"

"Alright, look. I went but when she got there, I told her ass to back off and I left. We didn't even go into the theatre together."

"Oh my fucking gosh."

"Bella, baby, it's not that serious—"

"Why!"

"She, look, she umm…"

"Spit it out, nigga. Why the fuck were you about to go on a date with my damn roommate?" I used air quotes when I said about.

"She was trying to blackmail me, Bella! Damn!"

"Blackmail you? What the hell does she know about you that she could blackmail you with, nigga?"

He closed his eyes and scratched his head, before taking a deep breath. I didn't know if I was ready to hear what he had to say.

"She thought she saw something, and even though I tried to explain to her that it wasn't what she thought it was, she told me she would tell you. And in order to keep her from doing so, I agreed to a date."

"What did she think she saw, Santino?"

"Why? It wasn't anything! She didn't *see* anything, Bella!"

"What. The fuck. Did she think. She saw." I broke my sentence up, because I was holding back from knocking this nigga out.

"Me and another girl."

"Doing?"

"Nothing!" he shouted and then grunted. "We were walking together, kind of but not really. We were coming from the same place, and it looked like we were together, but we weren't, baby."

"You're a liar!" I shoved him into his roommate's closet.

I tried to punch him, but he grabbed my biceps and shook me violently.

"I'm not lying to you! She saw me at the Paris hotel, and got the wrong fucking idea, Bella! I didn't do anything!"

"What were you doing at the Paris hotel?"

"I went with some friends! And you got your damn nerve questioning me and shit when all you do is run back home and fuck another nigga!"

I saw he was still bothered by me sleeping with Dean.

"Santino."

"And then you never wear your fucking chain I got you! I ain't wanna say shit, but since you're interrogating me I'm deciding to speak the fuck up!"

"I don't wear it because he broke it and I need to get a new chain."

"That nigga broke some shit I paid for and you didn't tell me?" he stuck his finger into his chest and raised a brow.

"Yeah, but it's okay beca—"

"No it's not fucking okay! I swear I'm knocking that nigga out on sight!" He walked to his bed and sat down, before dropping his head into his hands. "Bella, I can't do this shit with you. Either you be with me, or you be with him. I know I said I would wait but I can't anymore. I love you, and now every time you go home, I'm gonna be wondering if he's sliding up in you and I can't handle that," he spoke softly.

I turned his lights off, allowing his laptop screensaver to be our only light. Making my way over to him, I pulled my shirt over my head and then stepped out of my shorts and panties. Huelo wasn't here, and I hoped he wasn't coming back anytime soon.

Standing in front of him naked, I let my golden-brown hair down, and caressed his chin hair as he let his hand travel down my stomach.

"I love you, mami." He looked up into my eyes as he pressed his full lips against my belly button, while holding my waist.

I said nothing as I pushed him back, and straddled him while pushing his sweats down. He watched me while rubbing up and down my thighs and back, and once I got him out and positioned his head at my opening, I slid down.

I felt confident enough to fuck him like this because I'd gotten on birth control before coming back. My mom urged me to, I guess knowing I was gonna be sleeping with Santino. She didn't care that I assured her that we always used condoms.

"I'm on the pill," I whispered to him. His head was thrown back in pleasure already, so obviously he wasn't concerned.

I moved my body up and down on his rod, controlling how softly and often he hit my spot. He lifted his head back up as he gripped my hips, pushing me all the way down on his dick, causing a whimper to burst through my lips.

"You drive me crazy, you know that?" he grunted as I began to rock my hips back and forth on him.

"Mmm, ahhh," I cried out.

I pressed my right hand into his abs and let my left rest behind me on his thigh, as I bounced on his dick like a professional jockey. Once he lifted up to suck my nipples, I was done for, spilling my juices all over him.

Putting me on all fours, he pressed my face into his pillow, and then got off the bed to completely remove his boxers and sweats. He made his way inside of me, and held my ass cheeks as he glided in and out with precision. His slow strokes were driving me insane, and I loved every minute of it. The feeling of his strong hands groping my body while he worked my middle was enough for me to have back-to-back orgasms.

"Ahh! Ahh!" I called out once he gripped my shoulder and began pummeling me.

Our skin was smacking together loudly, so I was sure anyone in close proximity could hear us… well me. He was going in on me from behind, while sucking on my ear because he knew I loved that shit.

"Tell me it's a wrap," he growled in my ear, slowing down his pumps which made me cum. He was playing with my clit as well, making my body go through all kinds of changes.

"I-It's a wrap," I whined.

"You gonna leave him?" he inquired, groping my breasts and leaving a hickey on my shoulder for sure. "Huh?" he slammed into me a couple of times and pulled out slowly. I came way too quickly when he did that.

"Yes, yes I am!"

I heard him chuckle lowly before rising up and pounding into me doggy-style. I damn near ripped a hole into his sheets as he fucked me like it would be the last time.

"Ah fuck!" he called out, letting me know he'd be exploding soon.

"Mmmm, ah!" I shrieked in a high-pitched moan as I released on him, and he was right behind me.

After panting heavily for a little, he slid out of me slowly, and then picked me up to carry me to the shower. He placed a mat down for us to stand on, before cutting on the water. We stepped inside, and stood closely together so the water could hit us both.

"I'm glad we came to an agreement, baby," he kissed my forehead while holding my face.

"Me too. I love you, Santino."

176

CHAPTER SIX

Anton

"So he's healthy and should be here pretty soon. He's supposed to come in a week, but you never know with these babies," my alleged baby mama, Violet's doctor said.

I didn't believe it was my child, but I was gonna come through for her until I could prove it. I didn't want to assume and miss out on anything that happened in his life, so it was better to just be here when I could.

"Great, can't wait," Violet half smiled and struggled to sit up. I helped her and she refused to look at me.

She was salty because I still didn't believe this was my child but I didn't care. I was being honest. It wasn't like I was just attempting to get out of something because I didn't want to accept responsibility. I genuinely believed the kid wasn't mine. If I actually thought it was, I would never accuse her of lying.

Violet and I met one night at this bar inside of Treasure Island Hotel on the strip. I took her home, smashed, and then left. She let me hit every now and again after that time, but it wasn't even consistent like that, and I always strapped up using my *own* condoms. So how could she really expect me to believe this kid was mine?

She took me denying paternity as me calling her a hoe. I wasn't even trying to come at her like that, I just wanted her to see where I was coming from. She had no facts of any kind to support me being the father of her baby, and that was all there was to it. And once the damn DNA test proved it, I would be free of her ass.

"Ready?" she raised her brow at me before snatching the door open. I hadn't even realized that she had gotten dressed already.

"Yeah."

We walked out of the room, and after she chopped it up with the nurse in the lobby area, we left out. I opened my car door for her, and she slipped in after sighing and rolling her fucking eyes. She always did that shit and expected me to press her to find out what was wrong. Too bad I really didn't give a damn.

"Violet—" I stopped talking when she burst into tears. "What? Why are you crying?"

"Because I hate you! You did this to me and now you're treating me like I'm some random slut that's trying to trap you!"

"Violet, you don't understand that I deal with shit like this all fucking day. I got two other girls yelling the same thing you're yelling and I know for a fact that they're lying."

"And what the fuck does that have to do with me, Anton?"

"Not necessarily you, more so me. I guess you can say I'm a

little scarred from my past situations with these other women. Not to mention that I always strapped up when I fucked you, Violet."

"Condoms break."

"They do, but every time I pulled out the condom was good. I check them every time to make sure so if it did break, I could let the girl know."

"So even when you're drunk and/or high, you know if the condom is intact?"

"I mean, yeah, I do this shit all the time." She had me second-guessing myself now, because I had definitely slid through on her while high and drunk off my ass.

"Okay. Just take me home, please."

"Did you still wanna stop and get food?"

"No." She folded her arms across her chest and stared out of her window as I cranked up the car.

Once I got this kid tested, I was gonna work on getting the others. I was done with these hoes plaguing my fucking life. Between them fucking with me, and Tasmine dropping my ass like I never meant shit to her, I was going through it in my personal life.

After dropping Violet off at home, I went to meet up with Oden and Truman at the dealership, just so I could check on the progress of the windows being fixed before class. I was still puzzled on who could have gotten at us like this, but Oden was sure that it was Billz. He was getting a plan together and everything. I felt he should just approach the nigga and see first. He'd be able to read him and tell if he was lying.

"Damn, shit is almost back to normal," I said walking up to Oden and Truman who were standing outside of the dealership, inspecting the place.

"Yep, and I decided to take your advice. I'm gonna talk to Billz as soon as he gets back from his honeymoon."

"Nigga married that fine ass bitch he's been fucking for years?" I chuckled and shook my head.

Everybody knew Marie was only with Billz because he had money. She, like all the other bitches in Nevada, wasn't fucking with Billz before he became *Billz*. But as soon as he took that empire from his father, she was right in his face and his stupid ass fell for it. In her defense, though, the pussy was good.

"Ain't no way I'm marrying a bitch who didn't want this dick before I had fat pockets," Truman shook his head, saying what I'm sure both Oden and I were thinking.

"You talked to Khyle?" I glanced at Oden as Truman burst into laughter. "I guess that means no."

"You damn right I haven't. I'm done with her."

"You ain't even tried, Oden. You had a bitch that you fucked before in your room, at the hoe crib, and claiming you didn't fuck. Not to mention you smashed her best friend and her sister. Of course she's not gonna believe nothing went down that night. It's unfortunate but true. You think two sad ass attempts to get her back was gonna do the trick? Khyle ain't like these weak bitches out here who ask how high when we say jump. You know that too, that's what you liked about her."

"Fuck," he said under his breath as he shook his head. "It's just I didn't do anything, Tony. Why the fuck should I plead guilty?"

"Just do it if you love her, which I know you do. Listening to Truman's ass gon' have you old and lonely, fucking young bitches who steal from you when you pass out," I taunted, making Oden snicker lightly and Truman wave me off.

"Man, what about baby girl with them eyes?" Oden looked to me, referring to Tasmine.

"She's tripping."

"And you thought that one *sad ass attempt* was gonna get her back? Oh wait, you didn't make any fucking attempts. You didn't even try to find out why she suddenly changed her mind. I bet one of your baby mamas got to her," Oden put me in my place. I clearly needed to follow my own advice.

And now that he mentioned it, it was odd that Tasmine had just out of nowhere felt that way about me. Moreover, her body language and facial expressions told me a totally different story than the one her mouth was telling.

"I'm gonna get her. You just make sure you get Khyle. And Truman, I think you may have fucked it up with Pilar."

"I don't even care anymore, bro. I actually like living freely and shit." He texted something on his phone.

"Oh, okay. Because I didn't wanna tell you that I saw her out on a date with some big buff muthafucka."

Oden and I burst into laughter at the sight of that nigga almost snapping his neck to look over at me.

"He's fucking with you, Tru. Relax."

"He wasn't gon' do shit anyways. That buff nigga would have snapped yo' skinny ass in half, Truman."

Oden and I cracked up even further at my insult.

"Don't underestimate me, man. I may be skinny but I got them hands for any nigga that want that issue."

He wasn't lying either. For a nigga that looked like he needed to eat a Subway foot long or two, he sure knew how to get down if needed.

The three of us talked and joked with one another for a little longer, before I had to jet and go to class. When I got out, I remembered that Tasmine always went to the library around this time on Thursdays. She said it was her way of keeping what she'd learned in her head before partying for the weekend. I really didn't understand it, but she was strange like that. We both were kind of weird. I chuckled at the thought as I trucked it to the library.

I found her on the second floor, with her books and papers on the long table, and Khyle across from her. She looked good, even though she was dressed down in jeans and an oversized sweater. Her hair was up in a ball, which I liked because it really brought out her beauty. I guess because her hair was out of her face.

"Evening, ladies," I smiled at them.

"Hey, Tony," Khyle looked at me uncomfortably before turning her attention to Tasmine.

"Khyle, would you mind giving me a minute with Tasmine?"

Khyle gave Tasmine a look, asking her if it was okay. Tasmine glanced up at me, and I put my hands in the prayer position to silently beg her. She smiled a small smile, before telling Khyle it was okay. Once Khyle had moved somewhere else, I took her spot across from Tasmine.

"What brings you here, Mr. Nickerson?"

"I knew you'd be here and I missed you."

"You did?" she asked softly, her eyes sparkling. "I mean, and?"

I laughed at her odd ass, and she had to join me after a while.

"Yes, I missed you, and I wanted to talk to you. You know, about what you said to me that day in the parking lot by the South Hall dormitory."

"Nothing to talk about."

"Why did you all of a sudden not want to date me anymore, Tas? I thought we were on our way to becoming couple of the year, and then boom."

"I told you that we want different things."

"And I don't believe you. We discussed what we wanted and agreed that we would work towards being in a relationship, baby, so how did we end up on two different pages suddenly?"

Her golden-brown skin was so beautiful, and I just admired it as she tried to get her thoughts together to answer my question.

"I'm gonna ask you something, Tony, and I want you to answer it honestly. If I feel like you're lying, then I will continue to push forward without you."

"Shoot."

"Who is Amethyst?"

Fuck my life.

"She's a stripper that works for my nightclub."

"And? Don't lie, Anton."

She was serious as a damn heart attack. Fuck fuck fuck me.

"Okay, and she umm, we had sex a couple times, but that's it. As soon as you and I become one, she's gone."

"When did you start fucking her? Because I wasn't aware that while we were talking, you were gonna be fucking other women."

I knew this shit was gonna happen. Something in my gut told me to clarify the rules with her, but I didn't. I didn't because I never thought she'd find out, and because I actually thought it was cool to do me until we became official. Apparently, that wasn't the deal at all, and now I was kind of panicking.

"This past winter is when it started, Tas. But I thought that until we became official, we could do us."

"Oh really? So, if I told you I fucked Reuben during winter break, you'd be okay?"

"You fucked that bitch ass nigga?" I got more hype than I had intended to in this quiet ass library. "I see what you're saying. I'm sorry though," I softened my tone.

"She has you in her bio and everything, Tony. And you talk to her on the phone. I thought you only talked to me on the phone."

"I'm sorry, but how do you know all of this?"

"Your little fuck buddy is a show off on social media."

"And you saw this, so you… ooooh, okay. I get it. Wow. Okay. Tasmine, baby, Amethyst is noooothing like what you think she is. I swear I fuck her at the extra spot I told you about and that's it. I only picked up the phone when she called me because she was cool."

I couldn't believe that bitch was behaving like that on social media. Sometimes it pays to be active on shit, because you learn so much.

"So right now, in this moment, you want to be my boyfriend? Which means only fucking me, only talking to me on the phone, and only touching me. That's what you want? That's what you're ready for?"

"With you, yes. More than anything." I thought about this girl way too much to not make her my first girlfriend. I didn't even know you could have another person on your mind that frequently until her.

She got up from her chair with a stale expression that I couldn't read. She rounded the table, and then slid into my lap, before cupping my face and kissing me. I wrapped my arms around her body to hug her tightly, as our kiss became even more passionate.

Now that I had my big baby, all I needed to do was prove I didn't have any little babies, and get rid of these hoes who felt like we were together. It wouldn't be easy, but the shit was gonna get done.

CHAPTER SIX

Shayne

"Lloyd, I have to go," I giggled as he kissed down my stomach. I really wanted to let him give me head, but I had to get home so that I could shower, change, and make it to rehearsal.

"Give me a second, you know that's all I need," he grinned before latching his mouth onto my clit.

Throwing my head back, I caressed his smooth curly hair as he went to town on my middle. The way he could make my body feel was something serious, and something that I didn't want to share. But the only way that could happen was if I were to break it off with Pierce. I didn't even bring up us being serious anymore because I didn't want to hear Lloyd's mouth about me having a nigga at home.

"Lloyd," I whimpered, feeling his tongue flick over my button before he began sucking on it again. "Ahh!" I called out, exploding more violently than I had expected.

Pulling away from my box with a smile on his face, Lloyd licked his lips, before turning me to the side and biting one of my ass cheeks.

"Sexy ass," he grunted, as I laid there out of breath.

When he left out of the bedroom, I went into his bathroom to clean up a bit before going home for a shower. After getting myself together, I slipped on my Givenchy slide-ins Lloyd got me, and gathered the rest of my things.

I didn't talk to him for four whole days after he stood me up and I had to go over to Marisol's. But I healed quickly as fuck when he brought me these Givenchy slides at my job. Shit, I damn near had forgotten what I was even mad about in the first place.

"Coming back later?" he quizzed as I walked by him in the living room.

"Probably not, I have a busy day."

I was tired of being so available for him, so from now on, I would keep him guessing and wondering like I did the rest of these niggas. Until Lloyd was mine and only mine, he was gonna get that side nigga treatment. He wasn't the only one who could ignore calls and texts. When I was done with him, he would be in love with me.

"Oh, alright then," he nodded and gave me that look he always gave me when he wasn't feeling something that I'd said.

As I walked out of his new spot, he started towards the bathroom. A smile crept over my face because I was sure that my little game was working. The less I gave the more he was gonna want.

I got to my apartment that I shared with Pierce about 20 minutes later, feeling myself. Today was gonna be a good ass day. I was gonna shower, eat a big breakfast, and then head to rehearsal for the show this weekend.

I swear I loved my job, because I loved anything that had something to do with dance. And to think my daddy said dancing would take me nowhere but the gentlemen's clubs. Looks like he was wrong and I was right, as usual.

I entered the apartment and went straight to the shower. Once I was all clean, I got out to brush my teeth and then went into the bedroom to get dressed.

I was so happy that Pierce wasn't home. I knew that was shady to say, but it felt good to be alone when I came from Lloyd. I wasn't sure if it was because I felt a bit guilty from being out with another man, or if his touch really repulsed me. Whatever the case was, his absence at the moment had me swaying my hips as I got dressed.

"Look at you," I smiled into my full-length mirror as I checked myself out. I was in tights and a tank top, still killing these bitches on their best day.

When I'd had enough of admiring myself, I grabbed my keys, phone, and purse, before heading out of the door.

***

Seven hours later...

"Today was so brutal," my co-worker in a sense named Blair said.

"Girl, my body is gonna be sore as hell tomorrow, I already know," I smiled at her.

I'd obviously met Blair when I got hired on as a dancer for the Harrah Hotel show, but she seemed to be the only one I clicked with. She was white, beautiful, and she didn't give me those stank faces whenever I walked by, or whenever someone complimented me in the hotel. These other bitches didn't like me, and they didn't have to come out of their mouth to say it for me to know.

"Mine too, but I already have the oils for my honey to give me a nice ass massage."

"Doesn't sound like a bad idea."

Blair and I continued conversing as we made our way out to our cars. After finally exchanging numbers after all this time, we parted ways.

By this time, it was around 8:30pm, so the lights on Las Vegas Boulevard were in full effect. I loved driving down and just admiring all of the beautiful hotels and shops along the street, especially during the week when there was no traffic. One day, I would be living in a penthouse suite in one of these hotels, ringing bells for my maid to bring me lunch. Hopefully, Lloyd would be the nigga to provide that for me.

I pulled into my apartment's community, and sped around that bitch to get to my space. They told us not to because it was unsafe, and kids sometimes played outside, but I didn't give a fuck. Maybe if I clipped one of them little rascals, people would pay more attention to their damn children.

I hit the alarm on my car and checked my phone as I made my way to the door. I had texts from everyone, even Lloyd, but none from Alanna. I guess now that the bitch had her weak ass nigga back, she didn't need me. It was cool though, ain't like I missed her meek ass either. I sucked my teeth as I listened to the lies that circled my head. I loved Alanna, she just annoyed the living daylights out of me.

"What the…" my voice trailed off when I entered my place.

The room was tinted red because of all of the red candles lit. There were rose petals all over the living room, and a table in the middle with plates, flutes, and a bucket of champagne on ice. Before I could speak again, Pierce entered the living room smiling from ear to ear. I could tell that he'd just gotten his hair cut because he looked so handsome.

"Pierce—"

"Sit down for a second, Shayne."

I hesitated for a moment, before dropping my purse onto the couch and sitting next to it. He walked closer to me, wearing that same damn smile. I didn't know what this was, but most importantly I didn't know why I was about to cry.

"Pierce, what is all this for? I feel dirty, I just came from work, and I need a shower. You—"

Him dropping down on one knee caused me to choke almost. What was he thinking? I hoped he was just down there to be eye level with me, and not to do what I think he was doing. He had to be out of his mind to wanna marry me with the way I'd been treating him for so long.

"Shayne, I've never met someone like you, baby. And I know we've had our share of problems, due to all kinds of shit, but I know we can work through it all. I don't ever want to be without you, so I'm wondering if you would be my wife." He opened the ring box, and a much better ring than I had expected sat inside. "Well?"

I was gonna take this time to be honest and finally let him know my true feelings, but money was tight for me, and I would have nowhere to stay. I could probably move in with Lloyd, but that was a big probably. On top of all that, the look in his eyes did something to me, and I just couldn't hurt him.

"Yeah, yes, I will marry you."

He gave me that sexy grin of his, before sliding his hand behind my head to pull me in for a kiss. For the first time in a long time, chills ran down my spine as our mouths made love. Pulling away, he scooped me up bridal style and headed towards the bathroom.

"We can shower together and then eat, since you feel dirty," he chuckled, and so did I. "Then you can put the ring on."

What the hell was I doing with my life?

CHAPTER SIX

$\mathcal{I}$t was Thursday, which was most people's Friday, including myself, and I couldn't be happier. I planned to go to the nail shop and then come home to just relax and recharge, because this weekend was gonna be full of parties. Life was good right now, but I would be lying if I said I didn't miss Oden.

It was so hard seeing him around campus or at parties, and watching all these random groupie bitches hang off of him. I hated the way they touched him, hugged on him, or did anything with him. But, he was no longer my concern and I was sure time would change how I felt soon enough.

"Khyle!" Huelo called after me. We had two classes together, Women's Studies and Political Science. We were currently walking out of the latter.

"What's up?" I smiled up at him, and he just gazed down into my eyes for a few.

I knew he liked me, and I guess I was starting to like him a little bit too. It wasn't the way I liked Oden, but maybe I just needed some time.

"I was wondering if you wanted to go somewhere tonight. Since there is a party every day this weekend, I thought we could do something today."

"Sure, we could go to the movies tonight. Nothing new on Thursdays, but I will look up something and see. What time?"

"Around 7pm, so I can have you for most of the night," he bit down on his lip.

Huelo was pretty sexy, but a very big guy. He stood at around 6'3 and was very muscular. I wasn't sure if it was from playing all that football, or if it was because he was Tongan. Maybe it was a mixture, but I would hate to see him pissed off, that's for sure.

"Okay, I will see you then."

I sashayed away, headed towards my dorm so I could put my books down, and meet up with Tasmine and Bella for the nail shop. Perry wasn't coming along because we didn't hang with her too much anymore after what she'd done to Bella. I felt kind of bad for her even though I shouldn't have, because I knew she was doing whatever it took to fit in. I talked to Bella and she said she would forgive her, but she needed to suffer for a few more days. We were suffering too, because we had to hitch rides with people or take Ubers when we went to parties now. I know that's shady to say, but it was fact.

"Hey, you ready?" Bella asked me as soon as I got into my dorm room. She was sitting on my bed, and Tasmine was on her own.

I loved that Bella was comfortable enough to be chilling on my side of the room because it felt like our friendship was growing. I was starting to believe God traded Emery in for Tasmine and Bella, and I was not complaining.

"Yes, just let me pee and put my books down."

"We were thinking we could all go to dinner tonight since we're not going to any functions or anything," Tasmine said as soon as I opened the bathroom door.

"Uh, I can't!" I called out. I always peed with the door open, so they weren't caught off guard by it at all.

"Why not?" Bella frowned.

I flushed the toilet and then came out into the room to wash my hands.

"Because unlike you bitches, I have a date," I taunted.

They were actually better off than me because they both had boyfriends. Shit, Bella had two of them in a sense, because she hadn't dumped Dean yet. She said she would when she went home next weekend, but something told me she was scared of him.

"A date!" they shouted in unison.

"Bitch, I knew Oden was gonna have you bouncing on his dick in no time," Bella giggled.

"Actually, no. My date is with Huelo."

"Oh, he's liked you for the longest. I bet he came in his pants when you told him that you'd go," Tasmine joked, making us laugh.

"Well, I hope not. But then again, maybe that's best because he won't be fucking me anytime soon."

I was turned off by sex in a sense. I felt like having sex with Oden caused me to become more attached to him because it was so good. So there I was, dickmatized, and in love. Damn it was hard to break free from that, still is, but I'm working at it. As far as Huelo, I couldn't even imagine letting him between my legs. I wasn't gonna be one of those girls who got fucked by and attached to every nigga she chilled with.

"I hear you," Bella sighed.

After tying my hair up into a bun, we all gathered our things and left out for our much needed nail trip.

***

Tonight I was wearing a long sleeved black top that had a deep dip in the back, making it impossible for me to wear a bra. I paired it with some jean shorts, and some black peep toe thigh high boots. I put body waves in my hair, and of course my makeup was flawless. To most people this was getting dressed up, but after living here in Vegas for a while, this was starting to just become my style. I was going for more adult looks these days.

"Damn, do you want my pepper spray? You're definitely gonna have to fight him off, chica," Bella circled me, smiling.

"No, I should be fine. Huelo isn't like that, at least I hope not."

"He better hope not, because if Oden finds out he did something to you it's a wrap," Tasmine bucked her eyes.

"Oden is no longer a part of my life, so what happens to me is no longer his concern." I grabbed my small purse and put the strap over my shoulder. "See you later. Keep your phones close in case I need you."

They both nodded with smiles as I walked out of the room.

Huelo had already texted me almost 10 minutes ago to tell me he was outside, so I was rushing a little bit. I didn't like to leave people waiting, but I wasn't ready when he hit me up. Getting onto the elevator, I made sure I was still looking good, before stepping out onto the first floor where he was.

"Damn, the wait was worth it," he spoke lowly once he saw me walking towards him.

"Thank you," I smiled shyly, before hugging him and kissing his cheek with the side of my mouth so my wine-colored lipstick wouldn't get on his face.

"Welcome." He shook his head as he scanned me from head to toe a couple more times.

He looked nice in his white button up with faint blue lines going vertically and horizontally across it. His jeans were a light blue, and his Adidas were all white.

He opened the glass door of the building for me, and once we were outside, we started making our way to his car to head out.

"I can't get over how good you look," he said once he pulled out onto the road in the direction of Regal Cinemas.

"Thanks, Huelo. You look nice too."

Nothing else was said as he drove to the movies. It was kind of awkward, but my thoughts pulled me away from where I was at the moment. For the first time in a long time, I was starting to miss Oden to the point where my chest was hurting a little bit. I didn't know if it was seeing all the couples out here for the weekend or what, but right about now, I would love to hug him or kiss him. Or even see him run his tattoo-covered hand over his big curly hair.

"Ready?" Huelo asked before exhaling heavily.

"Oh, of course, yes!" Damn, I didn't even realize we were here.

We both got out of his car, and went inside of the theatre so he could buy the tickets. Afterwards, we got in line so that we could hurry and get our snacks before the movie came on. We were a little late, my fault, so we had to be quick.

"Damn, baby, what I wouldn't give to have you sit on my face," some guy who was somewhat handsome walked in front of Huelo and I, licking his lips.

"No thanks," I replied politely. I glanced up at Huelo who didn't pay it any mind. I'm not saying I wanted him to haul off and beat the guy's ass, but damn. He wasn't gonna say anything? Brian and Oden would have checked that nigga.

We got our snacks and then went into our movie. Even though When the Bough Breaks was old, we both had yet to see it so we agreed that it would be our movie of choice. It was pretty good, but I didn't care too much for the ending per se.

"Enjoy the movie?" Huelo asked me as he cranked his car up.

"I did, just not the end part."

"Oh yeah, I agree. Surrogate was crazy as hell though," he chuckled and so did I.

"Are you hungry? Fridays inside of the Orleans is open until

2am." It's only 9:30 my nigga.

"Actually, no, I'm not— yeah, let's go."

I changed my mind because he looked a little bothered by me turning down his invitation. He was a very shy guy despite his size, and I wasn't sure if I was the right girl for him. I could be abrasive and feisty at times, and that seemed like it would hurt his feelings. I couldn't be dealing with any sensitive ass niggas.

"Cool."

We got to the Orleans hotel in no time since the streets were clear. And getting a table at Fridays was just as easy since it too was pretty empty.

"So Huelo, when was the last date you went on?" I asked once the waitress dropped our drinks off and took our orders.

"I went on a couple last semester, but none this semester. So, I will say my last date was like a week before Thanksgiving. When was your last date?"

For some reason, I didn't expect him to ask that.

"Let's see, about a month ago," I nodded, sipping my drink. There Oden was again, dancing around in my mind with his fine ass.

"Oh yeah, you were dating that guy."

This nigga knows he remembers Oden's name.

"Yes, I was."

"What happened with that, if you don't mind me asking you?"

"We just didn't work out. Nothing big, really. He wanted one thing and I wanted something very different." I felt myself getting emotional.

"Damn. I bet we want the same things."

"Oh yeah?"

"Yeah, we both want to be married and to have kids, and to be successful in our careers of choice."

The mention of kids reminded me of my abortion. Bella was right when she said it would haunt me. Just the thought of having a baby after killing one seemed so wrong.

"You're right, we do want the same things out of life."

"Unlike with your ex."

"I think we wanted the same things out of life, but I'm not sure if we were on the same page with what we expected from one another, that's all."

"A man like Oden doesn't deserve someone like you, so I'm happy you left."

"How long have you been umm, playing football?" I changed the subject.

We ate dinner, and it was nice except for when he brought up Oden and how he was nothing like him. I was kind of disappointed with tonight because I thought my like for Huelo would grow, but it actually dwindled. He was a little too timid for me, and too worried about the next nigga. I was now understanding Oden when he would tell me not to bring Brian up when I was with him… it was weird. Why do you care so much about another man that I used to date?

"Well thank you, this was nice." I stood at my room door, waiting for Huelo to leave.

"It was. What are you doing Sunday night?"

"Bella."

"You're doing Bella?" he laughed.

"No, I'm sorry. Umm, Bella and Tasmine have this thing and I already said I would go so yeah, I'm gonna go do that on Sunday." Horrible lie, I know.

"Right, okay. Well I should see you at the parties tomorrow and Saturday."

"Yep!"

We hugged and then I went inside of my room.

"How was it—"

"I don't wanna talk about it," I told Tasmine and she burst into laughter as I gathered my shit for a hot shower.

When I got out, Tasmine was whispering on the phone with Anton, making me smile. Damn did I miss those days.

Picking up my phone, I saw that Oden had called me. Of all the nights to call, he chose tonight. I turned my lip up when I saw he'd left me a voicemail, because I hated voicemails. Tapping his name on the visual voicemail screen, I hit the speaker button so I could hear out loud.

Tevin Campbell's "Can We Talk" burst through, prompting Tasmine to sit up in her bed with a frown while laughing. She told Anton she would call him when she was almost ready, so I guess she was going over there, and then she came and sat next to me.

I started to write you letters, but I wanted to be more clever. I wanted to get down and sweet talk you. But just like a baby I could not talk. And I tried to come closer but could not walk. And I think of it every night.

Once the part he wanted me to hear was over, he turned it down to speak into my voicemail, and Tasmine and I were on pins and needles listening in.

"Khyyyyllllleeee," he slurred into the phone, obviously drunk; high, too, knowing him. "Baby, I miss you, baby. I can't fucking sleep. I'm out here, by the fucking umm, the shit you stay up in, calling you. I don't know what to fucking say, man." It got quiet for a second. "I'm sorry about that Keesha shit, baby, and I'm begging you to forgive me. I'll do whatever you want. I will rub your feet. I don't like sucking toes but I'll do it."

Tasmine and I giggled at that part, but lowly as if he could hear us.

"I'm just miserable without you, Khyle. I know you said you don't love me and shit, but I still love you and I can make you love me. I tell you what," he slurred. "If you umm… fuck was I gon' say? Yeah, if you let me hold you tonight, just hold you so I can get some sleep for once, I will leave you alone for a couple more weeks. Okay? I love you. Call me back. I'm gonna be sitting out here all night. I'm getting out of the car to sit out front."

He hung up and the voicemail ended.

"Tasmine, why the fuck are you crying?" I asked.

"Why are you crying?" she retorted before we both laughed.

"I can't go out there."

"Why?"

"Because he cheated on me."

"Or is it because you feel like people will judge you for taking him back? If you didn't care that he fucked your sister and your best friend, you shouldn't care about this. And I kind of believe him about nothing happening."

"He said she touched it. And how many things am I gonna let him get a pass on?"

"I think he's learned his lesson by now, Khyle. But it's up to you, I have somewhere to be, boo."

I thought about it for a little bit, and then just threw on this t-shirt dress and some Rihanna slides. I removed my shower cap and redid my bun, before grabbing my little purse, my phone, and my ID.

Making my way downstairs, I saw him sitting outside of the building on one of the little squares. He was wearing grey sweats and the grey hoodie to match, with some gray and white Jordan 12s. He was drinking from a bottle, just staring at the South dorm across the way. When I came outside, he didn't notice me. I walked around from behind to face him, and he sat up slowly as if he couldn't believe it.

He was so fucking fine, and damn did I miss him. I hadn't seen him in forever it felt like, and just the scent of his cologne had me my heart beating rapidly.

CHAPTER SIX

Oden

"*I* don't even know why I came out here, Oden." Khyle kept her arms folded across her chest as she stared down at her pretty feet.

"Because you love me?" I bent my neck a little so I could look into her face. She just shook her head at me, catching the tear that was on its way down her cheek. "You looked nice tonight," I sniffled due to it being a little nippy outside.

"What?"

"I saw you leaving with him. Big burly nigga with the short curls." I took another sip of the bottle of Brandy.

Seeing her look sexy as hell while with another nigga fucked my head up for sure. I had a mind to follow them to the movies and whoop homie's ass, but I knew that wouldn't get me anywhere with her. My main goal was to get back with Khyle, not beat on my chest to show the world how manly I was. Especially since right now I was feeling like a straight up bitch.

"Oh, well thank you."

"He touched you?"

"Why does it matter? I mean if he touched my pussy in my room for all of two seconds, would it be a big deal? No, it wouldn't if I had a little to drink, right?" she cocked her head. I hadn't seen her this close up in so long, so I was admiring her beauty for a minute.

"Please tell me you're fucking with me and that this nigga didn't really touch your pussy, Khyle. Please." I ran my hand down my face. My hair was stuffed back into my hood.

The fact that he may have even so much as seen what she had between her legs, had my body overheating.

"No, he didn't, Oden. But it wouldn't be a problem if I let him because I'm single. Something you weren't when you let that hoe put her hand on your dick." She wiped her tears again. "Did you have sex with her that night too? Now would be the time to tell me."

Just as I was about to speak, I saw Anton pull up, and Tasmine walk to his car. As soon as the passenger door closed, he sped off.

"No, I didn't fuck her that night. She was trying to suck my dick, and I swear I was almost falling asleep because I was that twisted. However, I kept telling her to leave and I thought she had, so I started to pass out. Your phone call is what kind of stopped me from dozing, and helped me realize that her ass was still there trying to get some shit started."

"So if I hadn't called, you would have fucked her basically. And probably raw, too, if she was in control."

I understood why she felt the way she felt, but honestly, that night I didn't even plan on fucking Keesha. I was so gone that I was just going with the flow. I would have never even allowed her to ride home with us if I were sober, and I would have had the driver take me home before going to the hoe crib with Anton and Truman. I just got caught up in some shit that I didn't stop, and I was regretting it like crazy.

"Khyle, I love you." I grabbed her arm to pull her closer. She tried to move away but she wasn't strong enough. As soon as I got her up to me, I hugged her body tightly. "Take me back, please. I didn't do anything," I whispered, kissing her neck.

She was silent, but then I felt her arms circle my torso to hug me back.

"This is the last time you fuck up, Oden. If anything, and I mean anything happens with you and another woman, it's over forev—"

I cut her off by pressing my lips against hers, and then shoving my tongue into her mouth. I'd missed kissing her, so I was making up for lost time right now.

After pulling away, I pecked her once more and then led her to my car. I hit the alarm so she could get inside, but she stopped when she saw something in her seat.

"Oh, I meant to take them out of the car with me but I forgot."

She grabbed the roses and inhaled the scent before smiling. She then turned to me for a kiss, before I helped her in.

"I hope you had a horrible time tonight," I said once I cranked my car up.

She sighed and laid her head against the headrest.

"Well, I didn't. I had such a good time that I almost thought about getting into a relationship with him."

I laughed because I understood her rude ass humor by now.

"Oh yeah?"

"Yep."

"So is it okay if I make love to you tonight even though you like him so much? That wouldn't be a problem, would it?"

"No," she spoke so lowly that I could barely understand.

I took her small hand into mine, and just held it until we made it to my place. When we got inside, I hit the lights, and she immediately started scanning the room with her eyes as she moved further into my townhouse.

"No one has been here but me and the homies, so quit looking for whatever you're looking for."

"I know you're not that stupid. I mean, you're stupid for jeopardizing the best thing that has ever happened to you, but I hope it stops there."

"Stupid as fuck for that you mean," I replied, making her grin.

I led her to the bathroom, and we both undressed one another. As she turned the shower on, I brushed, flossed, and rinsed. I hated the taste of alcohol in my mouth, especially when I was attempting to sober up.

We got into my big ass shower, with three showerheads, and just let the water cover us completely. I moved closer to her, and gripped the sides of her face to stare down at her. I'd never been in love before, but damn could I tell that I was in it. It's true when they say you'll know it when it hits you.

"Oden, I forgot to tell you."

"Tell me what?"

"That I love you too."

I sucked her lips while playing with her nipples, and rubbing all over her body. Every time she moaned into my mouth, my dick got harder. Sitting her down on the built-in shower seat, I dropped down and propped her legs up. I started with slow, deep, sensual kisses on her middle, as she shivered under my touch. I then let my tongue swipe between the folds, before collapsing my mouth around her clit.

"Oden," she cooed, as I pressed her thighs into her stomach, sucking the life out of her center.

She gripped the handles on the seat, as her chest heaved up and down lightly. I continued snaking my tongue over her bud, and switching back to sucking because I knew she loved that shit.

"Oooh," she sniveled, quivering a bit when I dipped my tongue into her opening and brought it back up.

Burying my face in deeper, I let my mouth become one with her pussy, as her juices dripped down my chin just the way I liked. Listening to her voice shake as she moaned uncontrollably was my favorite part of fucking her.

"You're drenched down here, baby," I mumbled against her lower lips before diving back in.

"Ah! Odeeeennnn!" she cried out, releasing.

I kept eating, feasting on my favorite meal, as she stared down at me like she was about to cry. It took no time to yank that second orgasm out of her, and once I did, I rose to my feet. Picking her up, I sat on the shower seat, and then brought her down into my lap to take my dick. I was happy to know she hadn't been touched, because her pussy was virgin tight and giving me a hard time.

"Bounce on it," I groaned as I sucked the shit out of her left nipple, making her whimper.

I held onto her torso as she moved up and down slowly, making it easy for me to keep going at her nipples. Her small hands held onto my shoulders as she began to bounce faster, coating my dick with her nectar completely.

"Ah, fuck," I moaned before pulling her lip into my mouth. "This is gonna always be my pussy," I growled before kissing her, bouncing her on my rod a little faster, and making her scream into my mouth a little. "I missed you, baby."

I sat back, still holding her sides, and just watched her move up and down my pole. I loved seeing that pretty face with those full lips. She always licked her lips while she rode me, and that in combination with seeing her perfectly round breasts move about, always help me bust. Not to mention the pussy stayed sopping wet while gripping me.

"I'm about to cum… fuck."

"I need to-to get off," she whined, just before cumming so hard she shook.

"Nope."

I sat up and hugged her body, before humping upward feverishly. She was digging her nails into my back while I bit down on her shoulder. We began calling out together as I fucked her mercilessly, and moments later, we were exploding together. We sat there kissing for a few moments, and then I picked her up off of my dick so we could actually shower together.

This would be the first and last time I lost my girl. I put that on everything I love.

CHAPTER SEVEN

Truman

"*L*ife is perfect," I smirked at Oden and Anton, as we sat in the VIP of TAO Nightclub inside of the Venetian hotel.

TAO was big as fuck, inspired by Chinese culture, and stayed popping until like 5am on the weekends. I loved their VIP sections because it reminded me of our glassed one back at Palace, meaning it was away from the 'regulars' per se. If it had glass it'd be even better.

"For us, yeah," Anton chuckled.

I knew what he was referring to, but I would never admit to missing Pilar. Little did they know, I was damn near on the verge of crying like a bitch some nights. The way I fixed that though, was laying up under Chiina.

And speaking of Chiina, I knew she thought we were getting serious, and shit, maybe we were. I ain't know what the fuck I was doing right now, and I didn't like that feeling at all. I was used to having control over my shit, and right now it was like I wasn't in charge of anything in my personal life.

"Yeah, for us," Oden snapped me from my thoughts, grinning. I ain't seen that nigga grin that wide lately unless a bitch was in his face.

"Ole lovesick ass," I taunted him and he shrugged.

"I was never into the player life, I was forced." He bobbed his head to the Jeezy track playing over the club.

"Forced?" both Anton and I said, snapping our necks in his direction as he chuckled.

"Yes. I wasn't about to be chasing these hoes, so I used their asses for what they were good for, and threw them to the birds. I've always said if I found the right one, I would do right. I just hadn't found her until Khyle."

"Then how did your dick get in Keesha's hand, bro?" I squinted my eyes.

"Hell if I know, I was twisted." He turned to us cheesing, before we all cracked up at his fake ass.

We all got up to overlook the club, and them niggas were going wild down there, right along with the many strobe lights. As I scanned the crowd, I swear I saw Pilar dancing up on some nigga. Now granted everybody down there almost looked like ants, but I knew my bitch and I knew that damn dress.

"Aye, Pilar is here with some nigga," I said, keeping my eyes locked on her.

"Nigga, what? How the fuck can you see anything? I couldn't tell you if my own mama was down there dancing," Anton scoffed.

"We're two totally different people. I know that damn dress

because I dropped a couple grand on it after she begged me for it. Now she's out here popping her ass on another nigga in it? Got me fucked up." I started off but Oden gripped my shoulder.

"And what you gon' do when you get down there?" he inquired.

"Whoop that nigga's ass, fuck you mean? She knows better than to be out here freak dancing on some other nigga! Everybody in Nevada knows Pilar is mine, and right now she's embarrassing me."

"Do not go down there, man." Anton shook his head as he kept his eyes on the dance floor.

"Instead of doing this, Tru, how about you go over to see her tomorrow to talk. Why cause a scene? It's only gonna make her angrier," Oden explained as I kept my eyes locked on Pilar.

When the guy pushed her head down, bending her over, I almost lost it so Anton and Oden grabbed me up.

"Nigga, have you even apologized to her?" Anton frowned, holding me by my collar.

"Fuck off me!" I shoved him. "I don't apologize to nobody!"

"Then prepare for that to continue to happen, Truman," Oden pointed down at her and the guy. "If you love the girl you can't continue to act like this."

"Act like what, nigga?" I got into Oden's face, and he glanced off, laughing as if I were a joke. That made me madder.

"Aye, you're drunk, so I'm gonna let you slide, Tru. But you're acting like a little ass boy is what I mean." He stared me dead in the eyes. "Little boys cry and stomp their feet when they don't get their way, instead of accepting their faults and trying to make it better. The girl caught you cheating on her twice, and you haven't done shit to try and rectify that."

"Don't act like you ain't just cheat on your bitch."

"Watch your mouth when you're speaking about my girl, nigga. And I didn't cheat, I was in a setting I had no business being in while in a relationship. But even though I didn't cheat, I was damn near on my knees, begging like the Temptations to make it better. I wasn't playing house with strippers, expecting Khyle to just show up on my doorstep one day."

"Whatever, man."

I looked down at the dance floor again, and saw Pilar and the guy making their way through the crowd like they were leaving. I raced down the one million stairs hoping to catch them, and once I got down there, I saw they were heading out.

"Truman!" I heard Anton and Oden calling after me but I didn't care to turn around. Pilar had me twisted.

I finally caught up to them once they got out into the hotel, so I pulled Pilar into me.

"Truman? What the fuck?" she frowned, pushing me off her.

WHAM!

I punched that nigga she was with right between the eyes, causing him to fall and slide on his ass across the marble floors. Before I could go in for some more, security had me hemmed up, slamming me into the nearest wall.

"Pilar!" I hollered loudly as fuck when I saw her kneeling down, tending to that nigga. "Pilar!"

"Tru, calm yo' ass down, man. He's just a little twisted, can you let him go, we'll take him," Oden pleaded to the security guards who were calling the real police on me, while holding me against the wall in cuffs.

"Back up, sir."

Oden and Anton stood there shaking their heads at me like I was the dumbest nigga in the world. And as I looked over my shoulder to see Pilar walking out with that nigga while rubbing his back, I felt just how I looked… stupid.

It seemed like every day I was fucking my life up and doing dumb shit. It felt like since that Christmas party, my life had spiraled out of fucking control, and I couldn't get a grip.

As the real police took over and escorted me out of the hotel to get into their patrol car, all kinds of shit ran through my mind. This was the last day of me being on some bullshit.

CHAPTER SEVEN

Shayne

Lloyd and I were at Prime Steakhouse, this nice restaurant inside of the Bellagio hotel. As usual, he'd pissed me off again by not answering his phone when I wanted him to, so this was his way of making it up to me. I wasn't sure how much longer I could go on just being his friend. I had never been so ready to be in a relationship with someone in my life.

"You look beautiful," he commented as I scanned the menu. I was still trying to be upset, because I didn't want him to think that a nice dinner would be all it took to get me back on his side again.

"Thanks," I replied dryly, thinking about how I'd lied to Pierce and told him I had a show tonight. Thank God he had to work.

"So you're gonna be upset like this all night until I fuck some sense into you?" he cocked his head, licking his full, chocolate lips.

"What makes you think we're gonna be sleeping together tonight, Mr. Gardener?" I laughed to myself as if it were the funniest thing ever. We were most likely gonna be fucking one another tonight.

"I mean I assumed, but I guess not. I ain't tripping though." He leaned back in his seat to continue looking over the menu himself.

"Oh, so you don't care one way or the other? We haven't had sex in a week and a half, but that's fine? You're smashing that many other bitches?"

"Shayne, calm yo' ass down, shawty. Who said I was fucking other bitches? Have you ever seen me with another woman?"

"What about Elodie?"

"The one all the way in Birmingham, Alabama? Yeah, she's satisfying my needs every night, you're right."

"Don't get smart."

"I'm not. I just don't understand how you can sit across from me like some scorned wife, when you're the one who has a man."

Lloyd knew nothing about Pierce proposing to me, and I wanted to keep it that way. Until I could figure how I was going to be supported, Pierce was gonna continue to be my man, and Lloyd was gonna be my side nigga.

"Here you go," I rolled my eyes.

"Exactly. You wanna run yo' damn mouth about shit, but when niggas bring it yo' way it's a problem. Shut yo' mouth sometimes and just enjoy the moment."

I stared at this fine ass nigga with my eyebrow raised for a moment, wondering who the fuck he was talking to. His beautiful curly hair was so shiny, and went perfectly with his deep chocolate skin. I could see his muscles that looked like they wanted to break through his top to reveal themselves to us all. He was so sexy, and I was turned on by the way he had just talked to me, but I wouldn't let that be known.

"Whatever, nigga."

The waitress showed up about five minutes later with our drinks, and then took our food orders. We were quiet for a little bit just sipping them, and looking at everything else but one another. I couldn't take it for much longer though, so I decided to speak up.

"I'm sorry." I reached across to touch his big hand.

He took my hands into his, and just pecked them lightly.

"I know. But ain't too many more times I'm gonna allow you to get smart with me, or press me about what the fuck I do when I'm not with you. When you leave your nigga, let me know, and depending on what I'm feeling like at the time, we can maybe work towards something."

I just nodded, not in the mood to argue. Plus, he was right. I would never let a nigga clock my moves like I did him, especially if the dude had a girlfriend.

As he lifted my hand to kiss it again, I saw Earl Jr. walking to a table with Alanna. She was dressed like I'd never seen before, and smiling like I'd never seen before either. That dirt ass nigga must have put something in her food for her to be so stuck on him. He was still parading his fiancée around town on television events and shit, while Alanna sat in the background like a fucking fool.

"Excuse me, baby," I scooted from my chair and got up, headed over there. I didn't know why I cared so much about Alanna's stupid ass affairs. "Well isn't this nice," I smiled once I reached their table.

"I don't want any problems, Shayne."

"You can kiss my ass. I was looking at Alanna, and therefore *talking* to Alanna muthafucka."

"Shayne," Alanna stared up at me with her mouth twisted. She looked so pretty, but the sight before me made me sad. She was taking whatever this nigga gave her. She was so weak!

"Relax, I just haven't talked to you or seen you in such a long time. I almost thought you were dead, but I'm happy to see that you aren't."

"I have umm, just been busy you know. Earl Jr. had to travel so he asked me to come with him and stuff," she grinned at him, before looking back up at me.

"Oh, okay," I nodded slowly. "And did you travel with him and his fiancée? Or did he fly you on a separate plane, and get you a hotel room separately from them too? Or no, maybe it was one big threesome!" I shouted even though I didn't mean to.

"Baby, the appetizer is here," I felt and smelled Lloyd hug me from behind and kiss on my neck.

"Could you please step away from my table, please," Earl Jr. put his hand up like he couldn't stand the sight of me.

"Aye nigga, calm yo' ass down, she's leaving. And move yo' fucking hand, it's making me uncomfortable," Lloyd snapped.

"Excuse me?" Earl Jr. rose from his seat, scanning Lloyd like he was about to do something.

Lloyd stepped closer to him and gritted, "I said sit yo' ass down, and calm the fuck down before you never see a muthafuckin' football stadium again homie."

"Earl," Alanna spoke up, because she knew Lloyd was nothing to play with. Anyone Oden Bishop called a friend was just as nutty as his ass.

"Yeah, listen to yo' girl, because you about to get fucked up, bruh."

Earl Jr. stared into Lloyd's eyes for a little bit longer, before finally sitting back down in his seat. Lloyd laughed lightly at him, before taking my hand and leading me back to our table. We sat down, and I could feel him watching me as I filled up my appetizer plate.

"What?" I frowned.

"You're fucking crazy, shawty," he chuckled.

"No I'm not, that situation just irks me." I glanced over at Alanna and Earl Jr., laughing while drinking champagne. She was so stupid.

"Understandable, but tonight I want you to focus on me."

"Okay, baby, I'm sorry. I don't even know why I gave them any of my attention," I forced a smile.

For the rest of the dinner, I paid attention to my boo and not their annoying asses. I was done with Alanna for good.

After dinner, Lloyd and I went straight to his townhouse. It was very nice, much nicer than the apartment he was in. He had to be making money because I swear it felt like he'd just gotten that apartment last week, and now he was here.

We both started undressing as soon as we got into the bedroom, and once I was in my bra and panties, I went into the bathroom. After relieving my bladder and washing my hands, I came out to see Lloyd sitting on the edge of his bed in the dark. He was toying with my engagement ring while staring at it.

"How did you get that?" I asked, walking closer to him but slowly.

"Rolled out of your purse. You're getting married, Shayne?"

I knelt down in front of him and caressed the side of his face.

"No, baby, I'm not getting married."

"Then why do you have this shit? Don't tell me another nigga gave it to you as a gift."

"No, no. Pierce asked me to marry him, but I'm not gonna marry him, Lloyd. You know that. And once I tie—"

"Up some loose ends. I don't wanna hear that shit. Here." He moved my hand from his face and pressed the ring into my hand. "I don't even know why I'm tripping," he scoffed, lying on his back.

I put the ring back into my clutch and snapped it closed. I then removed my undergarments, and crawled onto his huge bed. He just watched me, not saying a word as I pulled on his boxers. He lifted a little so that I could get them down, and once they were off, I threw them to the side. I sucked his lips as I rubbed on his dick to get it hard, which literally took me about 15 seconds. Once it was damn near comparable to a brick, I kissed down his six-pack and took him into my mouth.

CHAPTER SEVEN

Santino

$\mathcal{M}$y homies and I were sitting outside of the gym after having an intense ass workout. I swear I loved football with all my heart, but my body hated that shit at the moment. An ice bath sounded like heaven right now, but since these damn dorms only came with showers, that shit wasn't happening. Hopefully my baby would be up to massaging her man.

"How did yo' date with Khyle go, Huelo?" Trevor looked over at Huelo, smirking.

I didn't say shit because Bella had already told me Oden and Khyle were back together. And the worst part of it all was that she got back with him the night of her date with my boy.

"I didn't do too well, man. I was nervous as fuck for some reason," Huelo scoffed.

"You? Nervous? Nigga, all you do is talk and get in people's face. Since when are you nervous my nigga?" Trevor fussed.

"Since he got in the presence of some pussy he wanted," I chimed in, making him shove me lightly.

"It was like every time I wanted to talk, nothing would come out so I would just stay quiet. She would try to talk to me but I just didn't have shit to say. Well, I did, but I didn't know how I guess. And I kept bringing her ex up."

"Nigga, you a bitch," Trevor teased, shaking his head and downing some of his water. "I would have had her ass bent over in the back seat fucking with me."

"She wasn't gonna fuck him the first night," I defended her.

I didn't know Khyle like that, but I had hung around her before with Bella, and she just didn't strike me as the type of girl to bust it open on the night of the first date. Now, her sister, possibly, but not her.

"If she would fuck one nigga in the bathroom, and leave with another, shorty would fuck him the first night," Trevor corrected me.

"Wait, who did she fuck in a bathroom?' Huelo frowned, just as surprised as I was.

"Y'all ain't know? Bitch came to a party with some tall ass nigga, was dancing and kissing all on him. Then she went upstairs and got fucked, while the tall nigga was waiting on her."

"Man, where you hear this bullshit?" I sucked my teeth, shaking my head as I stared at the upperclassmen dorm across the way.

"My homegirl, Raye. She saw Khyle with the tall nigga, and then she said she went upstairs behind Khyle, to use the bathroom, but Khyle slipped into a bedroom. Raye said when she came out of the bathroom, she walked into the bedroom just being nosey, and heard Khyle getting fucked in the bathroom within the room. And Raye said when she went back downstairs, she saw the tall nigga sitting there, so it couldn't have been him that Khyle was fucking," Trevor elaborated and had Huelo and I speechless.

"So she's a hoe," Huelo scoffed. "If I had known that, I wouldn't have taken her ass out, I would have just smashed."

"Oden ain't wifing no hoe, man, something has to be wrong with that story," I frowned. It wasn't looking too good for Khyle, because she was definitely sounding like a slut.

"I mean look, her damn sister gets around, don't she?" Trevor raised a brow. "She's fine as fuck though. I'd still smash her sister. I'd make her change her ways though, and wife her," he grinned.

"A chick like Shayne wouldn't even let you breathe her same air, nigga," I laughed. "She's out there but she's picky with it. Only a certain caliber of niggas can hit."

"That's now, but when I make it to the NFL, I bet I can hit."

I shook my head at Trevor, before looking over at Huelo who was staring off, seemingly disappointed by the Khyle story.

"You good, man?" I asked.

"Yeah, yeah, I'm straight. Just glad I heard this before I asked her ass out again. Thanks for that information, Trevor, even though it was *after* my date."

"Aye nigga, Raye only told me because I informed her you were taking Khyle out. So there was no way to say anything before."

Huelo saying he almost asked Khyle out again caught me off guard because I thought everyone knew she was back with Oden.

"You know she's back with Oden anyway, so there wouldn't have been a second date, bro."

"When did she get back with him? Our date was just two damn days ago!"

"About umm… two days ago."

"Wow." He laughed angrily and looked off for a moment. "Cool."

"Aye nigga, I thought you said Leena took her ass back home already," Trevor tapped on my arm, and when I looked his way, I saw Leena walking up to where we were.

"Are you fucking serious?" I mumbled so only my friends could hear me, as I rose to my feet. "Leena."

"Hey, baby! I was supposed to go home today, but I decided to stay back so we could have some alone time together. Crystal was always trying to come with me to visit you."

"Leena, I'm busy this evening. Maybe—" I stopped myself as I looked down into her disappointed eyes. "Come here, let me talk to you." I pulled her away and checked my surroundings to make sure Bella nor none of her friends were around.

"What, baby?" She caressed my face once we were on the side of the gym, hidden. "Is something wrong?"

"Leena, you know we're not in a relationship, right?"

"Right now, no, because you want to focus on school and football. I know this already, baby, but I still think we can spend time together when I come out here."

"Leena, I fucks with you, like I really do but, remember the girl Bella I told you about?"

"The skank that you got pregnant, who aborted it before messing with another guy?" she raised her brow while folding her arms.

Yeah, I kind of trashed Bella to Leena a little bit because I hated that she was with Dean. Every time I saw them at school back in Arizona, it pissed me off. I wanted to fuck him up on plenty of occasions, but I knew it would be for nothing. At that time, I couldn't be with Bella due to my parents forbidding it, so what would come of me knocking Dean upside the head?

"Honestly, what happened was that I got her pregnant, and upon finding out, I left her and told her to stay away from me. She tried to talk me out of it, but I dissed her. So, she got an abortion, and then some months after, she got a new boyfriend," I told the truth.

"Okay, good to know she's not a shady bitch, but why are you telling me this, Sanz?"

"Ahh," I grunted lowly and ran my hand down my face. "I'm telling you all this because at that time I was young, immature, and had to abide by all the rules my parents enforced. Now, I'm grown, more mature, and I follow my own rules. By saying that, I have always loved Bella, and I've always wanted to be with her. She's finally giving me a chance to and I'm gonna take it."

"Hold up, so you wait until you leave the state to make the bitch your girlfriend? Why, Santino?" she shot daggers at me. I kept quiet, but she figured it out. "Oh, the bitch goes to this school, huh? Where is she! Where the fuck is Bella!" Leena shouted so loudly that people walking by, saw us and stared.

"Aye, calm the fuck down!" I hemmed her up against the building wall. "Leena, we were never in a relationship, so it was possible that I would meet someone anyway. I would like for us to be cool, but if you can't accept that then I don't know what to tell you."

"Is that why you came here instead of USC?"

"No," I half lied. "I came here because this was a good school. I knew it would look good for my after football life if people saw I'd gotten a degree from UNLV."

I could have gone to California, but I preferred Nevada's school to theirs. Bella coming here was just a big bonus.

"USC is just as good."

"Leena, go to your hotel. *Please* go to your hotel, and calm yourself down before driving home to Scottsdale."

"Don't act like you care about me," she started off but I grabbed her arm.

"I do care, but I also want you to know that I love Bella and I won't be changing my mind about her, so don't try to convince me to."

"Fuck you, Santino." She snatched from me and rushed off.

Leena was crazy as fuck, and so was Bella. This situation had me a little on edge, I must admit. Not just because if they met it'd be the brawl of the century, but because I knew if I lost Bella this time, it'd be for good, and I really don't think I could survive that.

"Fuck!" I shouted. I looked to my right and saw some people staring at me frowning. "Fuck y'all niggas looking at!" I barked, making them rush off.

CHAPTER SEVEN

Tasmine

"So when you asked him about Amethyst, what did he say?" Khyle questioned as we sat inside of Magliano's having lunch. We didn't usually dine at such expensive places, well expensive for a college budget, but Khyle offered to treat us since Oden had broken her off this morning.

"Yeah, what did that nigga have to say for himself?" Bella sipped her drink, while Perry just smiled shyly before glancing at Khyle.

For the first time, they were hearing why I suddenly stopped talking to Anton after Christmas break. I think I was too embarrassed because I felt like the same thing that had happened to me in high school was happening yet again. I didn't want people to know that I was dumb enough to give my body away twice to men that were playing me. But now that Anton was my man, it was nothing for me to spill the tea.

"He just basically said she was some hoe that he was smashing. He says he didn't know that he wasn't supposed to sleep with anyone else since technically we weren't together."

"You believe him?" Khyle asked.

"Yeah, niggas are dumb. But if he tries that *playing dumb* shit again, he will not get another chance from me."

I wasn't playing around. I promised myself that I wouldn't be weak and that I would have some pride when it came to these niggas. It was easy to cower under them, and let them run all over you in order to keep them. But Tasmine Randall was not about them games and bullshit anymore. I refused to be with anyone who wasn't a man, and men knew how to keep it in their pants and act accordingly at all times.

"That's what I said. Oden has gotten way too many passes from me. If that nigga even gives me a cold I'm dumping his ass," Khyle sucked her teeth as all of us burst into laughter, even Perry.

"Damn, bitch, a cold?" Bella grinned as she ate some of her ravioli.

"Yes, a cold," Khyle giggled, flashing her beautiful smile and flinging her long ass hair. "But nah, he's just on thin ice. From sleeping with Shayne and Emery, to bringing a bitch home and letting her even *think* they were gonna fuck, you would assume that I wouldn't want him anymore."

"But you do," I reached over to touch the *Bishop* necklace that she was wearing again. "I don't think he's gonna mess up again, though."

"You don't?" Bella frowned. Not in a way that said she disagreed, but more like she was wondering how I came to that conclusion.

"Wait, she didn't tell y'all how the nigga called her and played Tevin Campbell's 'Can We Talk' in her damn voicemail?"

"Who- who is Tevin Campbell?" Perry finally opened her mouth, pushing up her glasses.

"R&B from like before we were born, chica," Bella answered.

"Before we were born?" I cocked my head at Bella.

"Yes, bitch. We were born in '98, and Can We Talk' came out in '93. That's my jam, don't question me." Bella swayed in her seat as we chuckled. "But anyway, what the fuck? You just told me he was really sappy with it. I ain't know the nigga took the Drake route."

"I mean it was nice," Khyle shrugged, chewing her food.

"More than nice. Bitch went to his house and fucked him in the shower," I let the table know, and Bella giggled.

I noticed Perry's brows dip for a second before returning to their normal position. Either this bitch was a freak, crazy, or a crazy freak. I was just waiting to walk into a strip club and see her ass wearing contacts and flinging around a pole.

"Well, I'm just happy that we're all happy in the personal life department," Bella lifted her lemonade as if it were wine before taking a sip.

"Ain't you still with Dean?" Khyle raised her perfectly arched eyebrow.

"I won't be when we I go home sometime soon. I'm gonna sit him down and just tell him that I need to focus on school."

"I think you should mention Santino," I looked into her eyes.

"Why? All Santino wants me to do is break up with Dean and I will. Dean doesn't need all the details. Plus, chica, if I even let S-A-N come out of my mouth, Dean will go nuts. Can't even mention hand sanitizer around his ass."

"Okay, it's gonna bite you later, Bella."

"Tasmine, you always say that. You said that Khyle doing you know what would come back to haunt her, and it hasn't."

"Because no one knows but you guys, and I know you won't tell," Khyle chimed in.

"Exactly, chica."

"Thank God, because Oden would be pissed about the baby being gone," I said, and Bella and Khyle nodded.

The four of us finished eating lunch, and then went to the fashion mall. We were just window-shopping, but Khyle got us all some new stilettos, well just Bella and me. Perry didn't want anything. All she did was stay quiet like usual, stare at Khyle, and laugh here and there if something was *really* funny.

We came back to the dorm, and split up so that we could all take showers and get ready for tonight. Anton, Truman, and Oden were throwing another party, except this one was promoted as a pool party. I had the cutest thong bathing suit, but Anton didn't approve, so I had to wear my other one. It was just as cute and since my body was on point it was gonna be sexy, but I still wanted my thong one.

"Oden won't mind you wearing that one?"

I watched Khyle brush her hair down while wearing her bathing suit. The thong was a pretty pastel pink, and the bandeau top was the same color, with blue, yellow, and purple embroidery. We both bonded over the fact that we loved thong bathing suits.

"He said he doesn't mind because I'm his anyway. And trust me, no nigga will be bold enough to touch me or even look too hard with him there."

"True," I laughed. "If it were Huelo, that'd be a different story."

"Ugh, don't remind me. His punk ass. If that random nigga had have told him to move, I'm sure he would have."

I never took Huelo's big ass to be a bitch, but I guess he was.

"You notice Perry be looking at you all the time?" I had to say something.

"Yeah, but I just think she's admiring. You know like when you see a girl with a banging body, and you just admire it. You don't mean anything by it, nor are you jealous, you're just silently giving props."

"I don't know, Khyle." I pulled my bikini top up and tied it around my neck.

We dressed in front of one another all the time. I'd seen every crevice of Khyle and vice versa; Bella too. We've had many drunken nights together, and sometimes a bitch gets naked because she's so twisted. We never did anything like that, because all of us were strictly dickly, but we have sat in our rooms together, ass naked and drinking.

"What you think, she wants to eat my pussy?" Khyle chuckled.

"Maybe."

"Well, she does have a gap, and you know what they say about them gaps," she began playfully twerking.

"Ugh!" I laughed.

By the time Khyle and I done were patting glitter all over our body like some damn strippers, Bella was knocking at the door. I let her in, and then after Khyle and I put on our cover-ups, the three of us left.

"No Perry?" I asked.

"No, she's been a little glum since we left lunch."

***

And my bitch cold, she a centerfold. Put her on a stand, and she never told...

"Blasé" by Ty Dolla $ign played loudly over the pool area of the apartment building. There were a good 60 people here dancing, drinking, smoking; the same drill. All the girls were in bathing suits, and most of the niggas had on trunks, excluding Anton and Oden who said that wasn't their style. Truman's skinny ass was shirtless, showing off his tattooed covered chest as he shared a blunt with some girl that I'd been seeing him with a lot.

"Is that Truman's new girlfriend?" I whispered into Anton's ear as I sat in his lap.

"Nah, that nigga is just dumb," he replied before kissing my lips gently.

"Let's jump!" Bella said to us before kissing Santino, who was sitting on a lawn chair getting to know Oden.

"I'm good," I smiled, draping my arm around Anton. I wanted more lap time before I got wet, so I was gonna hold out for a little bit.

Khyle kissed Oden sensually for a little bit, and then stood up to remove her cover up. All the niggas that were nearby were damn near drooling at my roomy. And then when Bella did the same, I thought them niggas were gonna start screaming like some fans.

Oden grabbed Khyle by her waist, and brought her in so that he was face to face with her stomach since he was sitting. He placed a soft kiss on it, before turning her around and squeezing her ass. She yelped when he spanked her lightly, before she grabbed Bella's hand.

Khyle and Bella stood at the edge of the pool, before jumping together and falling under the water. All I saw were Bella's blond locks, and Khyle's black ones, floating, before they both shot up from under. They then swam to the edge, and placed their forearms on the concrete to prop their faces up to see us.

"Y'all look good together, no offense," Oden said, glancing at Santino.

"None taken, I agree," he chuckled.

"What y'all gone do about that compliment?" Truman shouted, lying his head against the girl sitting in his lap.

Other niggas were watching Bella and Khyle too, despite this backyard being covered with scantily clad women. My boos were just that fine.

"Nigga, shut up," Bella spat, before she and Khyle laughed.

"My man is here, stop trying to get me to cheat. I know my friend looks good," Khyle chimed in, as we all laughed.

"Not cheating if I'm here," Oden said, taking a pull on his blunt.

"What about you?" Khyle pointed to Santino with her fresh nails.

"I'm fine," he replied, cheesing. These niggas were nasty.

Khyle and Bella turned towards one another, and after Bella cupped Khyle's face, these bitches started tonguing it up. My jaw was on the floor, and it seemed like every nigga over here by us was nutting in their pants.

"Daammmnnnn!" a group of niggas sang.

The girls finally pulled away, and started giggling.

"Come here, Khyle." Oden stood up, ashing his blunt.

She climbed out like he'd asked, and walked up to him. She shrieked when he scooped her up, and carried her inside. Well, it was obvious what they were about to do.

Since Bella was alone now, and staring at me pouting, I pulled my cover up over my head and got into the pool.

The party continued to jump, as Bella and I swam and danced. Khyle must have been getting a damn pussy beat down because she still wasn't back.

I dipped under the water, and when I came back up, I saw that bitch Amethyst standing over my nigga talking. I stood there paralyzed for a few moments, almost in disbelief.

"Who is that?" Bella came up from under the water.

"The stripper, the bitch that was claiming him all over social media."

"Tony! Really, Tony?" she shouted when he stood up and walked around her. He came and kneeled by the pool then smiled at me. "You good?" he asked and I nodded.

"Oh, so this is why you don't wanna fuck with me?" Amethyst came and stood at the edge of the pool with her arms folded.

"Amethyst, take yo' ass on somewhere, please. Don't embarrass yourself."

"Yeah, bitch, don't embarrass yourself!"

"Bella!" I chuckled.

"I hate you— Ah!" Amethyst tried to push Anton, but he moved too quickly and her dumb ass fell into the pool, wetting up her club attire and trashy weave as everyone laughed.

Santino and Anton helped Bella and me out of the pool respectively, as that stupid bitch yelled obscenities.

"Anton, get every single one of these bitches under control, or you and I will not work. That includes your fuck buddies, fake baby mamas, or any ex-girlfriends."

"I told you you're my first girlfriend, Tas."

"I'm sure you have some women who thought they were your girlfriend."

"I promise, I'm gonna get it handled."

"Start with that," I pointed behind me, and shoulder checked him on the way to get my towel.

I watched Anton nod his head towards Amethyst, and some big tall nigga walked into the pool and grabbed her roughly. She screamed and fought, but it was pointless as he carried her out of the back gate.

"What happened?" Khyle finally came back out, hair disheveled, and hickies on her collarbone, inner thigh, and the area next to her vagina. *This nigga Oden plays no games.*

"Nothing," I said, watching Anton come back over to me.

If one more bitch ran up on me, I was throwing this nigga right to her ass. No man was worth this much damn drama, even if he was fine as fuck.

CHAPTER EIGHT

Perry

I stared at my phone, waiting for Snapchat to load the current story that Khyle had up. She was at that nighttime pool party with Bella and Tasmine, and the only reason I didn't want to go was because I wasn't in the mood to sit by and watch her with her boyfriend. For some reason the sight of them, and even the thought of them together, sickened me. I hated to hear her talk about Oden, and I hated when Bella and Tasmine mentioned them having relations. Ugh, it just bothered me like crazy!

I sat up on my bed and tapped the story once it loaded. I smiled as she talked about nonsense, and showed off her bathing suit. I didn't really care about what she was saying, I just wanted to see her face, her body… her. I hadn't noticed that I was smiling at her snaps until it switched to the next person and I felt my face drop back into its normal position. Feeling a little bit deprived, I went to her Twitter and then her Instagram to see if anything new had been posted since I checked 10 minutes ago.

My recent obsession with Khyle came out of nowhere and I

didn't really know where it stemmed from. I didn't want to date her or anything, because I wasn't gay, but I just wanted to be around her, and I enjoyed looking at her. The way she carried herself was so intriguing to me, and then to make matters worse, she was beautiful. Her lips were full, her eyelashes were long, so was her hair, and her body was very nice. I know her butt wasn't big and nor were her breasts, but she still seemed so perfect to me. I hated tattoos and piercings, but the dream catcher on her side, and the belly button ring were very… well… I don't like to use this word, but sexy.

"Ewe," I sucked my teeth as I stared down at the picture of her and Oden on Instagram.

Oden was a very attractive guy if you were into those rugged, thuggy types that carried loaded weapons everywhere they went. I mean personally, he was a bit too frightening, and I could never see myself being comfortable around a man that I was that scared of. The few times he did speak to me, I was so afraid of saying the wrong thing that I just froze up. The way he walked, talked, and moved was scary. You just knew that he didn't play any games, and that he despised bullshit. I guess intimidating guys were attractive these days. He was probably a monster in the bedroom. I cringed at the thought.

I got down off my bed, and threw some popcorn into the microwave. I guess I would just watch a movie or something since I had nothing better to do. Hopefully once it was over, Khyle would be back or would have some new posts up somewhere. *Who are you kidding, Perry? She's not coming back; she's spending the night with Oden.*

As I waited for my popcorn, I unlocked my phone and decided to tap the tab, which would show me all of the pictures Khyle was tagged in. When I did, my eyes almost fell out my head. There she was, in the pool, with her tongue down Bella's throat. How could she kiss Bella? A girl! She was disgusting!

Honestly, I hated to see her kissing anyone, but a woman? Was she serious? And someone she now called her best friend, even though she hadn't even known her a year. Just forget me I see. I was almost mad enough to curse.

I paced the room angrily, trying to think of a way to calm myself down. The microwave beeping stopped me from moving, so I made my way over to grab my popcorn. As I shook the bag up and down so the contents wouldn't be stuck together, an idea hit me. Shoving a handful of popcorn into my mouth, I hurriedly chewed it, before gulping some water down and going into the bathroom.

I knocked on Raquel and Siena's bathroom door, praying they answered. After Bella fucked them both up, they hadn't talked to me because they knew I had told on them. Luckily for Bella they didn't tell on her, so she didn't get into any trouble with the school. I heard through the grapevine that it was because they were gonna get her back way worse than how she got them.

"It's just me, Perry!" I shouted. I knew they heard the knocks because the music they had playing suddenly cut off.

"Go away, bitch, before I fuck you up!" Raquel barked.

"I know you're mad, Raquel, but I have something to tell you. It's something that will get you what you want for sure."

"Girl, bye! You ain't got shit we want but them history notes, and

I still ain't gon' let yo' four-eyed ass in!" Siena chimed in. I hated her more than Raquel.

"It will get you Oden Bishop!"

There was silence, and then finally Raquel pushed open the bathroom door. I stepped back so that I wouldn't get hit.

"Uh uh, talk." Raquel put her hand up to stop me when I tried to walk into her room. "I want Oden and you said you had a way to help me, so help me."

I looked into her face for a few moments, pondering on if I wanted to do this or not. It would be the ultimate betrayal, but I knew in the end I would get what I wanted, even though I didn't know why I wanted it.

I needed to stop being so nice, and start worrying more about myself like the rest of these girls do. All they care about is making themselves happy, so why shouldn't I do the same? Khyle, Bella, Tasmine, Raquel, Siena—they were all alike; just a bunch of super sexually active girls that wouldn't know real love if it slapped them in the face. Not to mention they were more selfish than the Grinch that stole Christmas.

Khyle. Khyle. Although I despised her actions, my infatuation was still at an all-time high. However, she needed to—

"Hello!" Siena yelled, standing behind Raquel with her arms folded.

"Okay," I licked my lips, moving my phone around in my sweaty hands. "Khyle got pregnant by Oden and when she found out, she didn't tell him. She instead got an abortion, and just acted like it never happened."

"So," Siena shrugged. "How will that help Raquel?"

"Well at lunch earlier, Tasmine mentioned that Oden would be very upset if he found out. So if he finds out, you know, somehow, he will leave her… leave Khyle."

I felt like shit for telling, but this breakup had to happen. Khyle shouldn't have been kissing a woman. That was nasty!

Raquel and Siena looked at one another, smiling, before looking back down at me. I hated being so short.

"How rude of me, Perry. Come on in," Raquel stepped back to allow me into her room. "I can't wait to see that bitch Khyle beg for his forgiveness."

CHAPTER EIGHT

Oden

I was lying on my back, watching Khyle ride me backwards. The sight of her sexy back, smooth round ass, and long hair was beautiful. I especially loved when she looked over her shoulder at me with her face all twisted up.

Licking my lips, I lightly spanked her ass, before gripping it into my hands. Sitting up, I groped her titties, and sucked on her upper back as she continued to bounce on my dick. I reached down the front of her to toy with her clit, while enjoying how wet and snug she was.

"Fuck," I grunted, feeling and hearing her pussy coating my dick.

"Oden," she whimpered, slowing down after she came.

I wrapped my arm around her torso, and began guiding her up and down at a faster pace as she cried out.

"Uuuh!" we both yelled together as we exploded.

I threw her down onto her back, and climbed between her legs, pinning her hands down. Kissing on her neck, I let my lips travel down until they were wrapped around her nipples. Her nipples were so sexy to me. I sucked them each hungrily, before coming back up and tonguing her down.

"Oden you're wearing me out," she whined in between kisses.

"I can't help it, baby. I'm so attracted to you. I love you and this body."

She gazed into my eyes innocently for a few moments, before offering a soft smile. I kissed her deeply once more, before rolling off of her and getting some small towels from the warmer. We both cleaned ourselves, washed our hands, and then returned to bed.

"I love you more, Oden." She caressed my face as we laid down facing one another.

"Impossible." I grabbed her hand and kissed the back of it. "And I'm sorry, Khyle."

"You don't have to keep saying that, Oden." She brought the sheets up over her body, but I moved them back down.

"I guess because I made so many promises to be better than the last, and I fucked up so quickly. The one thing you asked me for, I failed to give you in a sense by having that bitch come home with me. It just bothers me."

You would think Khyle was the one who had a nigga in her room with the way I was feeling. Every time I thought about the shit, it made me feel some type of way. I wasn't sure what exactly it was gonna take for me to get over it but, I needed to. I wanted her to know that I would never be in a situation like that again.

"Well, just make sure that from here on out, you don't entertain other women. Even if you just make them think you will fuck them."

"I won't."

I pulled her body into mine, and then pressed my lips against hers.

***

I had to come into Palace early today to make sure that our liquor order was doubled. We straight up ran out of liquor one night because we actually hit capacity, while a line was still wrapped around the corner outside. The club held about 4,500 people, so to be at capacity with people still waiting was crazy. Anyway, to prevent us from running out of liquor again, I wanted to up our next shipment. I just thank God when we ran out, it was about five minutes away from 5am, so we were closing. We just kicked everybody out to save face.

KNOCK! KNOCK!

"Come in!" I called out, standing up from behind my desk.

"Billz." My employee Scott came into my office.

"Aight."

I shut my computer off, and then went downstairs into the main part of the club. I could see Billz as I came down the stairs, admiring the empty venue with that same stupid ass smile he always wore. As I descended the stairs, he turned to look at me.

"Heard you've been looking for me," he folded his arms.

"Yeah, you must've been scared. And since I wasn't about to hunt for no scaredy cat ass nigga, I decided to put the word out."

"Scared? Never. I went on a honeymoon with Marie."

"She finally married you, huh?" I laughed louder than I wanted to. Marie was sexy as fuck, but a gold digger nonetheless. I wonder if Billz knew Anton smashed her. I would love to tell him but that wasn't my place to.

"Sound like a hater to me."

"Never, nigga. You don't have shit I want. But I did *want* to get at you and see if you knew anything about my dealership getting shot up."

"What? Nah." He shook his head 'no'.

I stared blankly at his ass because I knew he was lying. His constant blinking, and his fake confusion were dead giveaways. It was cool though, because I was gonna carry out my initial plan on his ass.

"You ain't hear nothing?"

"Umm, no… no I didn't. Probably was a job from the inside my nigga. If I wanted to get at you about that cheap ass Wraith, I would have done more than shoot up your dealership."

"I hope so. Luckily all they did was break the windows, so everything else was intact. Whoever was behind this was clearly an amateur, because honestly, it didn't really hinder me in anyway. Guess I should have known it wasn't you just by the sloppiness of it. You ain't got any niggas on your team working sloppily, right Billz?"

"No… I don't."

"Right, because that's just a reflection of their boss. You want a drink or something?" I pointed to the bar.

"No, but umm, thanks."

"Scott, you can let Mr. Montgomery out."

I stood there in the middle of my club and watched Scott open the door for Billz. I'm not sure what type of niggas he was used to fucking over and with, but I was in a whole 'nother class. When I was done fucking his shit up, this nigga would be on the street corners begging for change. That's if he makes it that far.

After making sure the club was ready to open up in about five hours, I drove to UNLV so I could put this test questionnaire thing into my teacher's mailbox. I told her I wouldn't be able to make class today, and surprisingly she told me to just drop the shit off in her mailbox before tomorrow morning.

As I was leaving the building, I saw Rachel walking with some girl. The night I invited her to the hoe crib to fuck her and a friend, I ended up standing her up. I instead just took my ass home and blocked her when she started blowing me up on Instagram. The only reason I knew that she'd stopped by outside of hitting me nonstop, was because Truman was there smashing some random. I shook my head as I thought about that nigga. Anyway, I hadn't seen her since, and if God was on my side, then she would walk right by me right now.

"Hey, Oden!" she gripped my bicep as much as she could with her small hand.

"Stop grabbing on me," I moved my arm away with an attitude.

I hated when girls who didn't know me like that, just touched me for no reason. Don't touch me, my got damn hair, or anything else, unless you don' at least sucked my dick before.

"I'm sorry, I just wanted to make sure you were doing okay."

"I'm perfect."

"Wow, so strong. I couldn't imagine being able to just move on with my life after experiencing something so heartbreaking. But then again, I'm a female."

"Okay, what the fuck are you talking about?" I frowned, thoroughly confused.

"Siena, give us a moment." She looked to her friend who stayed put for a few seconds before sauntering off. "You know, the baby," she leaned in, whispering.

"What baby?"

"Wait, please tell me that she didn't do this without your knowledge."

"If you don't hurry up and tell me what the fuck you're talking about, we're gonna have a big ass problem, Rachel!"

"Raquel." She rolled her eyes.

"Same damn difference."

"You got Khyle pregnant, but apparently, she had it sucked out. Or she took a pill of some sort, but all I know is that she was pregnant by you, and she killed it. I just thought she would have discussed something like that with the father."

Clenching my teeth together, I stared past Rachel with my chest heaving up and down subtly. What she was telling me couldn't be the truth right now, it just couldn't be. This bitch had to be lying like a muthafucka. Khyle would never do something like that. And why the fuck would I believe some hood rat bitch that clearly wanted me, over the type of person I knew my girl to be? Yeah, nah, fuck that.

"Yo, you're pathetic," I chuckled.

"What? I'm not pathetic. Khyle got an abortion, Oden. I'm not just saying this so I can have you, I'm over you, honestly."

"Oh yeah? And how did you find this information out? What, she told you?" I crossed my arms and squinted my eyes.

"No I… overheard her, Bella, and Tasmine talking while I was using the bathroom. I live right next door to Bella and Perry so we share a bathroom."

I admit the more she talked the more plausible it sounded, but Khyle wouldn't do something like that.

"Thanks." I patted her shoulder and walked off.

Instead of going to the parking lot where my car was, I decided to go to Khyle's dorm. When I was getting close, I called her to let her know I needed to be let in. By the time I got there, she was standing at the bottom of the glass building, holding the door open with a smile.

"Hey, baby—"

"Tasmine in your room?" I cut her off after giving her a very light kiss. I needed her to tell me that hoe Rachel was lying.

"No, is something wrong?"

"Let's go up first."

"K," she replied softly.

Once we got up into her dorm room, I made sure no one was in the bathroom as Khyle watched me with confused eyes. I knew people eavesdropped like a muthafucka on their neighbors since they shared a bathroom; Rachel just proved it. No way I could live like that.

"What is wrong, Oden?"

"Okay, someone told me something today, and I know it's not true so don't get mad at me when I ask you about it, aight? Only reason I'm questioning you is just to pretty much prove myself right."

"What the fuck are you talking about, boy?"

I ran my hand over my hair one good time as I looked off. I wasn't sure why I was so scared to ask her when I knew it wasn't true.

"Someone told me that you got an abortion. That I got you pregnant, and that you got rid of it."

Her facial expression told me the answer before she even opened her mouth. The way her eyes looked from me to the floor, and from the floor back to me, made it obvious just like with Billz earlier.

"Oden—"

"First I need a yes or no on whether or not that shit is true," I spoke calmly, because I didn't want to push her ass out of the window by her bed.

"You and I—"

"Yes or fucking no, Khyle!"

"Yes!"

"Are you fucking serious?" I laughed angrily, pacing a small area of her room.

"But Oden, we were broken up, so I couldn't tell you about it! And I don't see why I needed to tell you anything!"

"You don't? You really don't think that I should have known that you were aborting our baby? Please tell me that's not what you think, Khyle Luke."

"I could not have a fucking baby, Oden! I am 18 years old, I don't have a job, and I live off my parents. My parents who would probably run me up a flagpole if I came home pregnant by some fucking criminal!"

"Damn, is that all I am?"

"No, Oden, you know what I mean. You——"

"Nah, I don't know what you mean. But see, the reason you should have told me was because for one, it was both of our baby, and secondly, an abortion is very traumatizing for a woman, Khyle. Whatever decision you wanted to make, I would have supported you, and been there for you, regardless of whether we were together or not. If you wanted to keep it I would have been a father, and if you didn't, I would have comforted you through the process. But I guess since I'm a fucking criminal, I'm not capable of shit like that, huh?"

"Oden—"

"Nah, fuck you, Khyle. Go find you a nigga worth having a baby by."

I walked out of her room and she rushed behind me. As I made my way down the hallway towards the elevator, she yelled my name at the top of her lungs. There was no need for me to turn around, because she and I were a wrap… for good.

CHAPTER EIGHT

Bella

"Khyle?" I walked out of my room because I heard her yelling Oden's name.

"I'm gonna go catch him."

"Wait, what happened?"

I realized people in the hallway were watching, so I pulled her into the room with Perry and I. Perry was studying, but who cares? This was obviously important.

"Bella, I have to go before he leaves!" Khyle grunted, trying to pull away from me, so I hugged her tightly from behind, hoping to stop her. Oden was obviously angry, and I doubted there was anything she could do right now. "Bella, let me go!" she screamed loudly, making my ears ring.

"Khyle, give him some time to calm down and tell me what happened."

I glanced at Perry who was chewing on her pencil's eraser with her eyes bucked wide open. I had to look away when Khyle dropped down to the floor and began sobbing hysterically. Her knees were in her chest, and her face was buried in her arms.

"Tasmine was right," she cried, lifting her head up. Her eyes were closed, and her cheeks were drenched, causing her hair to stick to her face.

"Right about what, Khyle?"

"The abortion, Bella! He was so angry!"

"So what, Khyle! You're too young for a baby right now, and like you said, your parents would have been upset." I got down next to her and rubbed her back.

"He was mad that I didn't discuss it with him as the father, not mad that I wouldn't keep the baby."

I felt so bad for her. I mean none of us thought he would find out, and even now I was perplexed that he did. Who could have told him? The only people that knew about the abortion were me, Tasmine, and Perry. Tasmine would never tell, I damn sure wouldn't, and Perry could barely form a complete sentence when talking to Oden, so I knew it couldn't be her.

"Khyle, calm down." I brought her into a hug as she wept.

"He's never gonna take me back," she sniffled.

"He should. You took him back, so he should do the same, right?" She looked at me and nodded her head slowly. "Right so after he calms down a bit, just tell him that he needs to forgive you like you forgave him."

"I will," she half smiled, and it made me smile too, seeing that glimmer of hope in her eyes.

God, please let this nigga take her back ASAP.

***

I walked out of the bathroom from a fresh shower, and then dug into my drawer for some clean panties and a bra. I slipped them on, and right when I pulled my dress down over my head, Perry came in looking like she had something to say but couldn't find the words. I think she was just weirded out from seeing Khyle break down like that.

"You good?" I asked, swiping deodorant under my arms.

"Yes, why wouldn't I be?"

"I'm just asking, Perry. You've been looking like a deer in headlights ever since last night, so I just wanted to make sure."

"Oh."

Sighing, I said, "I just can't get over how Oden found out about the abortion."

"He's pretty well connected out here in Vegas, Bella. Probably someone he knew was at the clinic when she got the pill or something. Who knows with a guy like him." She shrugged, jumping up onto her bed. "Want a bagel sandwich? I didn't know whether you wanted sausage or bacon so I got one of each. You can have first pick."

"No thank you, Perry."

I checked my iPhone and saw that Santino had text me to let me know he'd gotten the hotel room for the weekend. We planned to spend the weekend on the strip together as like a little baecation. We weren't rich so that was the best we could do. However, we hit a little snag when we found out you had to be 21 to book a room on the strip. Luckily, one of Santino's junior class teammates turned 21 in the beginning of January, so he took Santino's money and booked it for us. He'd just dropped off the room keys, so we were about to go.

"Leaving?" Perry munched on her bagel sandwich.

"Yeah, I will be back Sunday night. And umm, if Tasmine isn't around do you think you can check on Khyle? Just make sure she's doing okay, she's pretty sad."

"Yeah, I can do that," she nodded repeatedly.

By the time I got downstairs into the lobby, I saw Santino's car sitting right in front outside, so I rushed out. Throwing my little duffle bag into the back seat, I slid in and pressed my lips against his.

"One more please," he begged in a low tone that I found to be so sexy.

His beautiful caramel complexion looked so supple, just like his curly hair, and his beautiful eyes beamed every time we made eye contact.

"Come on, hurry! I wanna see the room."

"Aight, aight."

He sped out of the school, pulling out onto Tropicana Avenue. He hooked a right onto Las Vegas Boulevard, and as we made our way down, I watched all the people visiting from out of town. The sidewalks were so crowded, filled with celebrity impersonators, club promoters handing out flyers, groups of friends, and couples holding hands. Sometimes I liked Las Vegas on the weekends… sometimes.

Santino pulled into the roundabout driveway of the Treasure Island hotel, pulling right up to valet. After getting a retrieval ticket, we walked straight in and to the elevators. I felt so grown up already, and we hadn't even done anything.

"This is gonna be so much fun," I giggled as we rode the elevator to our floor.

It finally dinged, and I rushed off with Santino on my heels, carrying our bags. I waited impatiently as he opened the door to our hotel, and once he did my mouth dropped. My head tilted back as I scanned the room in amazement. I'd never stayed in a hotel on the strip before; actually, I hadn't stayed in many hotels at all. When my family and I traveled to Italy and Spain, we stayed with family since their homes were pretty large. And outside of that, we didn't leave Arizona.

"It's not even that great, Bella." Santino set our bags down and leaned up against the wall to watch me.

"You don't think so? I love it."

"I've stayed in better hotels, mami."

"Oh yeah? When?"

"When I have to travel out of state for a game, did you forget? We don't exactly have dorm rooms at other schools."

"I forgot all about that. I love basketball season because I get to see you so much more." I made my way over to him, and slipped my arms around his waist.

"I like it too, but only because of you. I miss playing though."

He leaned down to kiss me gently as his big hands went right to lifting my dress up. Our tongues danced around one another, and we sucked each other's lips here and there. Pushing my panties downward, he dropped to the floor to help me step out of them. Before I could do anything, he bent me over the little writing desk in the room, and dropped to his knees to eat me out from the back.

"Baby," I whimpered, kicking my flip-flops off under the table.

I pressed my upper body into the desk as he sucked my clit, and licked between the folds. As he held my butt cheeks in his hands, I felt him push his face further in, flicking his tongue over my bud feverishly. Hearing him moan as he put his mouth to work made me cum so hard. Santino licked me clean, before latching his mouth back onto my button and sucking like a maniac. I scraped my nails across the wooden desk, as high-pitched moans escaped my mouth. Trembling, I exploded, panting heavily like I'd just run a marathon.

"Damn," he mumbled as he touched between my legs from behind.

Out the corner of my eye I could see him undressing, so I turned around to help him. Once he was in his boxers, I got down onto my knees, exposed his dick, and took him into my mouth. I knew exactly how he liked it, so I let my mouth get wet, and his head touch the back of my throat.

"Bellaaaa," he grumbled, tousling my golden-brown locks.

I reached up to move his balls around in my hand as I slobbered on his rod, letting as much of him go into my mouth as possible. I looked up at him while doing so, and his teeth were digging into his bottom lip. He looked like he was about to cry as I sucked the life out of him, speeding up then slowing down. I let the tip of him hit the back of my throat again as I hummed on it, and like clockwork, he came. I took it back and licked my lips, as he yanked me up and pushed my dress down to expose my breasts.

"Get up here."

He lifted me up and sat me on the desk, pushed his boxers all the way down, and then slid inside of me. Placing my legs in the nooks of his arms, he slowly pumped in and out of me while staring into my eyes. I loved when he did that.

Gripping the sides of my face, he pulled me in for a kiss while still gliding in and out of me. He put my legs onto his shoulders, before grasping my waist and pounding my center. I was knocking all kinds of shit over, looking for something to hold onto.

"Ahh! Uhh!" I screamed damn near as he beat it up.

Seeing him damn near bite a hole into his lip was so sexy.

"Fuck, Bella," he grunted, just before pressing one of my thighs into my stomach, and releasing into me.

He collapsed on top of me, and we immediately began tonguing it up. We stayed there like that on the desk, for a good five minutes, just kissing and touching one another, before finally getting up to go take a shower.

"For the first time in I don't know how long, we can sleep naked in the bed," he smiled as we walked out of the bathroom in our birthday suits.

"I know," I giggled as we climbed into the bed together.

"What you wanna do tomorrow? We can order room service for

breakfast, then walk the strip, and then have lunch on the strip too."

"Sounds good, baby. But isn't room service expensive?"

"Yeah," he nodded. "But I would give you the moon if I could, Bella. And right now, I'm able to buy you room service food, so I wanna do that."

"I love you so much, Santino."

"I know, and I love you too, baby. I swear nothing will ever come between us again. Not my parents, not other girls or niggas, and definitely not a baby."

"A baby. I want babies, but maybe after I work in my field of choice for two years. Then I don't mind having a kid."

"So it's set. When you graduate, you will work and make a name for yourself. And then once it's a good time to take a break to where it won't hinder you, we can make a baby. I wanna marry you first anyways."

Hearing him say the exact opposite of what Dean had said to that same plan, just further proved that Santino and I were meant to be. I loved him so much that it was crazy, and I just hoped that this time we could make it, because I wouldn't know what to do if I got depressed like last time.

"What's on your mind, beautiful?" he kissed my nose.

"I'm just hoping that this time we last forever like we'd always planned. I was very sad when we broke up, I don't know if you know." I hated to tell him, but I felt the need to.

"I did know that. I was sad as hell, too. I hated myself for being so immature, and I hated my parents for not letting me apologize to you and be with you. I also hated that you had to go through something basically alone."

I thought about the reason Khyle said Oden was angry. I understood now.

"Yeah. I didn't know you were sad about our last breakup. It didn't seem like it."

"Because that was a facade. I couldn't be at school, crying and shit. If I couldn't be with you I had to act like I was okay with it. My close homies knew the real though."

Hearing that he was just as sad made me feel a little better about our relationship. My mother always told me that loving a man more than he loved you was a recipe for disaster.

"Well, we're stuck together now, so we can be happy."

"That's right," he kissed me. "Order some room service for right now."

"We can go out though, it's only 1:34pm."

"We're not leaving this room today, Bella."

Nodding with a smile, I reached for the phone in the room to dial. As the line trilled, Santino dipped down under the covers and put my legs on his shoulders.

"Mmmm," I moaned once I felt his mouth against my clit.

"Ma'am?" the front desk lady quizzed.

"Fuck, umm, do you guys have pasta? Mmmm, uh!"

I had one hand holding the phone, and the other gripping

Santino's hair, trying to pull him away from attacking my middle. That just made him go ham, pushing my legs into my stomach and sucking my bud harder.

"Yes, we ha-have chicken, shrimp, or chicken and shrimp."

"Oh shit, oh my gosh!"

"Ma'am? Are you alright?"

"Ple-Please just send, ahh, oh shit. Please just send two chicken and shrimp pastas!"

I tossed the phone onto the nightstand next to me, and threw my head back to enjoy the orgasm that was about to rip through my body. I exploded, and Santino just lightly kissed and licked my center before coming up with a smile.

"I think I'm full," he said as he kissed up my body.

This weekend was gonna be crazy… crazy fun.

CHAPTER EIGHT

Anton

"About time you step up to the plate," Kai walked into the hoe crib carrying 'my son', switching hard as hell. It was noon, and she was dressed like she was about to hit the club.

"You right. Can I get you something to drink?" I offered, making my fingers form a gun to the back of her head.

"I'll have some wine."

"Don't you think you should have something a little more PG with him here?" I frowned, looking at the adorable chubby baby she bounced in her lap. Anton Jr. was cute, but he wasn't mine. I didn't know how she thought her light-skinned baby belonged to me when she was brown and I was dark skinned.

"No, he can't even talk. He won't know the difference between cranberry juice and a little red wine, Tony."

I scoffed and grabbed a water bottle from the fridge. I wasn't about to give her ass no damn wine. I don't know what the fuck she thought this was.

"Here." I handed the bottle to her.

"So I'm thinking I can bring him to see you periodically, and we can spend time together when you wanna take him somewhere."

"That works." I nodded, sitting down on the other end of the couch.

"Yeah," she sighed and began looking around. "So you're still sharing a place with Truman and Oden? Don't you think you have enough money to get your own spot?"

"Least of my worries."

Usually I would have told her ass to shut the fuck up by now, but I needed to keep it cool until I had what I needed.

"Well, TJ is almost one and you haven't paid anything for him. We need to get some kind of payment schedule down."

When she said that shit I couldn't help but to laugh. I really attempted to hold it in, but she was just so fucking out of her mind. She knew that wasn't my baby, but she was going to continue to act like she was 1000% sure and shit. So, I decided to play along for a little longer until my other guest arrived.

"Oh yeah, how much were you thinking?"

"Considering the fact that I know you make a lot of money, more than hundreds of people make in five years, I'm thinking $20,000 a month."

"The fuck?" I spat after choking on the water I had just sipped. I was dumbfounded by this dumb bitch, even though I knew I wasn't gonna be paying her a dime. Just imagine if I were the father.

"Hear me out, Tony. That will cover his clothes, food, a nicer place for us, a car, and maybe some security since people who dislike you may come after us."

"Kai, you never seem to amaze me, baby."

"I'm just trying to—"

KNOCK! KNOCK!

I hopped up and went to answer the door, feeling Kai's eyes on my back. After checking the peephole, I opened the door with a smile to welcome Selinda in. She was carrying her son Antonio, frowning up at Kai. Yeah, both of these hoes named their kids after me. Selinda knew Anton Jr. was taken, so she picked the next closest thing.

"What the fuck is going on, Tony? Don't tell me you believe this bitch's baby is yours?" Selinda snapped, adjusting Antonio on her hip, and pointing her long curved nail at Kai.

She was the only female I'd seen in person with curved fake nails. Every day I wondered how and why I fucked her, but then again, every man has had his share of mud duck bed buddies.

"Who the fuck you calling a bitch, bitch?!" Kai sat Anton Jr. to the side and stood up.

"You! Bringing that pale ass baby up in here claiming it's his! That nigga is darker than midnight, dummy!" Selinda fussed.

"Okay! Okay! Both of y'all shut the fuck up!" I barked, hoping to get shit under control. I didn't want to have to pull my gun out on these birds but I would. "How about y'all put the babies in here," I shook the playpen I'd bought earlier, "and sit on the couch so we can have a conversation."

They both glared at one another, before grabbing their babies and placing them into the pen. I stayed close by, making sure they didn't try to fight while doing so. Once they returned to their seats and waited for my next words, I sent a text on my phone.

"What the hell?" Kai frowned as Oden, Truman, and two nurses came from the back. "Get off me, nigga!" Kai shouted to Oden as he grabbed her arm. Truman did the same to Selinda, as they carried the two to the back. They fought them the whole way, but luckily, they weren't strong enough against my boys.

"Okay, can you open your mouth for me cutie pie?" one of the nurses smiled down at Antonio before swabbing him. The other one had just finished collecting DNA from my mouth.

Thank God these nurses worked for us for when we were injured, otherwise it'd be alarming to hear all the shit Selinda and Kai were screaming from the back bedrooms.

As I watched the nurse move onto swabbing Anton, I had to speak up. I knew deep down these kids weren't mine, but I was curious.

"It's not possible for him to be mine, right? I mean he's light skinned, and I'm dark. His mama is brown skinned," I laughed, but nervously for some reason.

"Well, not necessarily, Mr. Nickerson. I've seen light babies born to darker skinned parents and vice versa. It's all genetics. So, if either one of you have a light-skinned parent or grandparent, it's very possible to get a light-skinned child."

"What? Nah," I chuckled. My grandma was damn near white

skinned, but I wasn't about to say that shit.

"I've seen it happen many times. And once the kid was tested, they found out he belonged to the father."

"Yes, just about five months ago I had a case like that. Mom was light, so was the father, and the baby was brown skinned. The father had filed for divorce and everything, thinking the mother cheated. But in the end the baby was his," the other nurse chimed in as they began securing the DNA evidence.

"Yeah, so about how long will this shit take, you know?"

"Give us about five days, Mr. Nickerson. I don't want to rush this process and make a mistake."

"Thanks."

I helped the nurses gather their shit from one of the bedrooms, before walking them out. When I returned, I knocked on the door to let Oden, Truman, Kai, and Selinda know they could come out. I was a little surprised by how quiet the girls were, as I listened to Oden and Truman joke around.

"Come in, nigga!" Truman shouted.

I twisted the knob to see Oden and Truman chatting with their guns drawn on the women. I nodded to let them know they could come out, so Oden and Truman put their guns away. As soon as they did, Kai quickly turned her attitude back on.

"Where the fuck is my baby, you deadbeat!" she shouted as the five of us made it to the living room. After scooping Anton Jr. up, she hugged him to her body. She'd been in that damn room for all of 10 minutes with her dramatic ass. "What did you do?" she grimaced.

"Got that young DNA test!" Oden laughed.

"Fuck you, nappy headed ass nigga," Kai spat.

"I would absolutely *never* fuck you," Oden shook his head. I could see how serious he was.

I noticed Selinda was silent as she picked Antonio up from the playpen. Hearing I tested that little nigga must have had her ass shook.

"Nigga, please, you give that dick to everybody! All of y'all do!" Kai yelled.

"And yet I still *never* gave it to you," Oden responded, prompting Truman to laugh.

"Whatever! And fuck you, Tony! When them results come back, be ready for child support court!" Kai stormed towards the door, with Selinda walking slowly behind her.

"Bye, Selinda!" Oden and Truman said in unison.

She flipped them the bird before leaving out like Kai. As soon as they did, the three of us started laughing and dapping one another up excitedly. I couldn't wait until I got them damn results back.

After handling some business with the chop shop, the three of us went our separate ways. I drove straight to UNLV, because I wanted to tell Tasmine about what happened earlier. I knew she thought about the shit constantly, so this would for sure ease her mind.

Once I got to the school, I parked right behind the dorm, and then rushed around to see if I could catch someone coming out. I saw a few people hitting the corner, so I figured more people would be coming out, or maybe the door wouldn't be closed yet.

"Thanks, man," I tapped this big nigga on the shoulder and slipped in past him.

"Welcome, Tony," he responded. It wasn't odd for niggas to know me so I kept it pushing to the elevator.

When I made it up, I saw Khyle holding some books and her purse. She wasn't dolled up like usual. She was wearing some jeans, and a big light colored sweater. Her hair was disheveled, but because it was so long it didn't look bad. As I neared her, my mood literally dropped because the sadness was radiating off of her. Oden didn't want to tell me why they had broken up, but it must have been bad if *he* initiated it, because he was straight up and down in love with this girl.

"Hey, need some help?" I offered.

"Oh umm, no, no, thanks." She pushed open the door to her room, and I held it so we could both go in."

"Hi, baby!" Tasmine shrieked like she always did, jumping down from the bed to rush me. I picked her up to hug her, closing my eyes to inhale her scent.

"Hey, let me give you guys some privacy." Khyle pushed her hair behind her ears and grabbed her purse.

"No, Khyle—"

"It's fine. I have to go work on something anyway. I need to have some quiet." She shuffled through papers, dropping shit and everything, before finally just leaving.

"She's like that all the time?" I asked Tasmine.

"Yes, and every day I can't stand Oden more and more."

"Oden? Clearly she did something to him if he would break up with her, Tasmine. He was obsessed with that girl, so she must have fucked his daddy or something."

"Don't say that. And I didn't know Oden had a dad."

"Everyone does, baby." I pulled my hoodie and shoes off, before we both climbed onto the bed, putting our backs against the wall.

"No, I know he has a dad, but I didn't know he knew him."

"He knows him but he acts like he's dead, if that makes sense. But I didn't come here to talk about Oden."

"Well," she straddled my lap. "What did you come to talk about?"

"I got DNA tests done today on Kai and Selinda's babies," I smiled, running my hands up her nightshirt.

"Yeah?" she grinned widely as hell.

"Yeah, I did. And when it comes back as a 0% chance, we're gonna celebrate." I kissed her soft full lips.

"That's good, baby, and then after that, all we have to do is get a test for Violet's baby."

"Already got that in place. She should be giving birth any minute now, and as soon as he gets here, I'm having him tested."

"Good."

"But now I wanna test you." I flipped her onto her back, pulling her top off and tugging at her panties.

"Dang, babe," she giggled, helping me take my shirt off.

I stepped off the bed, hit the lights since both ladies had a lava lamp, and rolled down a condom. I actually didn't mind fucking in the light, neither did Tasmine, but just in case Khyle returned, I didn't want her getting shocked.

Climbing into the bed, I crushed my lips against Tasmine's while playing with her clit. She moaned every so often against my lips, before slipping her tongue into my mouth. Sitting down, I pulled her into my lap, pressing her back into my chest. I lifted her bottom half a little, and then pushed my way inside of her.

"Shit," I moaned, gripping her breasts in my hands and sucking on her neck. She shivered as if she were cold, as I slowly bounced her in my lap.

Grasping the sheets in her hands, she began winding her hips and moving up and down on her own, allowing me to just sit back and enjoy. I stared down in my lap to watch her ass jiggle, as she glided up and down my pole slowly. Seeing her nectar drenching my dick was every damn thing.

Keeping my eyes on her ass, I used one hand to hold onto her shoulder, and the other to grip her hip before humping upward feverishly.

"Tony," she whimpered, cumming soon after.

I acted just like she didn't and kept slamming into her until she came again. Lifting her up, I laid her flat on her back, and got on top of her. Pushing myself inside, I sucked on her lips while making love to her.

I had never had sex so passionate like when I was with Tasmine.

That innocence mixed with sex appeal that she had, turned me on. Seeing her beautiful eyes sparkle even in the dark, as I invaded her body, was something I could look at all day.

"Baby," she whispered, rubbing the back of my head as I kissed all over her neck.

Pressing her legs back into her body, I pounded her middle with force until we both released. Collapsing back down onto her, I pushed her hair out of her face and just looked at her for a minute.

"What?" she smiled, still panting.

"You don't even know how pretty you are, but I think that makes you even prettier."

Her eyes wandered all over my face, and her full lips parted but nothing came out, signaling she was speechless.

"Thank you," she finally replied.

"What, you don't believe me?"

"I do, I'm just not used to hearing it from someone I like so much."

"And that's unbelievable to me. You're definitely one of the prettiest girls at this school, and in Vegas."

"How would you know?"

"Just know I've encountered a lot of women. Not saying I've slept with them all, but I've met a lot and seen a lot, and you're definitely up there."

She said nothing, she just pulled my face into hers so we could continue kissing. Life was finally starting to look like something worth celebrating.

CHAPTER NINE

Shayne

$\mathcal{I}$'d just gotten out of the shower, and slipped into some warm pajamas so that I could relax my muscles. I was so tired from rehearsal, and needed to recharge before the show this weekend. Tonight was gonna be good because I had ice cream, a filled DVR, and Pierce was working late. I didn't ask any questions either, I was just happy he was gone.

I heard the doorbell ring as I sifted through my DVR list, trying to decide what I wanted to watch first. If this was Alanna interrupting my time, I was gonna curse her stupid ass the fuck out. Bitch hadn't talked to me in forever now that she was Earl Jr.'s mistress. Stupid ass bitch.

"Okay, coming!" I hollered when they rang it again.

I rushed to the door, and when I peeked out of the peephole, I saw my little sister standing there looking like someone she loved had died. I immediately began to panic, thinking something had happened to our parents.

"Khyle, what's wrong?" I snatched the door open.

She stood there looking at me for a second with glazed eyes. She was dressed plainly in skinny jeans and an oversized oatmeal colored sweater. She had on Rihanna's oatmeal Creepers to match, and her gold chain that read Oden's last name. She stuck her tongue into her cheek, and tossed her hair from one side to the other, messing it up more than it already was.

"Can I come in here for a second? Tasmine needed the room, and I umm, I didn't have anywhere else to go," she whispered basically.

"Yeah, come in." I stepped back to let her in, and after I locked the door I turned the heater on. It was always so cold up in here. "Are you hungry or thirsty?"

"If you have some tea, I'd like some," she nodded.

Her voice was so low that some words were hard to make out. I had to know what was wrong with her because Khyle always talked loudly and with a lot of attitude.

"I have some. With milk?" I questioned and she nodded. "Are you gonna tell me why you're looking so sad, little sister."

I poured some almond milk into a mug, and then added some agave, before putting it under the Keurig to brew the tea. As the tea fixed itself, I watched Khyle from the kitchen. She was hugging herself almost, and looking off to the side. Grabbing the tea, I walked it out and sat down while reaching it out to her.

"Thanks."

"Khyle, I'm not gonna ask you again."

She sipped the hot tea, and then began shaking her head slowly as tears started to come down her cheeks. Okay, now I was really worried. I tried to hug her but she moved away. She hated to be consoled, which is why you would never catch her crying in front of you. Khyle hated for people to feel sad for her.

"I did something really bad, and there is nothing I can do to fix it."

"What is it? Most things can be fixed, baby girl."

She laughed and sniffled before sipping the tea again.

"I got pregnant, Shayne. I killed it because Oden and I weren't together and because I'm too young. And we weren't together because he cheated on me with a stripper. We got back together, but somehow he found out about the abortion, and now he's done with me."

I massaged my eyes for a little bit because this was way too much information for one sitting. All these events had transpired and I'd had no idea. Khyle did call and text me here and there, but I've been so wrapped up in being engaged to Pierce, preparing for work, and chasing Lloyd, that I'd pushed her to the bottom of the priority list.

"Wait, Oden cheated on you?"

"Yes, during winter break, and it should have been the last straw. Well, he had a stripper in his room, and he swears nothing happened but who knows. I should have been done with him after that, but," she dropped her head, and tears fell onto her jeans.

"What, honey?" I rubbed her back.

Setting her mug on the coffee table, she dropped her head into her hands and said, "But he told me he loved me before he even knew that I loved him. And the whole time we were apart, I couldn't stop thinking about him. Then he wouldn't leave me alone, which made it harder for me. I just…"

"It's okay, Khyle. That happens to the best of us. We meet these guys and it seems like no matter what they do our heart still yearns for them."

"I'm not like that, Shayne. I'm not one of those girls who falls in love and go blind. I've never been like that."

"Because you've never been in love," I smiled and thumbed the tear away that was cascading down her cheek.

"I don't like it, nothing good comes from it. I can barely sleep through the night without waking up and crying. Do you know I asked God to help me get over him?"

"Damn," I chuckled. "You need Jesus to step in?"

"Yeah, and ASAP."

"Well, have you tried talking to Oden? Maybe that will bring you guys back together."

"I don't know if I want that. I don't like feeling all vulnerable like this. I like being careless and in control. I feel too attached to him. Like right now I would pay any amount of money to sleep next to him."

"Then try talking to him, Khyle. Sitting around is only going to make you miserable, and give him time to be with another girl."

"I called and texted him but he never answered."

"Girl, you better drop by his damn house!"

"I can't do that. What if a girl is over there? Then I will be embarrassed and have to beat her ass to save face."

We both laughed in unison because she was dead serious.

"Do what you have to do. But you want him back, it's obvious because you're wearing this little necklace still."

"Yeah, maybe. Speaking of jewelry, what is this?" She lifted my hand to inspect my diamond ring from Pierce.

"Pierce asked me to marry him."

"And you said yes? Shayne, I thought you weren't in love with him anymore?" her brows dipped.

"I know, but Pierce is like that dish you always get from a restaurant because you know it's gonna be good. And you're too scared to get something else in fear of it being nasty, so you stick with it. Pierce is just safe for me."

"What about Lloyd?"

"I really like him, but he doesn't pay my bills and take care of me. He buys me expensive gifts and that's about it. If I leave Pierce, where am I gonna go?"

"I don't know, Shayne, but you need to try to get on your own two feet. You deserve to be with someone you actually wanna be with, and Pierce deserves to have someone that wants him back."

"And he will get that, just not right now. I will land on my feet soon, and at that time I will leave Pierce. But until then, I'm getting married!" I grinned.

"Shayne," she shook her head with a smile. It wasn't a good smile, though, it was the worried kind.

After talking about men for a little longer, we decided to make some shredded chicken quesadillas since I had all the stuff needed to do so. We made some tortilla chips, and a pitcher of real pink lemonade to go with it. We ate the food while watching shows in my DVR, and before we knew it, it was late as fuck.

"Where is Pierce?" Khyle frowned, following me to my bedroom. I told her she could sleep in the spare, and that I would give her a nightshirt.

Damn, that's a good ass question.

"Where is the nigga?" I grabbed my phone from the bed to see I had some texts from him, Lloyd, and Marisol.

Pierce: *On my way now, finally. Shit ran late.*

Lloyd: *Pretty ass.*

I'd sent Lloyd a picture of me.

Marisol: *Hey boo, busy tonight?*

"He's on his way now," I frowned at my phone before locking it.

"Hmm, you think he has someone he's fucking with? Or is he being honest? I mean it is almost 1 o'clock."

"I don't know, he better not." I handed her the nightshirt.

She shrugged and then left my bedroom to go into the spare.

I brushed my teeth, and then lied down in my bed, staring up at the ceiling. This nigga needed to get here in the next 10 minutes, or I was going ape shit on his ass. As soon as I reached for my phone, I heard the front door open and close. Right when Pierce came into the bedroom, I turned the lamp on, making him jump.

"Shit, you scared me. Sorry I'm so late, baby."

"Where were you really at Pierce?"

"I was working, baby, I told you—"

"You work in an office setting! They do not need you working this late! Tell me the truth right now, Pierce, or I'm leaving you!"

"Shayne, calm down." He walked around the bed to my side. "I was working, I promise you. I'm in line for a promotion, and I stayed late as hell in order to catch up on some work. I had a lot of claims in my system, and I wanted to clear it before the weekend. Why would I cheat on you when I just proposed, Shayne?"

I shrugged. I guess because I was doing dirt I thought he was too.

"I'm sorry. Oh, Khyle is here."

"That's cool. I was gonna shower, you wanna come?" he offered.

I would have declined since I had my shower tonight already, but because I felt uneasy about him being gone all night, I wanted to be close to him.

I nodded my head and he kissed me deeply, before leading me into the bathroom.

CHAPTER NINE

$\mathcal{I}$ decided to take Shayne's advice, so here I was standing outside of Oden's townhouse, preparing to knock. I felt like I was gonna have a damn heart attack in a minute, so I stopped to take a deep breath for a second. After gaining some composure, I knocked and then looked down at my phone to check the time.

"It's 9:30pm," I said to myself as I waited.

I looked over my shoulder and made sure his car was there, and it was. I was paranoid so that was my sixth time checking. As I raised my arm to knock again, I heard someone unlocking the door before it finally came open.

There he was, shirtless, only wearing basketball shorts and socks, with his tattooed chest on full displayed. My eyes traveled from his chest down to his abs, before landing on the waistband of his Polo boxers.

"What's up, Khyle?" his sexy raspy voice pulled me from my lustful thoughts, and I adjusted my purse strap to save face.

"Am I interrupting something?"

"Just playing a video game."

"Oh, sounds like fun," I chuckled, but he just licked his full sexy lips, before running his hand over his wild curly hair.

He stepped back to allow me to come in, and when I did, I scanned the place like I hadn't damn near moved in when we were together. I guess I was looking for any signs of another woman, possibly a girlfriend.

"Are you thirsty? Hungry?"

"Some water, please. And no, I had a umm… I guess I haven't eaten today but I'm not really hungry."

"You haven't eaten? And you're not hungry?" He handed me a bottle of Fiji before we both sat down on the couch.

I didn't answer him right away because he started back playing the game, but when he glanced over at me, it reminded me to open my mouth.

"No, I haven't really had an appetite these days."

"Oh," he commented, chewing on some gum, sexily.

I watched the side of his handsome face as he played the game with the sound muted. He smelled so good. I hadn't smelled that cologne in forever. And mixed with his body's natural scent, it was so heavenly.

"Have you been good?" I quizzed after gulping some more water.

"I've been straight; working and going to school, same old shit. You been good?"

"I've been better," I chuckled lightly. He said nothing, just kept his eyes on the game, chewing his gum, and sucking his teeth when something bad happened. He was so fine. "So have you met anybody yet?"

I tried to make it sound like general conversation.

"Nope, not yet." *Yet?*

"Oh, so you plan to meet someone?"

"No, I never plan to meet anyone unless it's a business associate. But as far as women, shit happens and you just meet."

"True." I felt like I was about to cry. He didn't sound like he missed me at all. He hadn't touched me, and he was barely looking at me.

"And school is good? Like the classes and stuff?"

"Yep, gonna get straight A's like always."

It was so sexy to me how he always got A's. It made me work harder, but even then, I got one B last semester. I had some nerve calling him a criminal like he wasn't more than that.

I scooted closer to him and touched his hair, but he moved away from me. I remembered him saying only the woman he felt like he was gonna marry could touch his hair, and that when 'hoes' did it, he moved.

Backing away, I just stared at the video game on the TV, trying not to cry. I didn't want to leave because I missed being around him, but I didn't want to stay with him treating me like this. I sat there with him in silence as he played the game for an hour and a half, before I finally decided to leave.

"I better order an Uber before it gets too late," I said, breaking the silence.

He rose to his feet to cut the game and TV off, before wrapping up the cords and stuff to put them into his glass cabinet by the entertainment system.

"I mean it's late. If you wanna stay in the guest room you can. It's not really safe to take an Uber at this time, but it's up to you." He cut the lights off in the living room.

"Okay, I will stay in the guest room."

I followed him to it, and he opened the door for me. It was nice, and very plain, which is how guest rooms should be. Don't get me wrong, it was the bedroom that a lot of people dreamed of, but compared to where he slept, this one was bland.

"Thank you," I whispered with my back to him. When I turned to say something else, he'd backed out and closed the door.

Removing my clothes, I placed them on the brown chaise, before climbing into the bed wearing just panties. I laid there in the dark sobbing lightly for a little bit, before my body became tired, causing me to drift off to sleep.

Around 3am...

"Khyle," someone called my name.

I opened my eyes and looked to see a naked Oden, getting into the bed on the other side. He turned me onto my back, and then began pulling my panties down.

"Oden, what are you doing?" I whispered as I watched my panties get thrown onto the floor. "Shouldn't we talk?"

He laid down between my legs, and pressed his sexy lips against mine. Shockwaves traveled throughout my body as I enjoyed our kiss. I missed kissing him. I missed him, and by the way he was touching me and groping me, I could tell he missed me too.

"Uh," I gasped lightly as he pushed himself inside of me.

It was painful, so my body froze as he moved in and out of me while sucking my nipples. He pushed himself into me more, causing me to yelp in pain since I hadn't quite gotten used to his size again.

"Fuck," he groaned, picking his head up from my nipples and kissing me nastily. "You feel so good, Khyle."

He talked to me as I continued to whimper while digging my nails into his sides. He sped up a little, pounding into me, and finally my body began to welcome him more.

"I love you, Oden," I whined as he fucked me hard but slowly.

Suddenly he stopped, using his eyes to scan my face for a bit, before he pulled out and rolled off of me.

"Oden, what's wrong?" I asked, watching him get out of the bed and grab his boxers from the floor. "Oden." I crawled to the side of the bed that he was near.

He didn't say anything; he just left the bedroom.

I was so confused on what had just happened, not to mention I was sore between the legs now. I climbed out of the bed, grabbed my panties from the floor, and then went into the bathroom. I peed, which was uncomfortable, and then washed my hands. I left out of the bedroom and went down to his, but when I turned the knob it was locked.

"Oden," I knocked lightly on the door.

I stood there for forever it seemed like, before returning to the guest room and crying myself to sleep again.

***

I woke up feeling really tired, as I tried to remember where I was. When I saw that it was Oden's guest room, sadness overcame me as last night's events invaded my mind. Peeling the covers off of my body, I walked to the big window and closed the blinds because the sun was too bright. I then put my clothes back on, before twisting my hair up and coming out of the room.

"Good morning," I greeted Oden who was eating a bowl of cereal in the kitchen.

He was dressed in dark jeans, a navy blue thermal, and some navy blue Chucks. His hair was wild, curly, and luminous like always.

"Good morning."

"I can make you something else if you'd like."

"No, I have to be somewhere." He poured the milk from the cereal into the sink before running the water over it. "Look Khyle, I want to apologize for coming into your room last night. I thought— I'm just sorry."

"You thought what?"

"Nothing, just please accept my apology for getting into your bed and shit."

"Oden, I'm sorry for what I said about you that day, and I'm sorry about the abortion. I should have told you, but I was angry with you."

"Khyle, I have to go. So did you want a ride back to your dorm or what's good?"

"You don't miss me at all?" I began to cry as I looked up into his beautiful mug. "You're perfectly fine with us being broken up right now?"

"I have to be somewhere, Khyle, and I'm sure you have things to do as well." He walked past me, hitting me in the face with his cologne.

I followed him out of the townhouse, and just walked in the opposite direction of him as I ordered an Uber car. I sat there waiting for it in the sun, as he sped out of the parking lot with his music blasting as if he didn't have a care in the world.

I was back at my dorm about 20 minutes later, and as I was opening my room door, Perry came out of hers.

"Hey, Khyle."

"Hi." I looked over my shoulder at her for a second.

"How are you?"

"I'm great, Perry. Thanks." I walked into my room and she came in behind me.

I found it strange, but then again, I had been hanging with her for as long as I'd been hanging with Bella and Tasmine, so I guess it wasn't strange after all.

"I saw you kissing Bella on the Internet," she said as I began brushing my teeth. I simply nodded in response. "So are you guys gay now or something?"

I choked on the water I was rinsing my mouth with because I laughed.

"No, it was just fun and we were drunk." I began flossing. I didn't even know she talked this much.

"Oh. So are you happy to be single now?"

I spit my mouthwash out, and began gathering my things for a shower. I had to ponder over her question for a bit.

"Honestly, yeah, I am." I was gonna say no, which was the truth, but Oden had pissed me off this morning. "What happened to that guy you were dating?"

"Oh, it went south. Maybe if I looked like you, he would still be around and stuff, you know?"

"Not true. You see I don't have a man. Maybe if we both looked like Tasmine or Bella," I joked. "But honestly, if a guy only cares about looks, you shouldn't want him. And plus, you're beautiful, Perry."

"You think so?"

"Yes!"

"So if we were drunk you would kiss me too?"

"I guess so, I don't know. It's not really something I think about. I've never kissed a girl outside of Bella. I'm gonna shower though."

She nodded as I walked into the bathroom to clean myself. After finishing, I climbed out and dried off. I then put on my panties and bra in the bathroom, which I never did, but I didn't want to scare Perry off by being naked in front of her. After putting my short robe on, I came out of the bathroom.

"Do you think we can hang out more, Khyle?"

"We hang out all the time, Perry," I responded as I did my skincare routine. She stayed quiet until I finished.

I walked over by my bed where she was sitting, and grabbed the dress I'd picked out. As I removed my robe to put it on, Perry's eyes scanned me from head to toe. I just slipped my dress over my head, and sat down next to her to let my hair out of its bun. I combed it down, and then brought it to the side opposite of the one that she was on.

"You know Perry—" She cut me off by kissing my collarbone, and rubbing my thigh. "Perry, no." I shook my head at her with a confused expression. What the fuck did she think was about to happen?

"I'm so sorry, I don't even know why I did that. I'm not even gay." She shot up off the bed and paced the area in front of me.

"I know," I replied, even though I wasn't so sure if that were true. She was such a confused individual.

"I'm not, Khyle!"

"I know!"

"I'm gonna talk to you later." She jogged towards the door of my room and rushed out.

As I laid back on my bed, I saw I had a text from Brian and Huelo. Why not respond to them both? I had nothing to lose.

CHAPTER NINE

Truman

$\mathscr{I}$ walked into our chop shop located underneath the dealership, to see Oden and Anton discussing something. On my way over to them, I nodded at the lineup of nice cars ready to be shipped out. All of our shops had improved greatly, getting out five and six cars a fucking night. The money coming in was so much greater, but for some reason I wasn't as happy about the shit as I thought I'd be. I knew why, and I hated that shit. I wanted to lash out, but after getting arrested and sitting in jail for four days, I decided to keep it calm.

"They torched every single one, robbed them too," I said as I took a seat next to Oden.

He nodded, ashing his blunt, before smiling.

"You told them they could keep the money?" he questioned.

"Yeah, them niggas were happy as hell."

"We don't need it so I thought why not be generous," he shrugged.

Since Oden realized that Billz was the one who shot up the dealership, he had some of the guys from our team rob and torch his traps. I figured he should just kill the nigga and be done, but that was Oden; he liked for his enemies to suffer. And in a way, I kind of agreed with him because Billz thought he was the king of everything and everybody. So, the thought of seeing him hit rock bottom did bring a smile to my face.

"Does he know you smashed his wife?" Oden asked.

"Nah," Anton and I said in unison, prompting Oden's jaw to drop.

"Wait, both of y'all niggas smashed?" he pointed to us smiling. "I thought just this nigga Tony had."

"Shit, me too. I ain't know she let you hit, Tru," Anton laughed.

"See, you fucked her one time, I hit multiples."

I'd been fucking Marie for a cool minute, but stopped about nine or ten months ago. The pussy was good and shit, but she thought because of who she was in a sense, that I should be trying to wife her. I told her ass she was crazy, and now she was Billz's wife. Damn was he a sucker.

"Multiples? You're still fucking?" Oden looked to me and I shook my head. "Still rolling with Chiina, huh?"

"Yeah, I just wish I could have her *and* Pilar."

I stared off thinking about Pilar. We hadn't talked in forever. I'd been meaning to take my homies' advice and go get her, but I was too embarrassed to do so after getting arrested. But now that some time had passed, I wanted to holler at her.

"Nigga, no you don't. Multiple women are too much. All I need is Tasmine and I'm good, aight?"

"And let me guess, all you need is sexy ass Khyle." I looked to Oden.

"Don't be calling her sexy my nigga. And I'm straight. I don't need anybody."

"So you wouldn't mind if I smashed, right?" I fucked with him, causing Anton to grin while we waited for his answer.

"She wouldn't let you, but if you did, I think you know what would happen."

"How you know she wouldn't let me? As sad as she is, all I have to do is give her a shoulder to lean on and then make my move. I know that pussy is good."

"Keep talking that shit, Truman." He pressed his gun to my head, that I didn't even see him pull out. This nigga was bugging, but it was funny as fuck to see him sweating over her.

"Damn, I was just asking a question, chill."

Anton and I laughed, as Oden put his gun away. He then got up from the chair he was sitting in, and pulled his hood onto his head.

"I'm leaving. Just a heads up, I'm gonna have Petey and them intercept Billz's next shipment. Fuck y'all niggas and have a goodnight." He left as we continued to snicker.

I watched him for a minute over my shoulder, before turning back to face Anton.

"Why he don't just take her back?"

"I have no idea. I don't know what she did, but the nigga is acting like he can't even find the words to say what it was."

"Damn," was all I could say.

Anton and I talked for a little bit longer, before I just went home to sleep alone. I didn't feel like having some random hoe in my bed trying to converse after fucking. I was too damn sleepy for that anyway.

The next evening...

I sat outside of Pilar's new condo, mulling over all the shit I had planned to say. I was gonna go easy on her, instead of rolling up and demanding that she come back to me. That shit wasn't working, so I thought I'd try a nicer approach. After all, I was the one who fucked up.

I checked my appearance in the visor mirror, and then got out to walk up to her door. I inhaled sharply, and then exhaled, waiting for her to open up. It was after 6:30pm, so I knew she was home. She got off work around 5:30pm, so that was more than enough time for her to get here.

"Oh, hi," she answered the door, in a robe.

"Hey, P. Are you busy?" I stuffed my hands into my jean pockets. Why was I nervous? I spent years with this girl.

"I just got out of the bath. You can sit down while I change clothes." She stepped back to let me in, and I scanned the place as I made it to her couch.

"This is nice."

"Thank you."

I sat down and took the time I had alone to get my mind right. I just needed to be honest with her about my feelings, regardless of how bitch-made I felt it was. Shit, it worked for Oden when he got Khyle back, and that was the weakest move I'd ever seen. Playing Tevin Campbell? I chuckled lightly at my thoughts.

"I have some wine if you'd like," Pilar made herself known by speaking.

"Oh nah, I'm not in the mood for any alcohol, surprisingly."

"What the hell? I need to mark this day on the calendar," she joked, flashing her pretty smile and sitting next to me. The smell of sugar and roses hit my nose, bringing back a lot of memories.

"I know. Pilar, I came to talk to you about us. And before you shoot me down, I just want you to listen," I sighed. "These past few months away from you have had their good parts and bad parts. At the beginning, I won't lie, I was a bit relieved to be single and free to do what I wanted."

"And *who* you wanted," she sucked her teeth.

"Pretty much. But as time went on, I started to realize that I missed you, us, and being in a relationship. I missed hearing you tell me how successful I was gonna be in life, and how great of a man I was despite what my father thinks of me. The shit I got from you, I just can't get from anyone else. And I know hearing this so late after the fact probably doesn't mean shit, but I'm asking for another chance. I'm asking for real, because I want to be the type of nigga you deserve and brag to your friends about. I ain't trying to be smashing different women every night, I wanna be married and shit some day... to you."

She wiped one of the tears that left her eye, before glancing away for a moment.

"Truman, I love you and hearing this does make me feel good. But you're right, it's been a very long time since we broke up. I would think you would have wanted to try to do better sooner."

I knew she was gonna say that, and that's what had my ass nervous as fuck. She probably didn't love me like she used to, which was scary.

"I agree with you on that. I think I needed to grow up though, and really experience how life was without you. Yeah, it seemed like the shit at first, but at the end of the day, right here with you is where it's at."

She looked into my eyes with her mouth twisted a little. Whenever she was thinking about something, she always did that. I let my eyes wander over her voluptuous frame while she took her time thinking.

Tousling her long brown hair from one side to the other, she said, "I'll tell you what, Truman, I will give you a chance but you're gonna have to date me."

"Wait, you mean start over? Like from when I first met you?" I frowned.

"Yes. You need to call me, text me, ask me out, do nice things. All the shit you did to make me want to be your girlfriend the first time. I need to see *that* Truman Morrison again. If that's too much, then we're just gonna have to go our separate ways."

I looked down at her carpet while thinking. I had done a lot to get Pilar because I wasn't her 'type' from the beginning. She was fucking with some big tough nigga, more her type at the time, so my tall skinny ass had to go overboard. I had never worked so hard for a woman in my entire life. The shit I was doing to get her even started to interfere with me getting with other bitches at the time.

"Okay, I can do that, baby. So, since I'm here, can I ask you out on a date?"

"When?" she cheesed.

"Let's see. I'm pretty busy the rest of this week, because the club and the liquor line are doing way better, earlier than expected. So how about next Friday?"

"Okay, that works. Make it good, Truman." She got up and walked to her front door to open it.

"Oh damn, I have to leave now?"

"Yes, I have some documents to look over for work. But I will see you next Friday. However, my number hasn't changed so you can start working until then."

"Fair enough." I got up from the couch and walked towards the door. Damn, she was looking good and thick. I wanted to lick her caramel ass from head to toe.

Hopefully, I could next Friday.

I kissed her cheek, and held back the urge to squeeze her nice round ass as I hugged her. On my way to my car, my phone chimed, and I looked down to see Chiina. I needed to get rid of her, but I wasn't sure if the feelings I'd developed for her would go away too. Fuck.

CHAPTER NINE

Santino

"You don't need any fucking makeup for the movies, Bella," I sighed, falling back onto her bed. I just wanted to leave so we could have enough time to fuck in my room before Huelo came back.

"I'm not even doing what I usually do, Sanz. Relax."

I watched her put some shit on her lashes, and then put on some Chapstick before this other lipstick. She then went digging in another bag, so I got up and came behind her. Pressing my dick against her ass, I began rubbing my hands up her thighs, lifting the tight little dress she had on. I'd been hard as a rock since I walked into the room.

"Santino," she whispered once I slid my hand down into her panties and began sucking on her neck.

I plunged my fingers inside of her, and began moving in and out slowly while thumbing her clit. She was getting wet as hell, and I was beyond ready to just fuck her right here over this sink. She trembled from releasing, but I just kept going while sucking on her neck like a vampire.

"Oh, sorry," Perry walked in, making us both jump.

I quickly removed my hand from Bella's panties and she hurriedly pulled her dress down. Bella rushed off to the bathroom, so I just washed my hands while smiling at Perry's old snake ass. Bitch probably knew I was about to pull my dick out and fuck, so she purposely came in.

"Sorry about that, Perry." Bella came from the bathroom after cleaning herself up, and grabbed some new panties from her drawer before washing her hands.

"It's cool."

"Uh umm, let me just put on my lip-gloss, Santino."

I nodded.

Bella finished her face, and then we left out without saying another word to Perry. We continued to stay silent, all the way until we got into my car.

"I hope you have a new roommate next year."

"I won't," she laughed. "Perry is just confused and trying to fit in. I think we need to set her up with someone. I know you have some single friends, baby."

"Not any that are gonna fuck Perry. Well they *will* fuck her, but that's about it."

"Why? Perry is beautiful!"

"She is an attractive girl if you mentally remove the glasses and the horrible posture, but she's weird, Bella. The fact that she tried to blackmail me for a date was crazy."

"You know why she did it though."

"So you would have blackmailed your friend's boyfriend for a date, because some ugly ass hoes told you to?"

"No, but she's not me, Santino. She's trying to fit in, and she thought that Raquel and Siena were gonna help her do that. You don't know what it's like to feel like everyone is always talking badly about you," she pouted as I took off at the green light.

"Oh, and you do, Ms. Bacigalupi?"

"Yeah I do, nigga."

"Oh my gosh, baby. Yeah right. When have people talked about you, or pointed their fingers? Unless they were saying how beautiful you were."

"Never mind," she shook her head, staring out of the window.

"Exactly. It's never happened to you, so don't act like you can relate to Perry and her strange ass ways."

"It has happened to me."

"Give me an example."

I shook my head with a smile at her ass because she was so dramatic. Bella was very well liked in high school, and even is now in college. I don't ever remember a time where people were whispering about her as she walked the halls, unless they were complimenting her.

"When you got me pregnant, left me, and then shamed me in front of your friends when I tried to find out why."

I turned into the free space I saw without saying anything back yet. After putting the vehicle in park, I released my seatbelt and got out of the car. I made it to Bella's side, and opened the door for her, but kneeled down, stopping her from getting out.

"Bella, I'm sorry about that. I guess I wasn't thinking about what effect my actions would have on you. I was confused and very upset back then because I couldn't be with you anymore. I know it may not have seemed like it, but that's what little boys do; cover up their hurt with dumb ass actions.

I was in love with a girl that my parents forbade me to be with anymore, and then I had to see her at school every damn day. Do you know how difficult it was to see you and not be able to hold you or kiss you? And then you coming up to me trying to talk all the time pissed me off. I felt like it was keeping me from getting over you, when in reality you already had my heart so getting over you wasn't even possible. I hate to even think about what happened between us when we were 15, and I promise from now until forever, I'm gonna make sure you never feel like any muthafucka is whispering or laughing at you. Okay?"

"Okay," she half smiled and rubbed my hair a little.

"Give me a hug."

I stood up and helped her out of the car. Once she was out, I wrapped my arms around her shoulders and pulled her in, kissing her temple. She held tightly onto my torso, and we just stood there hugging for about five minutes.

"I love you," we said in unison before chuckling.

After she grabbed her purse from the seat, we went inside to see the movie.

***

"What you wanna do now? You hungry?" I asked Bella as we walked out of the theatre. I'd already texted Huelo and told his ass to find something to do outside of the room.

"I want pizza."

"Let me order it on my phone and then we can go get it."

"K," she nodded as I placed my jacket around her shoulders.

"Hey, lovebirds," Leena walked up, making me slip my iPhone into my jean pocket. Bella squinted her eyes in confusion before looking up at me. "Oh, you've forgotten who I am already, Santino?"

"Who are you?" Bella questioned.

"Leena, don't start."

"I was his girlfriend before he came here. No, actually, *while* he was here too. He just broke up with me by the way."

"Santino," Bella looked to me.

"Leena, for real? Girlfriend? You were my fucking girlfriend? I should push yo' ass into the street for saying that stupid ass shit."

I draped my arm around Bella because I could sense that she was about to walk her little ass off.

"Santino, you—"

"No, you need to get a muthafuckin' grip, Leena. I was fucking you, and we chilled on occasions, but don't be rolling up on me like you were my bitch when you know you never were."

"So if she's just some scorned fuck buddy, can we go? I want my pizza," Bella sighed.

"Anything for you, baby. I love you." I kissed her lips a couple times before placing my arm back around her and walking off.

"Santino, I am not the one!" Leena hollered to our backs.

"That's obviously why he was never your nigga," Bella yelled back, before waving to her. "You look dumb as fuck right now by the way."

We both laughed as we continued to the car, and once we got in, I finished ordering the pizza so it'd be ready by the time I got there to pick it up.

"I have to say, I was scared as fuck that you weren't gonna believe me, and believe her instead."

"Why would I believe her? I don't even know her. But I know you, and I know that you're serious about us. Not to mention, I've had Dean dangling in the background."

"I'm happy you trust me, and you need to cancel that shit with Dean ASAP."

I was surprised that Dean hadn't caught on yet, considering the fact that she never talked to him really while she was out here in Las Vegas; I made sure of it. I checked that phone faithfully, and the only time they texted would be in the early afternoon, and she would always leave him hanging after a couple meaningless texts.

"I am. He's already getting suspicious. He calls me all day, even through Facebook."

"Don't tell me shit like that if you don't want me to fuck him up. He broke your necklace so I had to buy a new chain, and now he won't leave you alone. You need to handle your part though, Bella. I need some comfort and the only way I can get it is knowing that I'm the only nigga walking around here thinking you're mine."

"And I am yours, I always have been. When I go home in a week and a half, I will tell him as soon as I touch down."

"Better."

"I will, baby."

"Well, we better go before Leena rolls up and tries to break one of my windows."

"And get her ass whooped," Bella snapped, making me laugh. I knew she was for real about what she'd said too.

Shit was finally starting to work out between Bella and I. However, I was gonna see that nigga Dean.

CHAPTER TEN

Tasmine

"I was actually able to pay attention to the game because of all them fine ass niggas on the team," my cousin Mia grinned as she, Khyle, and I walked out of the basketball stadium.

Poor Bella had a paper to write that she procrastinated on until last minute, so she was in for the evening and night. Santino was in her room *helping* her though, so I wasn't sure how much work she was actually going to get done.

"Yeah, there were some cute ones," I nodded, nudging her.

"Khyle! Tasmine!" Reuben shouted as he jogged over to us with his friend.

He played very well tonight, and I was happy that what I'd heard about him wasn't just bullshit. I'm not sure if he was as good as Santino was in football though.

"Hey, Reuben," I chuckled because Mia was eyeing him like a piece of fried chicken. "This is my cousin Mia."

"Nice to meet you, Mia. Khyle, you know Khalil, right?" Reuben pointed to his friend who was also a beast in basketball, maybe even better than Reuben. They were both freshman on the starting lineup, which said a lot about their skill level.

Khalil was very good looking, with his deep caramel complexion, low fade, and neatly trimmed facial hair. He was about 6'7 I believe, but not too skinny like most tall dudes. He and Reuben were almost about the same size.

"Not really, but nice to meet you, Khalil," Khyle shook his hand, as his eyes wandered all over her small frame.

"Same, baby. What you about to get into?" Khalil asked her.

"I have some studying to do, so this is pretty much it for me. The game was the highlight of my night I guess."

"Is there any way I can convince you to go get some food or come to a movie with me?" He cocked his head, as all of us waited for her answer.

"Khalil, thank you for the offer, but I'm not really in the mood to do anything tonight. I just want to study."

"Damn nigga, she shot yo' ass down," Reuben laughed, and I playfully hit his chest. Mia stayed quiet, looking like she was in disbelief at the fact that Khyle had turned Khalil's fine ass down.

"Can I get your number then, and hit you up?" Khalil ignored Reuben, keeping his eyes on Khyle.

She looked away for a second, and then tousled her very long hair.

"Khalil, I can't. I'm sorry. Have a good night you guys." Khyle turned away and started down the stone steps outside of the stadium.

"See you guys around," I said before grabbing Mia's hand and catching up to Khyle. "You okay, Khyle?" I inquired once I caught up to her.

"Yeah, I'm fine, why?"

"Because you just dissed that fine ass nigga back there. I must see this Oden guy, because if he's got you turning down niggas like him, he must be a godsend," Mia joked, making us all chuckle.

"Has nothing to do with Oden, I'm just not in the mood to talk to anyone; boys I mean. I just want to finish this semester strong, and keep my mind clear."

"This has nothing to do with Oden?" I questioned suspiciously. Khyle just smiled and moved her hair from her face.

"Only that he has me afraid to talk to anyone, but I don't wanna get into that."

"So you're sure you don't wanna come out tonight, Khyle? It's a celebration for Anton, and a lot of people are gonna be there so you won't even look at Oden." I hugged her from the side as we approached our dorm building.

Tonight, Oden and Truman were throwing a big ass party for Anton because the DNA results came back, proving that he wasn't the father of neither Kai nor Selinda's babies. Everyone knew it already, even them hoes, but now that he had proof, them bitches couldn't do anything. I was relieved as hell that he'd gotten the test done, because it was about time he got them out of his life. Now, all he needed to do was prove that Violet's wasn't his, and we'd be good.

"No, because even though a lot of people are gonna be there, I'm not in the mood to see Oden all up on some slut. Just imagining it right now is making me sick." Khyle leaned up against the pillar outside of our dormitory.

"Okay, well—"

"Stupid bitch!" someone yelled, right before an egg hit the pillar next to me.

The three of us walked to the edge of the curb to try and get a better view of the person across the way, standing in the yard of the South complex with a carton of eggs.

"This bitch got me fucked up," Mia started to walk off the curb, but I stopped her.

CRACK!

Another egg came flying, and Mia had to duck so that it wouldn't hit her. At that point I knew it was over. Mia darted across the small driveway-like area in between our dorm, and the South dorm, headed towards the girl. Khyle and I were right on her heels, and by the time we'd caught up, Mia was already straddling the bitch, fucking her face up.

"Amethyst?" I frowned down in disbelief as my cousin wailed on her ass.

"Mia, come on! Tasmine, help me!" Khyle shouted, snapping me from my thoughts.

We both had to damn near peel Mia off of Amethyst, as Amethyst covered her bloody face. She didn't know who she was fucking with, because if she did, she would have never tried anything in front of Mia's crazy ass.

"What the hell is your problem, Amethyst?" I shouted down at her dumb ass as she attempted to stand to her feet, bawling like a bitch.

"You know this hoe?" Mia barked.

"She's obsessed with Anton, Tasmine's boyfriend," Khyle explained.

"The bitch from Instagram!" Mia recalled with her eyes bucked, before trying to break free from Khyle to fuck Amethyst up some more.

"I will not stop until I get him! You don't deserve him! You left him here in Vegas to go wherever you went, and he was mine at that time! I will not stop!" Amethyst hollered through all the tears and blood that covered her face as she backed away.

I couldn't respond because I was floored. I didn't know shit like this really happened. She was straight up obsessed with Anton, and it had been evident since I watched that video she made of their phone call. I just couldn't wrap my head around the fact that this bitch had brought a carton of eggs here to throw at me. I did not know hoes like her existed outside of the films.

"What the hell did Anton do to her?" Khyle asked, finally letting Mia's little ass go.

"I'm wondering the same damn thing."

"Well don't let him do it to you," Mia half joked as we snickered lightly, still staring at the space Amethyst was once in.

I was not built for this shit.

The three of us went inside the dorm, and after Mia and I changed and cleaned up, we left to the party at Anton's fake crib. I didn't like calling it the hoe crib, so I chose to say fake instead. Plus, he hadn't been bringing hoes there lately, so the name no longer fit for him.

"I hope it's some niggas there that can show me a good time," Mia laughed, prompting the Uber driver to look at her through his rearview mirror.

"There will be plenty of people, trust me. The best parties are thrown by my man and his friends."

Me: Get Amethyst together nigga. I'm not playing.

Baby: I am, I've been busy. But she's been low-key so... why you hitting me with this right now?

Baby: And where are you?

Me: On my way. I'm hitting you with this now because my cousin just had to whoop her ass for throwing eggs at me, her, and Khyle.

Baby: Eggs? Lol. Wow. I got it Tas. Don't trip.

The Uber driver finally made it to the Wyatt townhouses, and after making sure our makeup was good, we got out of the car.

"Damn, he's living like this?" Mia nodded in approval as we approached Anton's door.

"This isn't really his home. This is a place he and his friends own together to host parties and bring women to. Anton of course doesn't bring women anymore."

"Why do they need to do that? That's kind of extra don't you think?"

"No, not when you realize who they are. Did you not just see a bitch throwing eggs at me over Anton? Imagine if she knew where he lived."

"True. And I have heard a few females mention Oden while back on campus, so I guess it is safer. And don't they do like some illegal shit that gets them major bread?"

"Just the club and liquor," I lied and she nodded.

"So Oden is gonna be here, right?" she cheesed right after I rang the doorbell. I could hear people talking and music playing from outside.

"Yes, but stop it, Mia."

"Stop what?"

"You just hung out with Khyle, how are you gonna come here and try to get with the ex that she's clearly still in love with? And he's very much in love with her, might I add."

"Then why aren't they together?"

"Because he's acting stupid and selfish right now, but they'll be back together soon, watch." I rang the doorbell again.

"That's fine. I'm just trying to test the dick out while I'm here."

"Mia," I sighed and shook my head just as some tall dark-skinned guy with curly hair opened the door. He was super fine.

"I'm Tasmine, Anton's girlfriend, and this is my cousin Mia."

"Yeah, Tasmine, I know. Sup Mia, I'm Lloyd."

"Lloyd? I don't mean to be in your business, but do you date my roommate's sister, Shayne?" I frowned. I remembered Khyle telling me how Shayne was throwing her relationship with Pierce away for some nigga named Lloyd.

"Umm, date? Yeah, I guess you can say that." He stepped back to let us in.

"Well nice to meet you, Lloyd."

"Likewise, shawty."

The house was full of people, but not like a shoulder-to-shoulder house party. This was more intimate, you could tell. There was definitely space on the floor to sit, and nobody was dancing; they were just listening to music, talking, drinking, smoking, and eating. It was a kickback, as Khyle would say.

As soon as Anton and I made eye contact, giddy smiles appeared on our faces. We gravitated towards one another like magnets, before kissing each other sensually but softly.

"Congratulations, baby," I said in a low tone. The results came back a while ago, but I still wanted to tell him congrats. "You met Mia already."

"Thank you, baby, and yes."

Anton led us to the couch where Truman was sitting. It was a long ass couch that curved, so it had space for a lot of people. I was surprised to see Truman there with his girlfriend Pilar. I was sure they had broken up, but they looked very cozy and very much in love.

"Back together?" I asked them as I sat next to Anton, with Mia on my other side.

"No," Pilar responded quickly. "We're *talking* I guess."

Truman sucked his teeth and shook his head before looking off angrily. She cupped his chin, and then kissed him lightly. Once that kiss turned into a porno flick, I focused my attention elsewhere. When I did, I saw Oden come from the back area where the building's pool was located. He greeted one of his friends, and then sat on the counter to light his blunt.

"Please tell me that's not Oden," Mia stared at him.

"Yeah."

"Damn, bitch, I'd be depressed about our breakup too. Look at them lips. I bet he can eat pussy good," she bit her lip.

"Wow," Anton scoffed. "Is that how y'all women talk when niggas ain't around?"

"Sometimes, just like y'all do." I kissed him. "Mia—" I tried to grab her when she got up to walk over to Oden, but she moved away swiftly.

"Don't worry, he ain't gonna talk to her," Anton assured me.

"Oden Bishop? Yeah right, and my cousin is bomb."

"Something is wrong with that nigga; he's been acting like a nun. Look, look," Anton tapped the side of my thigh.

I turned to see Mia smiling in his face, with him only returning half smiles. She then leaned up to whisper in his ear as he stayed seated on the counter with the blunt between his fingers. He said something back to her, making her smile fade, and she just stared at him for a bit before heading back over.

"Told you!" Anton chuckled along with Truman, before kissing my neck.

"What happened?" I questioned Mia once she sat down.

"Nigga talking about he's gay," she replied and Pilar, Anton, Truman, and I doubled over in laughter.

"Oh my gosh, he said that?"

"Hell yeah, fuck him," she pouted.

My night was made already, and it only got better as time went on.

CHAPTER TEN

Oden

"So y'all liking it out here so far?" I asked my homeboys Roone and Lloyd as we sat in the back of one of my chop shops.

"I'm liking the money and the women," Roone grinned, ruffling his dreads.

"Good. What about you, homie?" I smiled at Lloyd.

"This nigga don' found some bitch that's playing with his mind. I told him to say fuck it and throw himself into the many women here in Vegas."

"What, you?" I looked to Lloyd. This nigga was a super player, almost worse than Truman, so I had to know the girl that had him wrapped around her finger.

"This nigga Roone is exaggerating. She's cool, but she ain't got me bugging. I like her, and I would definitely like to see where shit could go, but I ain't sweating her."

"What's her name?" I quizzed.

"Shayne. Beautiful as hell with a nice little body, and a fiery ass attitude. Not to mention the head and pussy are fire as fuck."

I bucked my eyes at him, hoping he wasn't talking about the Shayne I thought he was talking about. But the description alone was enough to convince me, despite it lacking any specific physical features.

"Why you looking like that, O?" Roone furrowed his brows.

"Shayne is my girl's— my ex girl's sister."

"Yeah, she told me when we were out to dinner that you had a girl. I ain't believe the shit at first, but I was wrong."

"Lloyd, I need to tell you this because you're my nigga. I smashed Shayne, and not just once. I fucked maybe a cool six or seven times."

"Nigga, you fucked sisters?" Roone shot up out of his seat to dap me up, as Lloyd sat there silent.

"Yeah, I did, don't remind me. But Lloyd, I haven't fucked her in a long ass time, I don't even remember what the pussy was like."

I was lying like fuck. Shayne had some fire between her legs, but it wasn't as good as Khyle's, obviously. I think because Khyle was mine, well was at the time, and her pussy just felt different. Her shit fit mine like a glove, and every time I got inside it I knew it was mine. Her moans and sex faces, along with how hard she came whenever I let it sit inside… Fuck.

Sex with Khyle was just some unforgettable shit, and the fact that she killed a baby we made from that kind of hurt me. I'm starting to sound like a bitch ass nigga right now though, so let me stop.

"Damn man, fuck. Now we gotta run bitches by you to make sure you ain't fucked them?" Lloyd sucked his teeth.

"I wish I could take the shit back, trust me. I've been wishing that for a long ass time."

"I mean she is bad, and you said her sex was fire, so you gon' let all that go?" Roone looked to Lloyd. "She's bad than a muthafucka with that sexy light skin and long ass hair."

"I don't want a bitch that Oden fucked. Would you want a bitch that he fucked? I don't need my homies knowing how good my girl's pussy is," Lloyd hissed.

"See, I'm like a female when it comes to pussy. If the shit is good as fuck, I'll act blind to all the bullshit just so I can keep hitting," Roone nodded with a smile. I just laughed at his ass. "It's true. When females find out how good my dick is, they let me treat them any kind of way, because they know no other nigga can make them cum like I can. And I'm just saying I'm the same way when I get some of that rare toe curling pussy."

"I know what you mean. I ain't had none of that in a while," I bit down on my lip as I stared off, imagining Khyle's legs on my shoulders as she whimpered while getting fucked. Damn.

"I'm off her, man. I can't rock with that," Lloyd shook his head.

"Sorry my nigga," I said and he put his hand up to say it was cool.

"You think she'll let me fuck too, B?" Roone asked after a couple moments of silence, and then blocked the play punch that Lloyd sent his way. "Nah, but the last time I had some shit that made my toes curl, it was with this little Spanish shorty named Marisol."

I dropped my head, and both of them began groaning.

"You fucked her too, O?" Lloyd laughed.

"I actually fucked her *and* Shayne together before."

"I'm done with this nigga." Roone got up from his seat as the three of us laughed. "Nigga, you been living the life while out here in Vegas."

"Nah, I really haven't. I really haven't."

***

The next morning…

I stood at the back of the student union, and watched Khyle get her food from Subway. She looked beautiful, wearing a black dress with no straps that stopped in the middle of her sexy thighs, and some black Huaraches. Her hair was hanging down her back, sweeping her small round ass every time she took a step.

As she sat down, I wondered how many niggas had tried to get at her, and how many had succeeded. How many had tried to sample my shit? I say tried because I was sure none of them scored.

"Come on," I whispered to the men I'd hired, who were standing outside of the student union.

All ten of them walked in, in a single file line, holding bouquets of red roses. I stayed put as they walked towards Khyle, causing people to stop and stare at them. Khyle was sadly eating her sandwich, and so lost in her thoughts that she wasn't even paying attention. They finally made it to her table, and she looked up with her lips slightly parted, before setting the sandwich down.

The men began placing the flowers wherever they would fit, as

Khyle said something that I of course couldn't hear. As they walked away, she searched one of the flower bouquets for a note. By the time she picked her head up, I was standing right at her table.

"Oden, I…" she stopped talking, I guess realizing she had nothing to say.

"You like them?" I smiled.

"Yes, but what is all this—" I kissed her full lips like I'd been fantasizing about for the longest, cutting her off. She was into it, but then nudged me off of her and sat back down once people around us began calling out shit. "You can't just bring me roses and think everything is gonna be okay."

I took the seat adjacent to her, and pulled her closer to me.

"Khyle, I bought you this." I pulled a ring box from my pocket, and opened it so she could see the diamond ring. It wasn't too extravagant, but it was very nice and very expensive. "This is a promise ring, and it's to represent a promise that we have to keep to one another. I'm promising to never be unfaithful to you, to never lie to you, and to never break your heart. And I need you to promise me that you will be honest with me, and understand that I'm in love with you. Meaning that there isn't anything that you can't tell me or talk to me about. We have to be more than just lovers; we have to best friends, baby. Is that a deal?"

"Yeah," she nodded and wiped her tears as I slid the ring on. "You see I still wear this." She lifted the necklace I'd given her bearing my last name.

"I know. I'm happy about that shit, too."

I yanked her from her chair so that she was sitting in my lap, and then we began tonguing it up. We were hugging one another so tightly, that it was a surprise we could breathe.

"We just wanna say congrats on your marriage!" a group of people walked up to us smiling brightly.

"Oh, we didn't get engaged," Khyle laughed.

"Oh," the front-runner of them replied before they all pranced off.

"Ready to go make up?" I questioned Khyle and she nodded.

I had the flower guys pack the roses back up and take them to my townhouse where Khyle and I were going. As soon as they left, Khyle and I began kissing and taking one another's clothes off. When we got to the bedroom, I pushed her naked body onto the bed, and then spread her legs wide before dropping down. As soon as I was face to face with her pussy, I began French kissing it a little bit. She was moaning softly here and there, as I held her legs against her stomach.

"Oden," she rubbed my hair as I began to suck on her clit.

I flicked my tongue over it, before latching my mouth back on and sucking for dear life. She came, and tried to move away, so I gripped her ass and pressed her pussy into my mouth. I looked up at her to see her chest heaving up and down, while she gazed down into my eyes.

"Mmm," I moaned as I continued to feast on her drenched center.

I flicked, slurped, and sucked on her pussy for ages until her legs were shaking uncontrollably, and she was whimpering like a wounded animal. She sat up to suck my dick, but I wanted some pussy so I stopped her. Placing her legs on my shoulders, I gripped her waist and slid inside of her. Her pussy resisted me initially, but with force, I was able to fully get inside.

"Slow," she whispered.

"You ain't running this, Khyle." I slammed into her, and pulled out extremely slowly, making her cry out. "You want me to make love to you?" I asked her as I beat it up.

"Ye-yeah, ahhh, mmm!" she could barely speak, just before she came.

I placed her in the middle of the bed, and then lowered myself onto her before sliding inside. I pressed my lips against hers, and she wrapped her arms around my neck to hug me as I fucked her nice and slowly.

"Shit," I grumbled against her lips as I stroked her walls.

Holding her jaw, I sucked her full lips as she sniveled lightly. She was too fucking wet, and my dick could barely take it. You could for real hear that shit, and it was driving me crazy.

"Odeeenn," she whined, rubbing up and down my back.

I pinned her arms at her sides, and then dipped my head down so I could suck and bite her nipples while fucking her slowly. I was sucking the fuck out of her nipples, all the while enjoying the sounds of her cries. When I'd had my fix, I flipped her onto all fours, and began to lick on her pussy from behind for a little bit. Something about it glistening had me ready to feast again.

"I'm about to cum so hard, Oden!" she cried out as I ate her.

Once she released, I slid inside from the back, and just pounded into her forcefully, liking the sound of our skin smacking, and my dick beating her pussy up. Her smooth back was so sexy, so I bent down to bite and suck on it while slamming into her.

"I love you, Khyle. You know that? Fuck," I grunted as I kept my pace up.

The side of her face was pressed into the pillow, so I grabbed her by the hair and just began bouncing her on my dick, while I used my free hand to toy with her button. After doing that for a cool little minute, we were both releasing, and my kneecaps got weak. I had to bite down on her shoulder to keep from howling like a fucking werewolf.

"I love you too, Oden," she panted, before we both collapsed down onto the bed.

When I caught my breath about 10 minutes later, I put her on her back and went right to eating her pussy again.

CHAPTER TEN

Bella

I was back in Arizona with my family, and had only been here for some hours before Santino was texting me, telling me to call Dean to let him know the deal. He told me if I didn't do it, I couldn't come over and see him tonight. I definitely missed him, even though I'd just seen him yesterday. Plus, I didn't want to be with Dean so I might as well get the shit over with.

KNOCK! KNOCK!

"Come in!" I called out as I twisted my hair up into a bun.

"Baby girl, that little nigga is here. He's on the porch because I told him that he wasn't allowed to come inside," my dad peeked his head in.

"Okay, thank you."

I took a deep breath before getting up and grabbing my phone. I came out of my room and went down the stairs, hoping Dean wouldn't act up because my dad would for sure whoop his ass.

"Hey," I spoke to him once I got outside.

I sat down in the chair next to him, and stared straight ahead for a little bit. I didn't quite know how to start, and I could sense that he knew something was wrong. Not only was I acting strangely right now, but I hadn't been the best girlfriend while away from him in Vegas. It was hard to be when I had Santino breathing down my neck, and checking my phone faithfully. I didn't complain about it though because I understood. And I was just happy that Santino had agreed to our little arrangement for such a long time.

"Bella, what's going on with you?" Dean broke me from my trance.

"Dean, you know our relationship hasn't been the greatest for a while now, right?" I turned to look at him. He looked nice with his fresh haircut, but I could see the darkness in his eyes still. He wasn't right in the head.

"I know, Bella, and I've noticed that I've been biting your head off and pushing you too hard. But being away from you for a little bit helped me change some."

"I don't know, Dean. A lot of time has passed since we've been happy or since I've been happy. I haven't felt in love in a very long time."

"What? This didn't start until you went to school. You were fine with our relationship, and even agreed to marry me. But as soon as you went to that damn college you all of a sudden need more. Coming home with expensive necklaces and shit."

"Dean, I was unhappy before I left."

"Save that bullshit for someone who will believe it, Bella. You were perfectly fine before you skipped off to trashy ass Vegas."

"No, Dean, I wasn't! I didn't want to marry you! I never even wanted to be with you back in high school, but I felt like I had to because of how nice you were to me. I love you for how you helped me, but I never fell in love."

I was crying by now. I wasn't this type of person. I didn't like telling people things like this, because I knew it would break their heart. I knew Dean wanted to be with me, and it made me sick to have to tell him I didn't feel the same, and that I never had, especially because he'd helped me get back on my feet after Santino.

"Who gave you the necklace, Bella?"

I sighed, redoing my bun as I wondered if I should come clean or not. Suddenly my mind drifted to Tasmine advising me to let Dean know I was with someone else. I didn't want to, but after seeing how badly Khyle's secret abortion came back to bite her, I wanted to come clean.

"Remember Santino D'Stefano?" I looked over at him slowly. His eyes were squinted, but then they returned to their normal position as he laughed angrily.

"Do I remember? You're asking me if I fucking remember? Wasn't I the one who helped you gain some normalcy after he fucked you over?"

"Yes, Dean, and I appreciate that."

"That nigga fucked you, got you pregnant, and then kicked yo' ass to the curb. What do you think is gonna happen when he gets you pregnant again, Bella?"

"I'm not gonna get pregnant again, and when I do, he and I will be married."

"You think he's gonna marry you? Honestly? He hasn't even thought about you since the day he dropped yo' ass, but now all of sudden he's gonna marry you. Pull your fucking head out of the clouds, Bella Bacigalupi. He's only interested in you because you're some easy pussy he can fuck while in Vegas."

I was frozen as I looked into Dean's seemingly black eyes. I could almost hear him grunting as he looked at me from where he was sitting. I knew he wanted to pounce on me like a lion does his prey, but the fact that my father was possibly lurking stopped him from making such a huge mistake.

"Dean, Santino loves me. He loves me the way I want to be loved. He was 15 when he acted that way, and he has explained to me why. But even then, nothing you say will make me want to be with you. You treat me like a dog, you hit me, and you talk down to me. I don't like the way you love me, and that's all there is to it."

"He does not want you, Bella," he gritted.

"You don't know what the fuck I want," Santino's voice came through, and both Dean and I looked his way.

He was coming up the steps with his eyes locked on Dean, and his face balled all up. I knew he was angry, and I knew this wasn't gonna end well. Santino had explained to me many times that he was gonna fuck Dean up as soon as he saw him, so I knew no one could stop him in this moment.

"Aye nigga, you better stay back," Dean said, sounding a little worried which caught me off guard.

"Get back, baby," Santino instructed.

"San—"

"Get back!" he barked, just as Dean rose from his seat.

I slipped into the house behind my screen door, and before it closed good, they were fighting.

"Daddy!" I screamed.

My father came rushing down the stairs, and out onto the porch. Santino had Dean leaning backwards over the balcony of the porch, fucking him up. I actually saw blood flying, which was scary to say the least.

"Stop it!" my father hollered, snatching Santino off of Dean.

Santino yanked his body from my father, and tried to run up on Dean who was beaten severely, but my dad caught him. I watched Dean with wide eyes as he stumbled, trying to gain some composure. His lip was busted, and his teeth were completely covered in blood as he groaned.

"Don't you ever even look at her again!" Santino yelled, trying to get around my father to Dean.

"Go home!" my dad hollered at Dean, which I found to be odd. I mean, I knew he didn't like Dean, but I thought he would at least be on his side since he'd clearly lost. Not to mention the fact that my dad wasn't too fond of Santino either.

Dean limped towards the steps, and flinched when he thought Santino was about to get past my dad. I watched him walk off, while feeling slightly bad for him, because I could see how badly his ego had been bruised.

"De—"

My mom walked up and touched my shoulder to stop me from calling his name through the screen door.

"Bella, Santino is your man, do not do that." She shook her head 'no' slowly, to let me know going after Dean was a bad idea. "You assist Santino, not him."

I inhaled sharply before nodding my head.

Walking out of the house, I made my way over to Santino who was sitting down with my father standing in front of him.

"I can take it from here, Daddy." I sat in Santino's lap. He was staring down as if I wasn't there.

"Okay," my father panted before going inside of the house.

"I'm sorry, baby, I didn't mean to scare you. I've just been waiting to fuck him up, especially after all of the shit you told me." He raised his head slowly to look at me.

"I understand. Thank you for defending me. But remember you can't mess your body up, because when we have a family, we're gonna need that NFL money," I joked, making a small smile creep on his face. "I love you, Santino, and no matter what, I'm always gonna be on your side."

"I love you too, and know that I will die defending you."

I wrapped my arms around his neck before kissing his perfect lips.

Finally, we could be together with no outside attachments.

CHAPTER TEN

Anton

"Hello?" I answered my phone when I saw Violet's name flash across.

"You called me?"

"Yeah, how are you feeling?"

"I'm fine, Tony. Don't try to act like you care now. You spent one night in the hospital with me, and didn't even let the baby rest before you had your people come in and swab him."

"I'm sorry about that, it's just in the past people have tried to play me. And I knew if I let you get out that hospital— I mean, I knew if I didn't get it done then, it may be months before I got it."

"Unlike them, Anton Nickerson, ain't nobody trying to trap you. I swear if I knew you were such an asshole, I would have never let you touch me."

"Anyway, Violet, I called because the results are ready. Can you come over to my place in like two hours?"

"I'm not sure if you have forgotten already, but I've just given birth and cannot be traveling all around Nevada because some little boy refuses to take responsibility for his son. If you want us all to hear the results, you can come to my place."

"Alright, that works. And I'm sorry for asking, knowing you just had the baby. I apologize, okay?"

"Yeah," she sighed softly.

"See you later." I hung up, just as Oden was walking in all joyful and shit.

I was so happy this nigga got Khyle back because I was tired of seeing him down, and hearing him give out speeches about love every time one of the homies wanted to have a one-night stand.

"What's good?" He dapped me up before sitting across from my desk.

"Nothing much. I'm about to go to Violet's house so the doctors can read the results of that paternity test."

"Should I come with a cake and some balloons?" Truman walked in, closing the door behind him.

"Nah, Violet is cool so I ain't trying to do her like that. However, she's not cool enough for me to allow her to pin her baby on me."

"How does it feel to have Kai and Selinda off your back?"

"Nigga, I feel 200 pounds lighter. I almost feel like taking a jog around the block and shit. Having not seen their faces in a month has been heavenly."

Once Kai and Selinda got the results back, them bitches hightailed it out of my life. I hadn't heard from either of them bitches, to the point where I was starting to wonder if they were dead. But a nigga didn't care enough to really investigate, so oh well!

"I know that's right," Oden nodded. "Guess who Lloyd is fucking with? No, not fucking with, like damn near sprung off of."

"Please tell me it's not Kai or Selinda," I sighed.

"Yeah right," Truman laughed.

"Nah, nigga, Shayne."

"You told him that you hit that? And that she's Khyle's sister?" I bucked my eyes.

I couldn't imagine how Lloyd felt right now. I would never fuck with a bitch like Shayne though. She seemed like the type to get you hooked on her pussy just to leave you. I'm surprised Oden made it out, without getting sprung.

"Yeah, I told him, and he was bummed as hell."

"So tell me something," Truman smirked.

"Awww shit," Oden and I laughed in unison.

"Who was better, in everything? So out of Khyle and Shayne, who gives better head, whose pussy is better, and who takes the dick best," Truman grinned.

Usually I would tell his ass to quit it, but I was slightly interested.

"Nah, I'm not about to do that," Oden smiled.

"What the fuck, man! We yo' homies!" I shouted, chuckling.

"Okay, but y'all have to go first. Truman, who is better in all three, Pilar or Chiina? And Anton, who is better in all three, Tasmine or umm… shit… oh, Amethyst?" Oden cheesed.

"That nigga loves him some Amethyst," Truman joked. Hearing her name reminded me that I needed to get in her ass. "Aight, but out of Pilar and Chiina, damn. They're both pretty good, but Pilar's head game is better than Chiina's, so Pilar wins. It's just Chiina is young so she ain't as experienced in the dick sucking department. Her pussy is fucking out of this world though."

"Okay, okay. Now, Anton."

"Umm, shit, I'm gonna go with Tasmine. Sex with her is on some different shit. With Amethyst, fucking her is like fucking the rest of these hoes. With Tasmine, it's just… different, I don't know. Like, that's my girl, so I don't know but it's way better. So yeah, Tasmine is the best in all three."

"Alright, well, my answer is obviously gonna be Khyle. Like Anton said, it's just different with her versus other women, mainly because I love her. Now outside of that sentimental shit, Khyle wins hands down in all three categories regardless. Not that Shayne couldn't take the dick, but I love watching Khyle take it so much more."

"Damn, so you think Khyle will— I'm fucking with you!" Truman joked when he saw Oden glare at him.

We sat there talking about all kinds of shit until I had to go.

Leaving Palace, I went straight to Violet's house after sending the address to the nurses. When I got there, I saw their white van that they drove and that had me feeling good. I wanted this shit over with as soon as possible so I could deliver the good news to my shorty.

"Hello, Mr. Nickerson," the main nurse Phoebe spoke to me.

"Hey, how are y'all doing?" I asked as the three of us approached Violet's door.

"Pretty good, thank you," they both said simultaneously almost.

"Hey," Violet answered the door in some tights and a big t-shirt. Her blond curly hair was in a bun, and she wore no makeup. Violet was a beautiful girl, she just wasn't my baby mama.

We all sat down at the table in Violet's dining room, and once she put her son Athen down, she came over to join us.

"Let's hear this shit because I have plans tonight." I bit my lip thinking about hitting Tasmine from the back tonight with a clear mind.

"Okay, so you each get a copy of the results. You can keep them sealed or open them if you'd like, but I'm gonna read the ones I have here," Phoebe explained as she handed both Violet and I some sealed envelopes.

Neither of us opened them, we just clutched them tightly as we waited for Phoebe to pull the paper she was looking for out.

"Got it?" I inquired, anxious as fuck to get this done with. I planned to never see Violet's ass again.

"Okay, and according to these results here, Mr. Nickerson, you *are* the father of Athen Anton Nickerson."

I sat there frozen, staring into Phoebe's eyes, hoping that I would wake up from this nightmare I was having.

"What? Let me see this shit!" I snatched the paper and scanned it. There it was, 99.9%. Fuck! "How? I fucked you with a cap!" I grimaced at Violet. "Okay, I'm sorry, I'm just surprised. Violet, I'm sorry. I'm happy to have a kid, I am, but I didn't expect this. I just umm… wasn't expecting this."

Fuck me.

CHAPTER ELEVEN

Shayne

It was 1am, and Pierce wasn't home. He hadn't even called me to let me know he'd be working late. Speaking of working late, he'd been doing that a lot lately, and I was tired of it. I was done waiting for his ass to come home though. I had a way better man waiting for me, and since Pierce wanted to try and play somebody, I was gonna play his ass.

As I peeled the covers off of me, I heard someone knocking at my door. I loved my baby sister, but if this was her ass trying to get some sympathy for being dumped by Oden again, she was gonna have to sleep on it for now. I had other shit to do.

"Who is it?" I called out. No one responded, so again I yelled, "Who is it?"

Still got no answer, so I stood on my tiptoes to look out through the peephole. I saw Earl Jr., and didn't know how to feel. Firstly, I didn't understand why he was here, and secondly, I hoped he wasn't over here to tell me something had happened to Alanna. I despised her as of late, but I didn't want the bitch to die just because she didn't have a backbone.

"What the fuck do you want?" I yanked the door open. "And how the fuck do you know where I live?" I hissed.

"Did you forget that I was dating Alanna when she first became friends with you? I haven't forgotten where you lived." He walked in, looking around a little bit, before turning to face me.

"Again, what the fuck do you want homie?"

"I wanted to give you what *you* want."

"So you're gonna kill yourself?" I closed the door and folded my arms.

"I know the reason you ride me so hard is because you're jealous of the fact that I'm with Alanna. Pierce didn't quite make it to the NFL, and since I did, you want me."

I burst into laughter at this nigga and shook my head.

"Pierce may not have made it, but that would never make me want you over him. The reason I ride you so hard is because you ain't shit for how you treated Alanna."

"Oh yeah?" he stepped closer to me, backing me up against the door.

"Yeah, and you need to move the fuck back."

"I don't think you want me to," he smirked and kissed my neck, while gripping my body tightly.

"Stop, Earl, move!" I screamed.

He wouldn't let up and damn was he strong like a fucking bull. I began to panic because he was overpowering me, and I didn't want him to rape me. He yanked on my pajama shorts, pushing them down some, and then felt between my legs.

"Stop!" I cried.

Out the corner of my eyes, I spotted my glass vase with the flowers that Lloyd had given me sitting in them. Clutching the edge of it, I brought it over and clocked Earl Jr. upside the head.

"Fuck!" he shouted, holding the back of his head.

I grabbed another vase and cracked it over his back, causing him to yowl.

"Get the fuck out!"

"Okay! Okay!" he quickly twisted the doorknob and rushed out of my apartment, still bent over. I slammed the door behind him, and just stood there panting heavily, trying to understand what the hell had just happened.

I picked my phone up to dial Pierce, but of course he didn't answer. I then dialed Lloyd, who picked up on the second ring.

"Baby, can I come over there? I'm scared."

"Scared? What happened?"

"Alanna's boyfriend just came over here and he tried to rape. I had to hit him with the vase you gave me to get him off of me. He was so strong," I sobbed.

"Aight, relax. Don't drive over here though. I will come get you. Stay inside with the door locked, baby, and I will be to you in a little bit, okay?"

"Okay." I hung up the phone.

About 10 minutes later, Lloyd was at my apartment and I was getting into his car with a packed bag. I wasn't sure why I brought so much shit knowing I was gonna be going home in the morning, but hey.

We made it to his townhouse, and as soon as we got inside we went to his bedroom. It was late, and we were both tired, so it was time to call it a night.

"Did he hurt you?" Lloyd asked me, referring to Earl Jr.

"Just when he was groping me, but not like what you're thinking. I definitely hurt him more than he hurt me for sure," I chuckled lightly.

Lloyd just nodded before going into the bathroom.

I changed into a cool short nightgown, and as soon as I crawled under the warm covers of his big bed, his phone chimed. I reached for it, and saw he had a text from some bitch named Fiona. Fuck kind of name was Fiona? Wasn't that the bitch married to Shrek?

Since I knew he didn't have a code on his phone, I went in to look at it.

Fiona: *Don't forget about tomorrow baby. Goodnight.*

Me: *Fuck off.*

I smiled after pressing send, and then put his phone on vibrate. I heard it buzzing like crazy which meant she'd texted back, but I didn't care.

"Fiona? What the fuck are you planning to do with Fiona tomorrow?" I burst into the bathroom to see him brushing his teeth.

"None of your business."

"It is my business! I told you I didn't want you talking to other bitches! Stop keeping secrets from me!" I screamed. I was tired of this shit.

"Oh, like you kept from me the fact that you fucked Oden?" He dried his mouth.

My heart sank to the pit of my stomach when he said that.

"Lloyd, that happened a while ago, and I knew you wouldn't date me if you knew."

"Yeah, well you're right. I don't wanna date you now that I know. Excuse me," he brushed past me after hitting the light in the bathroom.

"So you don't wanna be with me even when I break up with Pierce?"

"Nope." He climbed into the bed.

"Okay."

I walked over to my duffle bag and zipped it closed, before throwing it over my shoulder. I wasn't about to spend the night with him for nothing. If he wanted to miss out on all of this because of Oden, then he could go right ahead.

"Fuck you going?" he spat.

"Away from here. I'm gonna see if Marisol or somebody can come get me."

"Get yo' ass back in the bed, Shayne."

"No, goodbye."

Before I made it out of his bedroom, he'd picked me up from behind and carried me back in. Closing the door behind himself, he locked it, and removed my bag from my shoulder.

"Let me go! I wanna leave!"

"No, you're not fucking leaving! I'm tired of yo' bullshit, Shayne! I'm not no muthafuckin' sucka, aight shawty?! Now you gon' lay down in this fucking bed and go to sleep. You ain't going back to Pierce, ever! What y'all had is a wrap! You're mine now and that's it!"

"You can't just tell me—"

"Lay yo' monkey ass down," he said through clenched teeth, scaring me and turning me on a little bit.

I walked to the side of the bed I usually slept on, and got under the covers. He got in the bed as well, and pulled me closer to him as we laid face to face.

"I'm serious," he whispered.

"Well then that means no more girls texting you. And how am I gonna let Pierce know about this?"

"I don't care how you let him know, but I can come along if need be. From now on, you're my girl. And you need to give him his ring back or pawn it."

"Lloyd, where will I live—"

"I got you," he pecked me gently but deeply.

We pulled away for a few seconds, before resuming our kiss. I had no idea how I was gonna pull this shit off with Pierce's ass, but I knew if I didn't do what Lloyd said, I would lose him for good.

CHAPTER ELEVEN

Oden: Hungry?

Me: Always hungry. Want some Raising Canes or Sonics.

Oden: Raising sounds good. I will bring it soon okay? Like ten minutes tops.

Me: Okay. I love yooooooou.

Oden: No you don't.

Me: Yes I do, so much.

Oden: I love you too pretty.

I smiled down at my phone before setting it on my desk. I walked over to the sink and starting to do my nightly skincare routine, because I knew after I ate, I was gonna be tired as fuck. Not to mention the fact that I was gonna be getting dicked down afterwards too.

After finishing up with my face, I changed into my nightshirt and some fuzzy socks to get comfortable. Tasmine was spending the night with Anton, so Oden and I would be here all alone tonight. I couldn't wait to just chill with him. I always looked forward to the time we spent together. And even though we'd hit more than a few snags, I felt like our relationship had become stronger. I was closer to him now, and felt like I could tell him anything. I was already comfortable with him before, but these days my comfort level was so much higher.

As I cleared my computer and books off of my bed, and set up the backrests for us, someone knocked on my room door. I had no idea who it could be because Bella was still in Arizona, and I knew Tasmine was probably getting sexed by now. *Lord, please don't let it be Perry trying to come over here and eat me out.*

"Huelo?" I opened the door smiling. "What's up?"

"I was wondering if you had the notes from yesterday's class? I wrote that shit down in my phone and it got deleted."

"Oh wow, that was a bad idea. It's always best to have a hard copy. But umm, yeah I have it, one second."

I walked away, expecting him to wait outside, but he came in, looking around a little bit. He let the door close behind him, and started to come in further.

"Where is Tasmine?"

"Oh, she stepped out for a second," I replied. "Okay here they… are." When I turned around he was all up on me on my side of the room. "Huelo."

"Come on, Khyle. I already know how you get down." He grabbed my face to try and kiss me but I moved away.

"What are you talking about?"

"Don't play that innocent role with me, baby. I know you like to fuck."

"Huelo, move. I don't know what the fuck you're talking about!" I shouted as he shoved me down onto my bed. "Stop!"

"I like it rough, too," he gritted as he pinned me to the bed and began to kiss on my neck. "You smell so good, Khyle. Damn, I've been dreaming about fucking you."

"Please, Huelo," I begged, feeling tears well up.

"Don't beg, that's making my dick harder." He ran his hand up my nightshirt, clutching the waistband of my panties before trying to rip them.

"Please Huelo, stop!!!"

TO BE CONTINUED

Join our mailing list to get a notification when Shvonne Latrice has another release! Text **SHVONNE** to **66866** to join!

To submit a manuscript for publishing consideration, email us at
fcpublishinggroup@gmail.com